ALAN HODGKINSON

A Sniper's Sun

Éditions
DÉDICACES

This book was professionally typeset on Reedsy.
Find out more at reedsy.com

Contents

Chapter 1	1
Back in the Bush	16
For the love of Christ	35
Day of the man named Bullit	45
Sky Pilot	65
Psycho-Vac	70
Death of a Real Life Hero	87
Father knows Best?	90
The VC in Aisle Five	100
Bodycount	114
A Gemini in the House	120
Stash	126
The Bridge	144
Sortie's	150
A Remf!	157
Lady in Silk	169
A Courthouse for San Refeal	183
Fatal Implications	186
Hot LZ	196
Notes to the City of Truth or Consequences	227
About the Author	229

1

Chapter 1

T he choppers began to set down. Jack's stomach tightened as bullets pelted the aluminum chopper skin.The LZ was too hot for a landing.The *eagle flight*, seven choppers hauling Alpha Company lifted into circling flight. In short time an aerial slight-of-hand unfolded. A UH-1 dropped down making a smoke screen across the wood line. With the vision of the enemy impaired, the choppers carrying Alpha Company finally set down. The guys disembarked and charged the muzzle flashing wood line. Bullets were like an angry beehive. The Pan American 727 skidded onto the tarmac at Tocoma International.

Another friggen hot LZ. Those at the headquarters' office who processed his departure paperwork at Dong Tam had warned him. *Go to the commissary, get a pair of slacks, penny-loafers and a polyester shirt.* Toss your military garb, and all vestiges of being in Vietnam *in the garbage.* But the protestors knew the plane originated at Saigon.Just check the Arrival/Departure displays. Even though he landed at home in disguise, the olive green duffle bag slung over his back gave him away. This homecoming war hero, among his ilk was greeted with mean-mouthed cries, cardboard signs and boos. *Why are you coming down on me? Tell Nixon, Mr. I'm Not a Crook,* he wanted to shout.

A beam of sunlight cast through one of the windows high overhead. The wood frame building, at least a city train station in size, contained its own brand of air pollution – a smog of sawdust. Though it made your lungs hurt to breath too deeply, it boded better than its cousin *LA* smog, Jack had been there. It at least smudged the place with the fragrance of pine.All of the timber cut to planks in the sawmill came from freshly harvested Ponderosa Pine trees. Upon flying in a plane around the Sierra Foothills, as Jack occasionally did with his friend, a pilot of a Cessna 150, you could see the bloodbath committed. Thousands of acres of onetime dense forest were clear cut in checkerboard patterns across the mountain landscape. At his sawmill workplace, Jack looked around himself at the crowded break-room table. Men did not remove their hardhats during lunch, but put their work gloves on tabletop beside their repast – hard to hold a tuna sandwich to dine on with heavy gloves. The several dozen men around Jack's age of twenty, and some up to ten years older, were all strangers. Jack had only been onboard for two weeks, and didn't expect a bottle of Champaign wrapped in ribbon with a welcome tag. These guys were blue collar, salt-of-the-earth like his father and grandfather before him. This hillbilly bunch could ignore him all they wanted, he adored them just the same.Jack munched on his blackberry jam and peanut butter sandwich, in deference, avoiding eye-contact with others at the table. After returning home from the 'Nam, Jack had no doubt he deserved more than a gas station job. At his hometown of Susanville, California, the best job you could get was at the sawmill. You could afford a house, a new car and a boat with powerful Mercury engine at stern. Working at a gas station just after returning home from the war, and later at a department store, over a year of minimum wage employment, Jack longed for a real job. His war buddy Albert fixed him up with a job here. One thing Jack did not take into account. In a helicopter shoot-down, his back was badly injured. His entry-level job at the sawmill deemed a *Sorter*. A fast-paced task, with a lot of lifting, was an all out assault on his back. Only several hours of taking planks with too many knotholes from a conveyor belt, throwing them into a bin, his back felt like living Hell with pain. Jack accepted this heavy price for a good job, going the distance eight hours a day.

At his downtown apartment after work, he nightly smoked a fat joint to kill the pain.

"You okay?" Audrey asked. I'm concerned about your back." Jack had divorced Skye, given up on Mia and Audrey had recently moved in with him. He felt very happy with her.

"I've got my GI Bill. I've decided I'm going to go to college at Sac State and get an office job for a career. My back can't stand this abuse much longer." Reclining on the couch, comfortably stoned, Jack allowed his memory to take charge. His mental clock went back a year and a half:

"And do you Jack keep thee only unto her so long as you both shall live?"

Flinching at the Presbyterian minister's voice directed at him, "I do," he blurted. Skye had handpicked him, her family minister, a fellow vegetarian and weekend visitor at their backyard pool in Rocklin where a hundred years or so ago, transplanted date trees perfectly lined the small downtown street, the most beautiful tree and undergrowth flower burgeoning town in the world, possibly contending with Cali, Columbia for first place. Jack had only seen sights of Cali in a travel brochure, but it looked beautiful. Despite the large area of shade from the midday sun bestowed by the boughs of an oak tree, once meticulously applied mascara now blotched at corners of the eyes of his bride to-be. And sweat formed on the minister's forehead faster than he could dab it off with a pocket napkin between delivering his diligently read biblical prompts. In addition to his wife soon to be, and this elderly cleric performing the nuptials, Jack as well was feeling the heat in his heavy three piece suit on this hot August day. He was far away from that place where on some days the heat was as responsible for as many dust-offs as the bombs and bullets. But, still, this in-your-face surrounding of foliage, and the otherwise pleasantly lingering bouquet of the carnation on his lapel, had him automatically glancing around himself and listening for sounds in the depth of the foliage. For Jack, lush and redolent garden settings came with a large price. Flowers, vines of them hanging from tree branches, tumbled to the jungle floor, white and pink and blue... perfumed flowers festooned vines so ravenous that over time they would swallow an entire building - Jack had seen this. He had seen bombed out and abandoned stucco structures left over from the French occupation, only discernible beneath heaping layers of tangled vegetation by their approximate shape. He had not only seen this, he had lived it for a very long year. His fellow platoon members and himself had plodded and forged their way through, sweating to the point of dehydration through stretches of undergrowth so dense that even machetes were rendered useless for those who attempted passage. Often heard utterances among guys in his platoon members suggested that the jungle and Charlie were one in the same. Allowing that the VC had earned a reputation as a warrior so Spartan in respect to his natural environment, that he had taught himself to blend ephemeral with the very shadows of those triple canopied stands of jungle, and that this place was home to many of the deadliest snakes in the world, and its canals and swamps had taken the lives of as many GIs as any number of VC snipers on a given day, this was no large stretch. And as hopelessly tangled and overgrown to the point of suffocation his memory was with these images of his year in the jungle, vivid details down to the shape of a leaf that distinguished one plant from another, or the number and color of petals in the flower of a tropical blossom - having stared for hours, sometimes days at the leaves and branches in his face that were his protective cover while pinned down by enemy fire - were something for which he would never forget.

Apart from such surroundings of trees and dense shrub that closed in on him like a tract of Southeast Asian jungle, Jack could go for weeks sometimes without thinking about the firefights that ensued along those heavily foliated jungle trails. And if this constantly looking over his shoulder, when he knew damned well there weren't any VC or anything remotely related in those bushes, was not enough, there was something else - not as menacing, but just as urgent.

"Now, both repeat after me. I promise to have and to hold, from this day forward."

"For better or worse, for richer or poorer, in sickness and in health," Jack mimicked. The arriving rattling and clunking of a car caused heads to turn from the rank a file of folding chairs. Jack as well looked as an older model sedan came down the dirt driveway. Dust settled on the neatly mowed lawn. Jack returned his attention to the minister who continued to quote from the Bible. The fragrance of the carnation grew more powerful, lifting in the humid air to the extent that Jack found himself entirely back into *that place*. Flowers, incredible vines of them hanging from trees, tumbled to the jungle floor around him, white and pink and yellow, perfumed flower festooning vines so ravenous they could swallow an entire building given the time. He had seen this - bombed out and abandoned stucco structures from the French occupation, only discernible beneath heaping layers of tangled vegetation by their approximate shape. Stretches of undergrowth so dense that even machetes were rendered useless, gave spooky credence to often heard utterances among his platoon members suggesting that the jungle and the VC were one in the same. Allowing that the VC had earned a reputation as a warrior so Spartan with his environment that he was ephemeral with the boundless shadows of those triple canopied stands of jungle, and that this place was home to many of the deadliest snakes in the world, and its deep muddy canals and quicksand like swamps had taken the lives of as many GIs as any number of VC snipers on a given day, this was no large stretch. And as hopelessly tangled and overgrown to the point of suffocation his memory was with these images of his year in that unforgivable jungle, vivid details down to the shape of a leaf that distinguished on plant from another or the number and color of petals in the flower of a tropical blossom - having stared for hours, sometimes days at the leaves and branches in his face that were his protective cover for hours on end, and sometimes days while on recon missions - were something he remained intimately familiar with, more so than any number of flowers, shrubs and trees he had grown up among in backyard America.

"And to cherish till death do us part," the minister's lethargy defying crescendo towards the finale' returned Jack somewhat back to the moment. An expectant palm hovered before him, causing him to stare a moment before comprehending. Hands fumbled in one pocket of his suit coat, the other. In seconds, he found the ring, hurrying for it to receive the blessing.

"With this ring, I thee wed," the minister returned the tiny diamond crowned ring. Placing it on Skye's waiting finger, Jack kissed his new wife.

"Those whom God hath joined together, let no man put asunder."

Applause rose from the gathering.

Standing clear of those now crowding around the drink table, Jack began searching for his buddy Ed. It was his car that had noisily arrived in the middle of the ceremony, so Jack knew he was here somewhere, but had not seen him around. His gaze momentarily landed on Monk with his pencil mustache and mirror sunglasses. This guy had the nerve to volunteer to be Best Man when Skye had informed him of her engagement. It wasn't even Monk's tactless manner of coming into your house without knocking, and helping himself to the refrigerator. You might come out of another part of the house after hearing someone moving about, and find him making himself at home on your couch, beer in hand, grinning at you from behind those stupid looking mirror sunglasses.Sunglasses inside the house?Yeah, Roy Robinson donned dark sunglasses on stage, but he was being cool and had earned the privilege. Monk wanted to be cool as well, but wasn't. It did not matter that he had timed his marriage in manner to avoid the draft. More power too anyone who could find an easy way to get out of that war. What had turned Jack forever against Monk, was his *too* nonchalantly uttered remark several months past, declaring the war in Vietnam a *fucking lost cause.* He continued to scan the gathering for Ed while he sipped sun warmed champagne. Jack noticed Skye talking to a man who was probably another one of her uncles or cousins. She turned to look in his direction and signaled with a hand to join her. Jack promptly glanced the other way, pretending not to notice. He had met all of her relatives that he wanted to before the ceremony. There wasn't one of these newly christened in-laws that he could even remotely *relate* to, and if he could avoid it, he would rather refrain from any further hugging, getting slapped on the back or being quizzed about himself, questioned what he did for a living. And for the man who asked what it was like in Vietnam, he was tempted to reply, *What do you expect me to say? You could describe it as a trip to the rodeo and back to be sure.* At the busy table before him, he smiled to himself to see his twelve year old sister taking advantage of the fact that everyone was too busy socializing to notice her, stealthily pouring champagne into a paper cup. Something sparkled in the bright sunlight. He looked up, shading his eyes with an out-turned hand. As soon as it came within hearing distance, he knew the aircraft - a Bell light observation copter, a *LOC.*These were increasing gaining popularity with the police and news media. Most prominently in his mind, this was the craft used by infantry battalion commanders. Like Colonel Marine, who while flying high above the fighting in his Command and Control Copter would yell such orders into his handset as, "Charge that goddamned wood line. I mean it. What are you waiting for? You don't want me to have to come down there." So they charged the wood lines and bunkers, and stormed the villages, mostly to appease the Godlike voice that roared out of the clouds, funneled into ground-based field radios.

Jack's sympathies went with the villagers. In fact, there were days when his sympathies spilled over to the VC, for whom helicopters ranked only second to the jets as prized targets. In fact, more times than he could remember, Jack had thought about how easy it would have been for him to shoot down the battalion commander in his chopper. Preferably, in case he survived, Jack would take him down over dense foliage. In such an area it would be most difficult for rescue craft to find this war criminal excuse for a battalion commander. For someone whose dumping of tons of artillery and napalm, decimated all life form below - women and children no exception, (Whose unfortunate presence in the realm of hand drawn bombing-site circles upon an aerial reconnaissance map was reported as *collateraldamages*), what better justice? Lost in daydreaming, a trace of smoke wafted from the muzzle of his M-16. Jack felt overjoyed to see a line of bullet holes formed across the craft's Plexiglas canopy. The colonel's helo began a free-fall. Jack flinched at the sound of snapping of branches and screeching of the aluminum hull as the copter plunged through a nearby canopy of forest. In seconds, an army of vines burgeoned out of the undergrowth, clambering over the now crumpled metal framework of the craft, multiplying, rapidly engulfing the disabled bird of prey, a gift from the sky for insatiable plant-life. He imagined the colonel either killed in the crash or eventually dying of his injuries, being slowly digested by the very jungle he had dedicated himself to decimating with bombs - warlord of the sky turned plant food. The helicopter shaped orgy of creeping vines burst into a pink and yellow pageantry of perfumed flowers.

"Jack!"

He glanced from the shimmering dot now disappearing into the horizon. "Ed!" Taking his good buddy's extended hand, he held it tight for a second. "I've been looking for you man."

"Up there?"

"Oh, there was a LOC."

"I understand. Just when you think things are getting back to normal, the sound of rotor blades are coming out of nowhere, and you find yourself in the middle of a rice paddy ready to pop yellow smoke."

"Got that right," Jack nodded. He started to tell Ed about his imagined confirmed kill, but decided it was enough simply to be in the company of someone who understood it all. "I was afraid you weren't coming."

"I should have turned left on Ridgeview instead of right," he muttered. "I ended up in Folsom before I realized I was going the wrong way. I finally found you though," he flushed, bobbing his head.

Jack knew the source of his war buddy's self-consciousness over getting lost. There came a time when Ed's squad had stripped him of his right to ever lead again, after taking them through waist deep rice paddy mud into some un-chartered reaches of no-man's land, so far off course that not even the re-supply copter could find them after dark. They ended up spending the night in some rat and snake infested swamp, wet, leech covered and hungry, and pissed off at Ed, after they learned of his striking an azimuth on a far away water-buffalo during their trek to link up with the rest of the company. As they neared the creature, it made its way to the other side of the rice paddy. Their compass-man, not paying attention to the animal's movement, ended up with his bearing proportionately skewed, finally straying off course through miles of some of the most unforgivable terrain in the Delta.

"I saw your car pull up," Jack remarked.

"I kind of hung out among the trees for awhile. I didn't want to just come walking into the gathering and having everyone look at me." As he spoke, Ed listed a little to his right as if he were favoring an injured hip. Among other things about this man, Jack was privileged to know about his good friend, was that an area just above his right hip had taken three AK-47 rounds. Ed looked over his shoulder when someone walked past just behind him. This set him in motion to scan the very presence of those around him.

Vicarious in his buddy's discomfort with crowds, Jack accompanied him in looking around. After a few minutes of this, he directed toward a place at the far end of the yard. "Come on, there's a nice quiet place, let's visit over there."

"I don't want to take you away from your reception," Ed held back.

"You're not taking me away from anything. Besides, at the most, there's but a half a dozen people here I even know. Anyway, most of them are here just for the champagne and cake." Glancing at the crowd of fifty people or more he confessed, "To tell you the truth, I would rather be in the company of a bunch of Viet Cong than this herd of non-combatants."

"I gotta go along with you on that - REMFs. Any brew around this place?"

"Fraid not. Just the bubbly." Jack lifted his nearly empty glass. "Or slightly spiked punch. Got plenty of that. Come on." He led the way towards the area he had indicated.

"I really can't stay long," Ed conveyed to Jack as they walked alongside. When they arrived at the secluded area, Ed looked around again. He rubbed the back of his neck with a palm for a minute. When you go through dozens of intersections, turning your head this way and that, looking for familiar landmarks and the correct road signs, your neck gets sore.

"You don't just *drop in for several minutes* for a close friend's wedding," Jack protested.

"I told Raynel I wouldn't stay long. You know how she feels about you. It's not that she doesn't *like* you, it's just that she disapproves of me keeping the company of Clyde Barker reborn. And some of the stuff you and I get into when were together."

Jack couldn't help but smile to himself to remember the latest incident that had set Raynel off. They had stopped at a traffic light, and Jack who was driving, did not notice when it turned green. A horn blared. When the signal cycled from red back to green, the horn honked again before Jack could even step on his gas pedal. Ed told him to hold up. He jumped out of the car and strode to the car behind, popped the hood open from the latch inside the grillwork and reached down in front of the engine. When his hand came out, he had a fistful of ripped out electric wires. He slammed the hood down, to reveal a now incredulous looking man behind the wheel who was clamping down on a large cigar between his teeth. Ed strode back to Jack's car and plopped down in the passenger seat. His hand was bleeding. Jack pulled a grease rag out from under his seat, giving it to Ed, who clutched it tightly in hand.

The light back to green, and a half dozen or more cars lined up behind him now, Jack started to drive off. He glanced into his rearview mirror on the driver's side to notice that the guy had jumped out of car yelling. Jack rolled down his window to hear better. "Yeah, run you motherfucker, 'cause I'll bust yer head if I catch you!"

When Jack stepped on the brake, Ed reached for the door handle. "Stay here. You cut your hand," he insisted, getting out of the car. Jack stopped just in front of the man who was huffed up, and baring his teeth that still clutched the fuming cigar. Jack did not feel the least bit intimidated by this overweight, out of shape looking excuse for a man who appeared about ten years his senior. "Watch your mouth. You're lucky my friend didn't drag you out of the car and beat your head into the pavement. He just got back from 'Nam. Sudden loud noises upset him."

"Well, that's his problem. In the first place, I don't feel an iota of compassion for anybody who went to Vietnam to kill Asians."

Jack reached and jerked the cigar from the man's mouth and replied, "I just returned from 'Nam myself, and I as well am annoyed by loud car horns - especially compliments of some moron." He crammed the bright amber of the cigar dead center into the man's goatee and gave it a twist, like the fat faced man's chin was an ashtray.

Some upstanding bystander called the cops, and they ended up spending several days in jail for that one. There were other such incidents - nearly every time that got together in fact. Jack did not begrudge Raynel for her feelings. Her reality required hewing your sails close to the wind. If you didn't keep your sail fast at all times, you ended up going off course or worse could capsizes. God forbid!Life was so full of uncertainties.

Ed's glance shifted to the gathering around the drink table.

Noticing his friend's shirt was wrinkled, and his slacks were too big around the waist, cinched by a large leather belt, Jack was surprised to see Ed was not wearing his rice paddy ravished combat boots that he rarely ventured from home without, regardless the occasion. Checking his buddy out completely, he exclaimed, "Wow, where'd you get the cool tie?" he asked about the wide strip of polyester that made its way less than halfway down Ed's chest - his huge neck taking up the rest of the tie. It was too busy with loud colors, an ugly tie in fact, and Jack was only humoring Ed.

"I bought it just for your wedding." He glanced down his nose the green, yellow and red decorated cloth. "You really like it?"

"Yeah. Really!" Jack lied. He had heard of an ugly tie contest in Sacramento.Maybe he would tell him, and Ed would certainly win first place with that ungodly looking thing around his neck, he thought with a chuckle to himself.

They were both quiet for several minutes, once again scanning their surroundings. "I heard they're starting to pull the rest of the guys out of the 'Nam," Jack broke the silence.

"Too late to do anything else anyway. That cock sucker Nixon," he grumbled. "I really gotta split. I just wanted to..." Ed reached into a front pocket of his jean pants. "I've got a little wedding present for you." He pulled his hand out of the pocket holding a down turned fist between them.

Jack opened his palm as Ed pressed the gift into his hand. Glancing down, he immediately recognized the small cigarette lighter.

"Every time you light up a doobie, think of me."

The small piece of metal in his palm could not have weighed much more than an ounce, but boasted tons of sentimental value. They had been in stand-down status for the night in the village of Bien Tre after a week long mission. Ed and Jack were out in search of a place they had heard about, that offered some all night pussy without the Saigon-tea routine, in route to which they were confronted by an old Vietnamese man who displayed something for sale, street venders common in 'Nam. American soldiers were rich compared to the Vietnamese. They always had a stash of cash in pocket. The man didn't want much for it in the first place, but Jack began to bargain him down. Ed quickly interjected and offered a piaster more than the original asking price. In a country where prices were routinely bartered down, but never up, the Vietnamese man made a shocked expression as he took the money and went on his way.

"You idiot, it's a buyers market here.People like you throwing your cash around ruin it for all of us," Jack had complained.

"You're just pissed off because I'm the one who got the lighter." Ed had flicked his new possession, displaying a triumphant flame. "Probably left on the bar from some guy who had too much to drink. I was at a bar in Saigon.Some guy in Green Beret uniform pulled out money from his front pocket to pay his tab, and staggered off into the night. I looked and noticed a wad of piaster had fallen out of his pocket. I grappled to the floor and picked up the bills. I came up with a wad of bills that came to around fifty American. I drank beer for the rest of the night on him."

"You're a fucking, lower-life-form scrounge, Jack replied.

"Yeah, and your best friend on planet Earth. I don't get any respect from you. I really gotta go," Ed mumbled, shuffling his feet.

"You sure you can't stick around longer?" Jack clasped the lighter with its serrated flame-adjusting wheel that had proven its worth time and again in providing instant fire to give life to countless joints in the months following that fateful day in Ben Hoa where Ed purchased the lighter. He slipped it into his coat pocket.

"Well, you survived 'Nam. Now, let's see how you do with wedlock," Ed smiled. "Did anyone tell you that after a year's up, you don't get to just pack up yer things and say, 'mission complete.'"

He was being funny, but from what Jack knew of Ed's nearly two years of marriage since returning home from 'Nam, he was more than likely wishing that marriage, like Tour of Duty had a year limit. They briefly embraced and Jack patted his friend on the back. "Drinks are on me when I get back from Colorado," he promised. They walked together towards the driveway. "Thanks for coming by," Jack added, "And thanks for the gift!" He stayed and watched as Ed got into his car and began backing out. Through the intermittent openings between the row of tall junipers, he grinned to himself as his friend veered one way then the other within inches of sideswiping one car or the other that flanked the narrow dirt driveway. At the sound of a step on the grass behind him, Jack spun around.

"Nervous?" Syke's older sister said. She took Jack's hand and pulled him up close. "Your bride sent me after you." She added, "I haven't had the opportunity of kissing the groom yet." Jack leaned until his lips met hers. She ushered him, arm in arm through the gathering, towards the same shady clearing where they had held the ceremony. He gazed upon his beautiful new bride at a distance, specially wrapped for him in an off-white, lace fringed gown, white high heels at one end, topped off with a halo of baby breath flowers at the other. *I should run for my life*, Jack thought. I should keep on running until I'm halfway around the Earth, back in that little French colonial town in the heart of the Mekong Delta, back in the arms of that unbelievably beautiful and charming girl for whom I had originally meant to spend the rest of my life.

As they approached, Monk, who had been speaking with Skye, lifted a can in salute.

"I've found the man of my dreams," Roma announced. "Jack is so irresistible to feast your eyes upon at in a suit." She pulled herself close to him.

"Go for it," Monk exclaimed. "I wouldn't be opposed to a straight across trade." He glanced to Skye with a mischievous grin. He meant what he said, Jack had no doubt. Skye was a catch to be admired. And Monk was very attracted to her, he made no secret. He had jumped for the concession of marrying Skye's sister Roma a year or so past. Jack had learned from Skye that Monk had asked her for a date during that time, and that she had turned him down. Next, he asked Roma for a date, and she accepted. He had married into the family of the girl he really wanted. The rest was history.

"Beer! Where'd you get the beer?" Jack asked.

"Inside the house. In the fridge. You want me to get you one?"

"You have to drive tonight," Skye intervened. "You're already toked-up, and you've been drinking champagne."

"Wow! Look how quickly she caught on to being a wife," Monk chuckled.

"May I be so bold as to crash this prestigious gathering?" A man walked up to Jack. "Skye told me you were in Vietnam." He sounded drunk.

"This is my uncle Stan," Skye said.

Jack shook hands with the young, pale faced, effeminate looking guy. "Yeah, I was there - just last night," he quipped. If this guy was a 'Nam vet, he would have understood that Jack was alluding to his nightmares that took him back *there*, every time he closed his eyes to sleep.

"My older brother was in Vietnam in sixty-six. He was a real live war hero. One time the VC shot a rocket into the side of his supply truck and hit the gas tank. He single-handedly put out the flames with a fire extinguisher."

Jack nodded. "Army, Marines?"

"No, actually Air Force."

Jack looked past the man to see his mother approaching. "No, she's not my younger sister. She's my mother. Really!" Jack turned and exclaimed to Roma as if he were in mid conversation with her. "What a coincidence," he pretended surprise at his mother's arrival. She stopped short of the group, taking in her newlywed son with a smile.

"Hi mom! Funny thing you should come along. I'm trying to convince Monk and Roma that you're really my mother. They think you're my younger sister. Won't you tell them that I'm your natural born son."

"Oh, you're making that up. If you weren't so big, I'd spank you right in front of everyone."

"Spank him," Monk grinned.

Jack gave a once-over to Uncle Stan whose suit was probably three times more expensive than his sharkskin suit that he had purchased in Hong Kong on R&R, and now wore for the first time his wedding. He thought, *am I supposed to be impressed by this moron's noncombatant brother who probably at most singed his eyebrows putting out the fire on a tanker truck? Who does he think he is coming on like he has something in common with me because of that?*

Jack looked to see his new wife who was talking to Roma and her husband, the little weasel with his mirror sunglasses. He glanced from them to his mother. Shifting his gaze to the larger crowd, consisting largely of an assortment of cousins, aunts and uncles to include his grandparents on his mom's side, he wondered, for that matter, what do any of these people know about 'Nam? He shuddered to think that people who had been so close to you all your life could instantly become strangers. I guess it's going to take some time to put that god-damned war behind me, Jack thought to himself. It's just going to get worse before it gets better, he figured. Rising inside was that sense of growing desperation one feels when stuck alone behind enemy lines. The VC have you surrounded, and they're going to have you for lunch.

2

Back in the Bush

J ack remembered having driven hundreds of miles through the middle of nowhere, only to find himself still in the middle of nowhere. "Welcome to scenic, flat ass desert to every horizon Nevada," he muttered to himself. The mind-numbing endlessness was only punctuated by an occasional rock that hit inside the fender well with the reverie shattering effect of a bullet hitting the helicopter floor when you least expect it. The darkness and solitude reminded him of his long hours on guard duty staring into the merciless tangle of jungle where he would start seeing things. Jack turned up the music. Glancing into his rear view mirror, he accelerated until the speedometer went to over a hundred, as if you could outrun those troubling images. When you are the only one awake in a dark spot of jungle in the middle of nowhere for a long enough time, you can easily stare a bunch of bushes, manifesting a half dozen black pajama wearing little men crawling towards your perimeter. Regardless of the louder music, Skye didn't as much stir. She had been so hyped about the wedding, only cross-tops and orange juice for breakfast, she had only slept a few hours last night. She certainly needed the rest. Still, he wished she would wake up so he would not be alone with his god-damned rouge thoughts. At least in 'Nam, you could get on the field radio and call in for illuminations to discover in bright view if you were really surrounded by the enemy. As it turned out in many cases, exposing the folly, of your mind playing tricks

16

on itself again. A car wailing its horn zoomed past in the in the opposite direction. Jack watched in the rearview mirror at its tail lights, cursing at the car for passing so close. When he returned his attention to the road ahead, he noticed that he was straddling the center line. He steered the car back into its lane. Skye finally stirred. "Too loud?" he implored. Turning the volume down, he felt relieved at the possibility of company.

"I thought I heard a car horn," she sleepily muttered. Sitting upright, she yawned. "Don't you have any other tape than that? I've been hearing that same song over and over again in and out of my sleep since we left Reno."

The Animals cried out the words from their song *We Gotta Get Out of This Place*, on all four of the custom speakers that Jack had installed especially for this trip. "Good song, listen to the words," he entreated her.

"I hear the words. Every single one of them. They're pounding into my head like elephant hooves. Why do you have to keep replaying that same song?"

Jack reached and turned down the volume.

"Jesus! You're doing a hundred," she exclaimed. "Slow down!"

"Don't worry. There's no speed limit in Nevada." When you departed city limits anywhere in the state, a road sign simply advised, *Resume Speed*.

"That's not what I'm worried about. What if we had a blowout, barreling at the speed of light?"

Jack gradually slowed to seventy-five to appease. He shook his head wryly.

"I have a good reason to be concerned. We're traveling on throw-away tires from the dumpsters behind gas stations you prowl at night. I asked you to get new tires for the trip, but no, you have to risk life and limb and run these to the ground instead of buying new ones."

Jack dimmed his lights for an oncoming car. The other driver did not return the courtesy. He again blinked his lights, to no avail. "Son-of-a-bitch," he growled as the car whizzed past. Major issues were building up inside of him. To start with, Skye's fears were measured in miles per hour; in spite of the years past, his fears were measured by the number of mortar attacks and ambushes he might survive on any given day. Jack wondered just how much of this irony Skye comprehended. The intelligence required to understand life's ironies, often comes with the ability to see your own fallacies. And Skye was an intelligent, sentient being. But did she fathom in the least the night the VC leveled a huge section of Dong Tam by blowing up the ammo dump of thousand tons of armament, and hundreds of them overrunning the perimeter of the base camp subsequently being blown to pieces as a result of their own heroic deeds? During Search and Destroy missions, did she understand why there was no enemy rifle fire during insertions of the Eagle Flights? The Americans would conduct patrols for hours, without contact, finally calling in the choppers for extraction. Only then did the VC come out of the woodwork, usually out of spider-holes, shooting up the sorties. Now they were sitting ducks during their slow lift-offs, heavily loaded with troops and their supplies. There was one early morning riverboat battle on the Rach Ba Rai, where the Fourth Platoon ambushed two sampans loaded with re-supplies. The enemy returned fire with B-40 rockets. The powerful recoils were such that the sampans capsized backwards. Jack's platoon continued firing into the ammo lauded boats wooden hulls until they exploded. He could still hear the VC screaming as they burned to death in the petrol flames atop the canal water. Jack shoved the tape back in, rewinding it to his favorite song. As he expected, Skye retorted to his tendency to withdraw from conflict with her by reprisal of ignoring him. She turned her head to the passenger window, where there was nothing out there to feast your eyes upon except darkness.

Headlights glared from behind. Jack glanced into his side mirror to see a semi closing in on him. He speeded up.

"What are you doing?" She wasn't going to let up.

"Some motherfucker in a semi is tailgating me. You know I hate to be tailgated."

"I really think that you need professional help," she sighed. "Why don't you just pull over and let me drive before you have a nervous breakdown." She daintily took something out of her purse. Jack saw it was a joint. He reached into a jeans pocket, and in a second held his lighter poised at the joint's diminutive tip. But repeated efforts of flicking the lighter, only succeeded in producing a lot of sparks. Skye finally remarked, "If that was an attempt to impress me with your fancy looking lighter, you have my condolences."

"Go easy on it. This sucker's been through a lot. I'm here to tell you," Jack remarked, speaking in the knowledge of the person who gave it to him. He shoved the gift from Ed back into his pocket. "Just needs a little adjustment probably."

Skye found matches in her purse and lit the joint herself. After taking a hit, she passed it over.

"This is what you call professional help?" He inhaled deeply from the joint, holding the smoke in his lungs as long as he could. In seconds, the numbing effects of the drug was moving up the back of his head, tingling his skull. There were times when he wished he could just dunk his brain in Novocain - but the weed was a close second. "My compliments to your supplier," he said, passing the roll-your-own back.

"It was from Monk and Roma. They gave me a whole handful of joints while you were visiting with your war buddy. A wedding present."

"That beats the hell out of the toaster/oven we got from my aunt Claudia."

"You still think about Vietnam a lot, don't you?" she asked, totally out of the blue.

He was stoned and off guard. "Yeah. Pretty much eight days a week."

"Don't you just want to just forget about it?"

Jack turned to look at his newly crowned wife to see in her expression if she was joking. "Is that question even legal in a court of law," he smirked. Taking the joint that she offered him, he inhaled from its rapidly shrinking remains.

"I just wonder, how can you think about the war that much, and never talk to me about it to me." He returned what was now but a *roach* to her. Skye took a final hit and coughed. When it gets to that point, the smoke no longer filters.

Jack rolled the window down a few inches for fresh air. "You okay?"

"I'll live," she coughed again. "Why won't you talk to me about it all?" she plied.

That lump came to his throat and he swallowed. Maybe he would tell her about the ambush in Can Tho, late November in Sixty-eight a day before his birthday, he regarded in thought. The rouge memory would hit him so hard, it would make his knees go out as he walked, and he needed several beers or a joint to calm himself. That ambush was something he had never talked about to anyone. It was so powerful in thought, that it couldn't have really happened. He subconsciously relegated it to a possible nightmare. It couldn't have really happened. Conveniently, you could sweep nightmares under the carpet. Just the mere passing thought of that harrowing occurrence made him flush."I, I uh. I was…" Sweat beaded on his forehead. Jack looked around from where he lay on the ground. Water glug, glug, glugged, compliments a AK-47 bullet hole in his canteen. From what he could tell, everyone else in the squad had been wounded or killed. Lucky me. Just a hole in my canteen. The only movement was a frog that hopped to and fro among the bodies of his comrades. Meanwhile, the enemy had split for parts unknown. "It looks like it's down to just you and I buddy," Jack was out of his mind sociable with the frog. Or he had thought those words to the frog, a detail for which he had never been certain."Fuck you," the frog had croaked in reply. The guys call the Mekong Delta frogs *fuck-you-frogs* because their croak sounded like they were sounding out in English to the words *fuck you*. The fuck-you-frog nonchalantly hopped away.

Gravel pelted the underside of the right fender.

"Jack!" Skye cried out.

He jerked the steering wheel to the left, bringing the car back to the asphalt. Watching the headlight illuminated section of road before himself for several minutes, he clearly remembered something odd as he lay there on the jungle floor, afraid to move least there were any VC still lurking about. He thought how much he envied that frog. It was so simple for him. All he had to do was hop away from it all, to the safe haven of the lily pond. Jack wanted to follow the frog, escaping with him to a simple, peaceful, lily pond existence. Those were his very thoughts that day as he lay pressed to the ground surrounded by his wounded and dead platoon members. He still felt that way. He could even accept a diet exclusively consisting of flies for the remainder of his life, if it meant distance from those friggen ambushes of life.

"After I finish college, I want to take some time off before getting a job, so

I can have a child."

Jack cringed at still another ambush out of the mother-fucking-loving blue. In addition to figurative and literal in nature, ambushes came in various sizes and shapes. "You want to what?"

"You act surprised," she turned in her seat.

"It's not as if we ever talked about this before," he muttered, eyes desperate for explanation switching back and forth between his wife and the road. "I mean we've lived together all this time, and you never, ever mentioned having a fucking kid."

"Well, that was different. We were *living* together. Out of regard for your potential off-spring who goes to school, and is quizzed about his parents from others, you want that kid to be able to say its mother and father is of the same last name. You don't have kids when you're casually living together. It's not proper. In days past, you were broke, and the extra responsibility would have made it worse. Now we're married. You didn't actually think we were going to go through life without having kids, did you?"

What the hell was I thinking? Jack wondered to himself. He could not help but notice that Skye was now using the plural in reference to the unthinkable. "Guess not," he replied. Considering the resolve in her tone, he felt that retreat was the only option. He would return to fight this battle on another day, when he might be better prepared.

"I know you want to live out in the country. We can do that. It'll be healthy for the kids to grow up in a rural environment."

Skye's proposal came obviously as a concession. Where a lot of topics had not been breached concerning their future together, Jack had spoken often of his desire to live in the country. His envisioned utopia consisted of about two thousand trees per human. Adults-only at that ratio would be even better.

The slowly growing patch of light on the bleak horizon was soon identified by a road sign reading *Winnamucca 18 miles*. Jack stepped on the gas. "Here comes an implication of so-called civilization. What do say we get a room in beautiful downtown Winnamucca?"

"I thought we decided to make Stateline tonight."

A SNIPER'S SUN

"I'm tired. Let's just call it a night and get a room there." Most of all, Jack needed a drink - several drinks.

"Okay. I can't argue with that. Let's stay at one of the casino hotels. I could enjoy a little gambling before I go to bed. I need to unwind."

* * *

At the crap table, some guy wearing a black hat, pearl buttoned cowboy shirt and a wide leather belt with a huge brass buckle boasting the bas-relief of a nude girl reclining seductively, was getting on Jack's nerves. Every time the dice came up seven or eleven, he led a chorus of cheers from others pushing up against the table. At each subsequent roll, he would first do a little dance with his reptilian cowboy boots."Do me a favor and go dosey-doe on a land mine, you annoying lump of cow dung," Jack muttered, his words drowned out by the rabble from the crowd. The man apparently didn't hear him. He went on to wander around the casino, eventually finding a quiet spot where a quarter slot-machine offered him an opportunity to continue gambling, away from the noisy scene at the crap table.

"You winning anything?" He looked from what had become a mind numbing blur of spinning cylinders, to see Skye at his side.

"Nah. I did fairly good at the crap table, but this money hungry machine is eating up all my earlier profits."

"Well, I'm forty bucks ahead and I'm going to keep it that way," Skye declared. "You ready to go to the room?"

"I'll be up shortly. You go ahead."That's Skye and her ilk for you, he thought. Forty friggen bucks? That will buy you someone candy bars for the month. Several thousand dollars, now we're talking real pocket change.

"It's our honeymoon," she protested.

"Come on. It's not as if we haven't been living together for over a goddamned year," he countered. Reaching into the tray of the machine, he scooped up a handful of quarters. "Here, play the machine next to me," offered her the coins.

"I'm tired, and I'm going to the room."

22

"I'll be up a half an hour or so. Warm up the bed for me." He dumped the coins back into the metal tray. Skye looked at her watch. "Do you realize it's nearly three in the morning?"

Jack nodded, continuing to feed quarters to the machine as quickly as it could eat them at each pull of the handle. After a minute, he glanced to his side, and behind himself, feeling good to discover Skye had gone.

* * *

"You thieving piece of shit," Jack exclaimed as he jerked the slot machine handle. The little cylinders that had been deceiving him for the past hour with prospects of a big payoff, now mocked him with a row of mixed fruit. I need rest, he thought, drained from the repeated surges of adrenaline with every near-jackpot, not to mention the very long day that he was surviving by dent of nervous energy at best. Staring at the glass enclosed cylinders, a faint reflection of himself gave the machine its own face. Jack stared back at those red, unblinking eyes. Here I am, he thought, visa-vise with the enemy. What I need is not rest, but more ammo.

When he reached the door to their room, he stooped until his vision was level with the lock. Pulling the door towards himself so that there would be no pressure against the bolt, he quietly inserted the key, twisting it so slowly that the only sound was his cadenced breathing. Next, he turned the knob with such care that the latch did not even click. Jack pushed the door open without a whisper of sound. He looked up and down the hall at no witnesses, and stood up. Upon toes that knew the amount of silence required to breach the perimeter of enemy-held territory, he entered the room, only after waiting long enough to let his sight adjust to the darkness. When his vision returned to the extent that he could make out the shape of the suitcase, he stepped in that direction. A warrior on night mission is a hyper-vigilant cat. The wooden floor beneath the carpet creaked. Jack froze. Listening to Skye's breathing until he felt certain she had not waken, he returned to the task at hand. In the dim light he could see that the suitcase was closed. He pulled, hoping it was unlatched - another clicking noise to surmount. The top lifted easily. Skye kept their cash in the nylon pouch at the rear of the suitcase. In seconds he was in possession of the stack of rubber band fastened twenty dollar bills. More ammo. He slipped out of the room.

Jack pulled the ball grip handle with the cuff of his palm so hard, the heavy chrome plated machine shuddered at its mooring. Heaps of quarters shifted inside. So close; but so far away. "That's my goddamned honeymoon money!" he muttered to the machine. An elderly man who had been glancing tentatively at every outburst from this crazed fellow gambler down the row of machines from himself, but was enjoying the generosity of a slot-machine very different from the one Jack played, finally scooped his coins from the chrome catchments tray, and swiftly disappeared. It wasn't about winning a jackpot. Even if he won a million dollars, it didn't matter, Jack would put it back again. This was a showdown. The showdown could not be assessed in dollars. The world is an unfair place controlled by forces in some backroom, and it came down to you against them. The Italian, the Jewish mafia wanted to bring the average guy to their knees by cleaning out their wallets. Simple as that. Jack found himself at war with those forces. He had been at war with dark forces. It wasn't about Pork Chop Hill. Pork Chop Hill was so much rock and soil. The reality was who would win and who would lose. That defined life on this planet. The winner gets all the respect; the loser should just curl up and die in pitiful defeat. As Jack continued jerking the machines handle angrily, a shadow cast over him from behind.

"Is there any problem here sir?" Turning, Jack saw a man in brown uniform. The name of the casino was embossed on an official looking shoulder patch. "There sure is. I've been putting money in this son-of-a-bitch all night and it won't give me any back." He returned his attention to the rectangular window that now displayed a bar and two plum. "No wonder they call these things one-armed bandits," he swore, again angrily shoving the machine with an open palm.

"You're going to have to stop that, right now!" the security guard raised his voice. "Just keep it up and I'll be forced to take you into custody, and have the city police come and arrest you for damaging casino property."

"What? Come on! I haven't damaged this damned machine. But it's cost me buckaroos a bunch."

"Well, you're alarming the other patrons." Jack could tell he was a Nevada hillbilly all over the place, and there was no arguing with him. "If you continue, I will have you arrested. Do you understand? In fact I would like to see some form of ID."

"I'm twenty fucking one," Jack grumbled, standing up from the stool to take out his wallet. Removing his driver's license from its plastic display, he handed it over. After studying the license a minute, the man returned it saying, "You're still going to have to leave." He stood with his legs spread, hands on hips. A long barreled twenty-two six shooter holstered at his side. Returning his cash-strapped wallet to his back pocket, Jack almost laughed to himself at the thought of a security guard, especially a casino security guard drawing a pistol on him - futilely *Attempting* to draw a pistol on him, that is. Jack would knock him on his ass before he even got it out of his holster.

"Fuck you and this whore casino pussy," Jack said under his breath, starting towards the elevator in retreat.

"Where do you think you're going? The exit is back this way!"

Jack stopped at the elevator door, looked over his shoulder. "I have a room here in the hotel," he retorted. The elevator door slid open and Jack stepped in. He didn't know if the security guard would come after him, and had no plan for what he would do in such a case. He didn't care. It had been a long day. He pushed the button for his floor. As the doors closed, Jack caught a last look of the security guard in his starched, casino issued uniform and chrome six-shooter, standing where he had left him. Though the ride could not have been more than a few seconds, Jack could not wait to get out of the small enclosure. Extremely claustrophobic, he in fact felt on the verge of panic. It was some sort of battle condition, he guessed. When you're pinned down behind a rice paddy dike and can't even lift your head, least you get shot, you end up with a hole in your forehead. He hurried out when the doors opened. When he entered the room, Skye was still asleep. She stirred as he sat on the edge of the bed and started taking off his shoes. He dwelled over the bad news he had for her. *The honeymoon is over my dear.*

"You just now get here?" she yawned.

"Few minutes ago."

"What time is it?"

"About four." He kicked one of his penny-loafer shoes off.

"Four!"

"Four-thirty or thereabouts." He kicked off the other shoe.

"And you're just getting back to the room?"

"Yeah. Remember that pretty waitress in the restaurant. See saw me gambling and lured me to her apartment nearby.I screwed her brains out into the wee hours. Oh what a night."

"In other words, you gambled every penny in your pocket, and finally came up to the room?"

"Something like that…" he started unbuttoning his shirt. "You got another one of those joints?"

Skye propped herself up. "You know, excessive gambling is an addiction."

Jack looked towards the window with its drawn gossamer white curtains. Blobs of colored lights splashed in short intervals from the several story high, neon-lighted, lasso spinning cowboy signpost in front of the hotel. That's the son-of-a-bitch who enticed me here in the first place when we drove into town he thought, with his *Howdy y'all come-on-down* in Bob Barker tone, appealing to anyone with a sense for adventure in tradition of the Old West, replete with Eureka! Gold Rush implications all over the place.

Skye found her purse bedside, and produced a joint. She even had matches handy and put a fire to the curare for him. Women are so accommodating, Jack marveled at his good luck for this partner in life. Meanwhile, he needed that brain dumb-down, now more than ever.

"How much did you lose?"

"Ouch, there stood crystal clear the question. "Everything," he confessed.

"Well, at least we have the stash in the suitcase," her voice lowered.

He accepted the joint from her, took a hit and returned it. "The stash included." Laid back so his head was resting on Syke's lap, he looked up, meeting her downcast eyes. Her face froze. He waited for her to lash out at him, but from her expression, what he had told her was just now sinking in. I got a little carried away."

Skye pulled herself out from under him, climbing out of bed. She was nude. She never slept in the buff, Jack thought. It occurred to him that she had been waiting for him, on this their honeymoon night. She paced back and forth across the room and stopped. Looking at him incredulous, "All four-hundred and fifty fucking dollars!"

He nodded. "Plus the several hundred I had in my wallet." Shifting his gaze to the ceiling, Jack wondered when it would ever end. The B-40 hit the chopper's engine and they went into a downward spiral. All Jack could think to do during the freefall was cross himself. As luck would have it, the chopper made a soft crash in a flooded rice paddy five or six hundred feet below. Several of his disks were crunched in his lower back, but he came out of it on both feet.After a week in the field-hospital, he went on to serve his seven month remaining Tour, but the pain in his back endlessly troubled him, especially with carrying a c-ration cans laden rucksack, two bandoliers of very heavy ammo, a utility belt with frag grenades galore, two canteens of water and a not very heavy M-16 in hand. Gad, a friggen ground-ponder with injured back.

"Now what are we going to do?" He heard the snap of Skye's purse.

"I've only got a little over fifty dollars. Guess that could get us back home…"

She's downright resourceful, Jack thought. He grimaced to himself. *I spaced-out the money in her purse. I could have turned everything around with that much more cash.*

* * *

Glancing to the rearview mirror, Jack cast one last frown at the little town of Winnemucca as they returned westward. He rested the palm of his right hand ever so lightly on the steering wheel. It was still black and blue from repeatedly slamming it against the ball grip of the slot-machine handle. But the *real* pain was in his God-forgiven brain. Pain, mental or physical was something to which he had grown accustomed a long time ago. He really didn't mind it that much. Good or bad, at least it was something that you could count on to keep yourself focused. "Can't wait to get out of this flat-ass, scenic-loser desert," he mumbled. Even at full power, the car's a/c struggled to keep up with the late afternoon heat. Since leaving the hotel, Skye had not spoken a word. There were better days to be sure. In Vihn Hoa, the rickety thatched roof buildings propped high above the muddy waters by skinny wooden stilts lined Kien Xiang Canal. Sampans and creaky skiffs some loading, others off-loading heaping cargoes of fish and produce, crowded the wharves and shorelines. This outer-perimeter security for the nearby division base camp, Dong Tam, in response to Viet Cong forces that had recently overrun Vihn Hoa, a company of American combat troops had set up camp on the edge of town for two months. During this stay, at a small restaurant on rue de Jardin is where Jack met Mia. "Give me mammary glands, big ones that stick out there like headlights on a '59 Cadillac," Stash exclaimed showing cupped hands about a foot from his own chest.

* * *

"A real German-American beauty, big bones and all huh?" Jack replied.

"She doesn't have to be American or European in any context. I think Vietnamese woman are just as beautiful, with the exception that they don't have a monopoly on tits. I'm a tit man."

"*Really*? A guy wouldn't know that from just talking to you at first blush."

The waitress arrived in response to Jack's call in his fairly good Vietnamese, for another round. Upon setting the bottles of warm beer on the table, she turned to leave. Jack had been flirting with her for over an hour. A natural for other languages, his ex-girlfriend in LA, a Chicano, he spoke to her in the Spanish. Jack as well spoke fluently in Vietnamese. Finally, grabbing the teenage girl's hand, he held it firmly but gently. "Hey, what'cha you say you and me ride off together into the sunset in my armored personnel carrier?" He said this primarily in English to amuse Stash, assuming by now, from her lack of acknowledgment to any of his one-liners, that the girl didn't speak much English, but she did. She knew English well, he discovered.

28

"I've had about enough of you," she retorted in perfect English, pulling her hand free. Picking up one of the bottles she had just brought to the table, she wielded it like a club and said, "If you don't quit bothering me, I'm going to break this bottle over your head."

Stash quickly grabbed one of the empty bottles still on the table and exclaimed, "Wait, don't waste a full one on him. Use this empty one."

Jack's relationship with the Vietnamese waitress eventually improved - considerably in fact. During his off-duty hours, they often strolled along the tree lined streets of the town, where Mia would often pointed out homes and shops of friends and relatives, or told of the history of Vihn Hoa's French occupation, followed by the takeover by the Viet Mihn, then the Viet Cong, then the Americans, retaken by the Viet Cong, and the Americans again. Even the military occupations were not so bad when you compared them with the mortar and artillery attacks, and subsequent heavy shooting that came with every retaking of the village. As she spoke, the sight of the bullet riddled and shell chipped stucco exteriors, and bombed-out remains of structures that were everywhere, gave vivid backdrop to her chronicles. These evening walks would terminate at the wood framed house she shared with her mother and aunt. They would socialize over tea, Mia translated when there were questions asked. Afterwards, she would take Jack to her room, just a wood frame bed behind a flimsy curtain.

Once Alpha Company pulled out of Vihn Hoa, he spent over a month fighting in other regions of the Mekong Delta. At the first opportunity, he returned on his own to Vihn Hoa. He spent his week of leave there with Mia before being sent off to another mission. That was the night he made the biggest decision in his life. He told her he wanted to bring her back to the United States. She acted overjoyed. But in her eyes he could tell she did not believe it. A week later, destiny in the shape of a piece of shrapnel to his knee from a mortar round, expedited his return home. In the hospital at Fort Ord, his love for Mia was being tested in the form of an attractive nurse who had been giving Jack more attention than the others in the ward. A guy in the bed next to him, who had lost an eye in a grenade explosion, summed it up well. "That Vietnamese pussy was great, but I can't wait to get back to Iowa. There's nothing like a virgin farmer's daughter in a hayloft. In 'Nam, I doubt there's even a ten year old virgin left.

Skye finally spoke. "I laid awake all night after you told me that you lost all of the honeymoon money thinking, how could anyone in their right mind do something like that? Then it occurs to me," she turned and looked at him for the first time since leaving Winnemucca. "There are definite signs that you aren't playing on a level field of operation."

I'm not *operating on a level playing field*," he corrected. And what are these signs?"

"There's plenty of them. Such as, you blowup at the slightest things, you drink too much, fight with everyone, and now I find out you have a gambling problem. In other words, I don't think that the extent of things that happened to you in Vietnam were not limited to physical injuries. As soon as we get back home, I want you to go to a doctor that specializes in problems like yours."

"I'm seeing a doctor," he replied.

"That's for your knee, dear. You should see a doctor for your other damaged body part…"

"Being?"

"God, do I have to spell it out.Your brain. Your friggen brain."

"What? What are you saying? I'm not crazy." He knew well that he was crazy as a loon, but felt certain that if you admitted it, you were indeed crazy - better to hang out in the safe place of denial.

"If you don't see a shrink, it's over. You understand?"

Jack felt assaulted at her words. The truth was that Before meeting Skye, every girl he dated eventually fled fearing that he might pull the pin on that mental hand grenade, and blow everyone up for a hundred feet around. If they were in a restaurant, and someone's baby was crying he would stare that couple angrily. He would go over and tip over their fucking table with all food and drinks dumping to the floor, and exclaim to them to *keep their retarded baby, offspring to retarded parents, at home at night. They should do* something about their stupid ass kid ruining all ambiance at dinnertime in the restaurant. Meanwhile, if anything amazed him, it was that Skye had held on for so long. Still, he protested. "Gad, we just got married." For a while, there was only the purr of the powerful Pontiac engine that he had tuned with new plugs and points for the now aborted honeymoon trip to Colorado."I didn't used to be this way," he finally stammered, "Not before I went to 'Nam." The sun began to drop toward the horizon, its light peeking through the top of the windshield. Jack pulled down the visor.

"That's exactly what I'm saying," she exclaimed. I've lived with you for over a year. I know you're a good man. That was a terrible experience for you over there in Southeast Asia. But you're going to have to get your act together. I mean it. I'm not going to put up with this shit! I don't pretend to know the extent of your problem. Maybe it's just that your attitude needs major alignment. Since you understand cars so much, maybe it's like a steering problem. You don't just keep fighting the steering wheel that pulls so bad that you can't even go in a straight line. You take it into a shop that has a machine that does realignment. So it is with your mis-aligned attitude. You go to a mechanic who specializes in that area to have it adjusted."

Skye's use of metaphor to diagnose him was disarming. His mental GTO was all over the road. She had his *MO*. Disregarding the pain it caused, Jack squeezed both hands on the steering wheel. Now that Skye mentioned it, there did seem to be a little pull to the left. He pressed his foot down hard on the gas. Quickly coming up behind a slow moving pickup truck, he looked to ensure the way was clear, and swerved into the opposite lane to pass. As soon as he came alongside, the truck speeded up. In the distance, another car sped towards him. As Jack increased his speed, so did the pickup truck. The oncoming car flashed its headlights several times, and moved to the shoulder, still coming fast. Skye screamed. The other driver continued racing him, but Jack finally edged ahead of him. Cranking his steering wheel hard, he cut back into the westbound lane. The car coming head-on flew past in a plume of dirt and gravel, its horn wailing. Glaring in the rear view mirror, Jack fixed his eyes on the driver of the truck. "That son-of-a-bitch did that on purpose," he cried, switching his foot from the accelerator to the brake pedal. In seconds, smoke began to billow from the rear tires of the pickup truck.

"What are you doing? What are you doing!" Skye cried. Working his brake and gas pedal just enough to prevent getting rear-ended, he managed to cause the other driver to have to keep hitting his brakes, each time skidding. When the truck rapidly cut off Jack, he swerved just ahead of him, blocking his way. Finally, he jammed his foot all of the way down on the brake, forcing the truck into a right angle slide.

Skye and the tires of the truck screamed in near harmony.

Except for the desert wind whistling through a poorly sealed wing-glass, all became silent. Jack reached to the space under his seat and pulled out a length of chain. "That's why I keep this handy," he muttered."For such emergencies. He opened his door and stepped out of the car.

"We're in the middle of the Goddamned road! What are you doing?" she cried.

He wound one end of the chain several times around his fist and turned to face the enemy. Heat from the asphalt, at the spot where he held his ground, rose through the thin soles of his worn penny loafers.

Both doors of the truck flung open at once. "You nearly got my wife and I killed with that stupid stunt," Jack blurted at the man who stepped to the pavement on the driver's side of the pickup truck. The passenger, a large, muscular man strode towards him, forward pointed shoulders leading the way. Stopping just out of chain length, Jack looked one way down the empty stretch of road, and the other. Nothing stood up all of the way to either horizon, except cactus and sage brush.

"So, what are you going to do, call the cops?" the man said.

Jack unwound a revolution of chain from around his hand to give it more length. "No, but I'm going to wrap this chain around your neck if you don't get out of my way. It's that motherfucker behind you that I've got a problem with." He lifted the length of tow chain from his side for all to see.

The driver stopped alongside his partner. He was holding a tire iron in one hand. *Great!* Jack thought. *Now I've picked myself a fight.* Glancing before himself to the pavement, he was relieved to see something to his advantage. His shadow stretched long before him. As the men slowly advanced, Jack backed into the narrow space between his car and the embankment off the shoulder of the road. They followed like sheep. The guy with the tire iron squinted and held his free hand before himself to block the sun. Jack swung a length of the chain in warning. The man dropped his hand, still advancing alongside his friend. Jack swung hard this time, wrapping a length of the chain around the man's wrist. It knocked the metal rod out of his hand. He cried out in pain. Doubling over, he grasped his wrist, his face contorted. His friend raised a hand to shield the sun from his eyes. Jack swung the chain at him. It whistled close enough to his head to give him a good scare. The man raised both hands like someone being held at gun-point and backed several steps."Come on Dennis," the driver called.I'm hurt."

The man stepped backwards all the way to the truck, jumped into his seat and slammed the door. His friend quickly followed. Jack let the chain go limp. He stood and watched as the truck engine revved, and lurched forward, tires chirping in loud report. It swerved around his car kicking up dirt and gravel from the shoulder of the road, with the driver's arm hanging out the open window, middle finger extended skyward.

Jack bent and picked up the tire iron, throwing it in the direction of the departing truck. "Hey, you forget this!" He yelled. It fell short of the tailgate, bouncing from the asphalt to the opposite shoulder of the road. Hope they don't have a flat tire out here in the middle of nowhere with no tire iron," he muttered, grinning to himself as he returned to his car. After settling back into the driver's seat and closing his door, he stashed his chain. He looked to Skye. Her face was red, eyes tear swollen. She turned away. He looked to see the truck speeding off down the empty stretch of highway. If it were not for Skye, he would chase the son-of-a-bitch. He would chase him all the way across the desert, if decided. And when he caught up with him, he would drag him out of his shiny red pickup truck and bash his fucking head into the pavement. But Skye didn't understand the injustice in the world, and how he needed to to deal with the incredible injustice on planet Earth.It was fucking unforgivable. Did she even understand? Nobody, at least very few people understood. He stomped on the gas pedal of his still running car. Tires squealed. After getting up to a little over a hundred, he let off to a comfortable ninety-five. Skye sat square, fingers rigidly interlaced on her lap, eyes fixed on the road ahead that rolled monotonously beneath the speeding Pontiac. Jack sighed. He had been through more pleasant mortar attacks than this encounter with what some people refer to as a *honeymoon*.

It took awhile, but Skye eventually turned to look at him. Her eyes were now dry, the redness gone. "I have to admit, you handled those two pretty well," she made a conciliatory smile.

"Give some credit to the sun. I had advantage of a Sniper's Sun. I just had to lure those guys in the right position to take advantage of it."

"A Sniper's Sun?"

"Yeah. It means the enemy has the sun behind him. If you're the one with the sun directly before you, it's a duck-shoot. You can't see them, but they can see you. We're talking strategic advantage. The sun in favor of the sniper, and you are blinded. How about that?"

"I guess there are *some* advantages related to the perilous open road to having experience in combat," she shook her head.

3

For the love of Christ

Jack stopped just inside the glass door to the hospital lobby. Not before surveying the scene before him a minute did he began his walk through the crowd of those with missing limbs, in wheelchairs, hooked up to respirators or guys just standing around with that thousand yard stare, compliments of too many months in the *bush* - I would actually kill myself before admitting to my girlfriend, out loud that I love her. Expressing yourself outwardly, placing yourself in the crosshairs, is tantamount to taking a bullet in the chest. Sweat formed on the back of his neck. Who am I, Jack thought, to come here and take up the time of the medical staff when there are so many who are in greater need of help than myself? As he crossed the large room, lifting each foot became more difficult with every step, like trudging across a flooded rice paddy knee high in thick mud. When he finally reached the elevator bank, he shoved the button hard. You don't want to stay in one place, exposed in the open too long. It takes only seconds for them to get a fix on you in the AK barrel target mount. Come on, come, he thought, banging the elevator button several more times with the ball of his palm. It startled Jack when the double doors parted before him, revealing a space not unlike the all aluminum interior of a UH-1. He stepped aside so that those in greater need than himself could board. Once inside, the doors closed and they were moving. Dread rose. When the choppers were descending into a hot LZ, bullets zinging wildly everywhere, you knew what it meant to be a tin-duck in a shooting gallery. Not until you could get both feet onto solid ground would you be able to fend for yourself. Seconds later, when the doors opened, Jack rushed out into the middle of the hall. His alarm subsided with the open space. Gazing uncertainly around at the white walls and acoustic ceiling, his sight settled on a sign giving directions to doctors offices and the Mental Health Clinic. *You're okay, you're okay now,* he thought to himself at the possibility of need for a psycho-vac. At the admissions counter, they gave him the zip-up and locked nylon pouch with his sacred medical records enclosed.

He could not see his own medical records, but anyone with a name badge, and a key for the pouch could. He made his way to the clinic here on the sixth floor, where he surrendered the pouch to another clerk. Several excruciating hours after his appointment time, Jack was finally directed to the doctor's office. "Have a seat," the man in a white smock said without looking up. Taking a cheap government chair with vinyl padding at the front of the gray metal desk, Jack watched as the doctor concentrated on a folder in his lap. He tried to get comfortable in the chair. Looking around, he noticed the only thing that even came close to an attempt to decorate the drab windowless room, on the corner of the desk nearest Jack sat a brass statuette of an infantryman. From his stance, the soldier was no doubt stalking the enemy. He held an M-16 in the readied. The sculptor had paid considerable attention to detail right down to the nylon canteen strap, and a string of hand grenades on the utility belt.Jack felt tempted to reach over and turn the little soldier around to see if the detail was as true on the other side. The doctor must be a 'Nam vet, Jack thought. Who else would have on display a statuette of a sweaty grunt busting his ass on search and destroy? Jack felt relieved that he didn't have to expose his best kept secrets to a friggen noncombatant.

"It says here that you have *two* service-connected injuries, in addition to your compliant that brings you here. Or is your problem that brings you here subsequent to other issues in some way?" The doctor stared with the eyes of a man who had not the time or patience for small talk. Jack wondered, what the hell was this guy bitching and moaning about? He considered that he was pushing his luck by adding still another complaint to the existing ones in his medical folder. He had given *sleeping problems* as the reason to make an appointment with the VA psychiatrist. Yes, Skye was right. He was crazy, kill yourself, kill someone else crazy, but that was his best kept secret. You even use the word *kill* when showing up on time for a doctor's appointment. They'll put you in a straight-jacket and ferry you off to the sixth floor of the VA hospital for *observation*, as they call it. This guy a possible danger to the peace loving public. Vietnam vets were a huge threat possibly worse then the atomic bomb. They had been unleashed from that unpopular war, trained baby killers, village burners – you name it. They had in concealment, pistols, knives, semiautomatic rifle with tons of ammo and considered everyone in their neighborhood, and around town the enemy. They were so twisted from their Tour in 'Nam that everyone was considered enemy. So, just give me some pills for my mental condition, I'll wash those down with beer, smoke a joint and try to sleep for several hours. The problem existed, Jack felt himself choking up even at the hint of self-disclosure. "I feel, you know, anxious - most of the time." Those very nerves where now instrumental in constricting his throat to the extent he could not begin to tell this official looking guy in a white smock about the nightmares, the uncontrollable anger, his jumping at every shadow. Meanwhile, insult to injury, nobody liked him - even his own parents. He was a possible serial killer because of his deployment to 'Nam. He wiped clammy hands on his lap. If the way the doctor raised his eyebrows was any indication, Jack had apparently communicated a mouthful, without need for words.

"Just take a deep breath, relax."

He took the prescribed deep breath. A simple feat. Relaxing, however, was something he did not know how to achieve. "I don't know what's wrong with me," Jack stammered.

The doctor's gaze returned to the folder. Is the Darvon we've been giving you helping your knee and back?"

Jack nodded slightly, thinking, sure, if taken in conjunction with beer and pot. Darvon was one of those high dose, aspirin pretend knock-offs. What you did was take the capsules apart, three or four of them. There were

37

tiny pellets inside. Those were the drug. You separated the pellets from the powder, which was plain aspirin, and gulped them down with a can of beer. Three or four of them with a beer, and a joint to top it off, did the job well.You didn't have to be a fucking Vietnam vet. You could drift off, mental and pain-free on the couch, and escaped the world and all of its issues.

"When is your next doctor appointment?"

"I don't have one. I mean I had one but missed, er, forgot about it." His knee began to ache at the suggestion of another visit with the guy who repeatedly poked his finger on the injured knee until Jack cried in pain, the motherfucker pumping his leg like someone jacking up a car to change a flat, ordering more lab work, more X-rays, finally admitting in so many words there was nothing that could be done for him with the exception of another bottle of Darvon for the pain. Additionally were the visits for his back injury. That bundle of nerves at the pit of his stomach ratcheted until he only saw red. What grip Jack had been able to maintain until now began to loosen. He wiped the blur of moisture from his eyes with a hand.

His psychological rescue person looked on calmly, as if this were all normal. Jack trembled and took another deep breath. This is great, he thought. You get wounded in battle, you come home shell-shocked and the government gives you free medical. They even pay for my gas at fifteen cents a gallon, coming all the way to 'Frisco from home. I'm absolutely, profoundly delighted for this VIP treatment.

Leaning forward, the doctor closed the manila folder and set it down on the desktop. He picked up a pen scribbling something on a pad. "I'm going to prescribe something for those nerves of yours. No alcohol with this stuff. Take one in the morning and one at night." Tearing the prescription slip from the pad, he handed it across the desk."I'm scheduling you to come see me again in thirty days."

Jack nodded. *Not in your life,* he rather thought. *Why would anyone in their right mind want to come back in here and put up with this abuse?* His contentions were validated when he dropped by the hospital pharmacy to pick up his prescription, and ended up waiting two hours. Two hours of my life is important to me. If I held up one of the medical staff for two fucking hours for some problem or another, they would without doubt call in the National Guard. Arrest and detain this guy - he's taking up two hours of unauthorized time and space. Examining the little cylinder container half full of pills while crossing the parking lot to his car, he read the label, *Diazepam*. He had heard this word before when he was in the hospital at Fort Ord. In a second remembering, he exclaimed to himself, "Valium!" The only way Jack had been able to get valium in the past was *on the street* in Haight Ashbury, and that at a premium. When he got into the car, before starting it, he took two of the tiny blue pills thinking, maybe I was a little bit too hasty in my decision not to revisit the hospital. As he crossed the Oakland Bay Bridge in the company of what seemed a million other cars, Jack began thinking about his slow-motion walk across the hospital lobby, like a scene in a Hollywood movie where something was very troubling on his mind. Something was going to happen next, and the death drums beat. Images of the faces of those men stuck in his mind. These were his comrades - his badly wounded comrades. One of the older veterans he saw there might have been Captain Maxwell - except that the captain did not make it back alive. The company had held up at a jungle clearing, where the captain unfolded his map, at his side three lieutenants and four radiomen with antennas spiraling for reception. After several minutes of conference, the captain stabbed with his forefinger at a place on the map, smiling most likely at the fact that the company had neared the chopper pickup zone, indicating the conclusion of a week long operation, the captain's first mission in 'Nam. He had grabbed the receiver from the company RTO, pushed the squelch and opened his mouth to speak. The crack of a single small arms round split the air. Instead of speaking, the captain gasped. He crumbled to the ground. The sniper's bullet had nailed him right between the eyes.

Something loomed large before Jack. Two red lights blinked, shining brightly. A panel truck stopped just before him. Jack jammed his foot into the brake pedal, screeching to a halt just short of a collision. He glanced to see dozens of cars stopped on both sides of him. Up ahead, a marquee with lighted red letters announced, *toll plaza*. Jack reached into a front blue-gene pocket for change. Traveling with the North Bay to his left, he could see the

Golden Gate Bridge in the distance. Just beyond that was the VA hospital on a cliff overlooking the mouth of San Francisco Bay. Jack weaved his way through the heavy commuter traffic, not so much in a hurry as trying to put distance between himself and that cold cement and poorly staffed edifice to marginal care for wounded veterans. But the imagines of those men in the lobby would not go away. One of them in a wheelchair, a guy about his age in the early twenties with both legs missing, another guy with an arm missing, or perhaps a bullet scare on the scalp, or cheek made Jack remember Bogart. He got the nickname from hogging the joint to himself, instead of passing it around to the others in the group as pot smoking protocol dictated. They were on a mission, just outside the town of Can Tho. Bogart had been assigned point position by the squad leader. From the size of the explosion, Bogart had stepped on what must have been a pirated 105 Howitzer round buried beneath the trail. Overlooking that tripwire that crossed the trail cost him both of his legs. Jack had been walking flank-point in the bush about ten yards to the side of Bogart. The ground had given way and Jack dropped into the opening. It was a punji pit. Fortunately, he landed on his feet in such a manner to push the pointed bamboo stakes safely aside. His head had just cleared the brim of the, at least six foot deep hole at the moment of the explosion. The ground shook and shrapnel zinged overhead. In the cloud of dust outside of his hole, someone screamed, "Medic!"

A horn had blared. Jack glanced to his right to see a car just inches from sideswiping him. Glancing back to road ahead, he noticed that he was straddling the white line. He jerked his steering wheel hard, returning to the middle of his own lane. For the time being, Jack forced himself to pay more attention to the road. Speeding to over a hundred when the traffic cleared, it wasn't long before he was crossing the Yolo Causeway, the section of I-80 that spanned square miles of sugar-beet fields. Glancing to his rearview mirror, he watched as a reddish blob remnants of the sun, settled into the haze of the now distant San Francisco Bay Area. He passed through Sacramento and in short time, on into the Sierra Foothills. Combined with the early shadow of nightfall, a rising moon made the mountain range before him a panoramic silhouette of crags and peaks. Jack eased his grip on the steering wheel he had been holding with both hands. Not only had the traffic dropped off considerably, but he felt very much in his element at night. You were secluded from the view of others at night. Does anyone realize? No one wants to be in full view in daylight or otherwise. You could get fucking shot in that clear view. And Jack enjoyed being on the move. You were not sitting there in plain sight where anyone could plug you with a bullet in the chamber. Am I freggin paranoid, Jack wondered. No I'm not. The world is a very dangerous place, and everyone is out to get me. In response to the gradual incline into the hills, he proportionately increased the pressure of his foot on the gas pedal. The large Pontiac engine responded commendably. A soft prickling sensation from the valerian root became evident, crawling up the back of his head. Jack grinned. He relaxed into the effect of the chemicals that now swept through his war-damaged body and mind, soothing frayed nerve endings, automatically readjusting his chronically mis-aligned attitude, as Skye referred to his stressed-out brain.

* * *

"You told him everything," didn't you?" Skye probed. She had a can of beer while reclined on the couch next to him.

"I couldn't possibly tell him *everything* in just one visit," Jack replied. "It would take for fucking forever for me to tell him *everything.*"

"Well, what did you tell him?"

"If you get me a cool one, I'll tell you everything – uncensored." Jack untied his shoes. He kicked them off from where he sat on the couch, while Skye fetched him a beer. Just as she returned, he remembered the doctor's warning not to drink with the valium. He had taken that double dose less than two hours ago. Skye put the can down on the coffee table before him. She had opened it for him and everything. Jack certainly didn't want to seem ungracious. Besides, he had developed a mighty big thirst after such an arduous day - not a thirst you could placate with mere water. At the other end of the couch, Skye took a long pull from her beer. Jack lifted his can from the table, holding it a second until the delicious prospects of a cool, satisfying drink obliterated all vestiges of the doctor's warning. He guzzled about half the can down.

"Well?"

It was six, and Huntly and Brinkly were coming on. Jack pushed the remote power on. "Uh, I told him about my trouble with sleep. The nightmares every night."

"And?"

"That's about it."

"That's it?" she retorted. "Did you tell him about your crazy driving, about your angry outbursts about your punching out people in the face?"

"Hey, he's the guy with the silk tie and university degree. It's not for me to tell him. If he wants to know about my mental problems, all he has to do is ask."

Skye was gnawing her way through the fuzzy coating for which the valium had mellowed him. "It was a short session. I'll tell him more later."

"When's your next appointment?"

In a month." Jack guzzled down the rest of his beer.

"In a month! Jack, you have to let the VA know how bad your problems are. Don't you think this isn't hard on me, having to be your baby sitter?"

Jack laughed to think. How can I reply to that? he thought. Looking across the small living room, he noticed with surprise his medals framed and hanging on the wall. "What's this?" he exclaimed, staring at the medals in frame on the wall.

Well, you've had them in a shoe box in the closet since I've known you. I took them to the frame shop in town last week, to give them a better home. I thought I'd surprise you."

"I can not tell you how much I appreciate your thoughtfulness. Now take them down," Jack trembled. Frayed nerves were hanging down and throwing off sparks like hurricane tossed power lines. The calming effects of the valium had all but vanished.

"Those are medals you won in the war, for heroism. I thought you would feel proud to have them on display."

"Profoundly." He bolted from the couch. Crossing the room in two long strides, he removed the stately looking framework from the wall.

"What are you doing?"

Holding the frame in both hands, he gazed at his nine medals, seeing them for the first time in neat rows, upon velvet, encased in glass. He looked at the Soldier's Medal. A violent splashing of water, and cries for help preceded a last, desperate sounding gasp for air. Reeves sank beneath the muddy canal surface. The only thing left at that spot in water was his steel helmet floating upside-down. Leaping into the canal from the shore-side, Jack instantly reached bottom. Finding Reeves after feeling around blindly for only seconds, he unlatched Reeves utility belt that weighed heavy with hand grenades. Finally jerking the two strings of M-60 rounds, a machine-gun assistant, over the private's head, Jack kicked hard against the canal floor, bringing Reeves to the surface and safely to shore. Only several weeks later, the stupid ass went and got himself killed in an ambush. Jack felt lightheaded, and his heart was racing from the rush of rouge thoughts. He glanced to notice Skye staring at him. "These are personal," he tried to convey. But there were no words possible. "I don't want just anyone who walks into the house to see them. If I start telling anyone who inquires the story behind one medal or another, I'll go off the rails. I'll go over the fucking cliff."

"You know, you're crazy as it gets, but I do see what you're saying. Can we hang them in the bedroom?"

"The bedroom," he thought for a moment. "Okay."

Skye rose from the couch. She stepped over to Jack, gently taking the frame away from him. He followed her through the bedroom door to the opposite side of the wall to where the medals had been hanging.

He turned one way, and the other. "Here's a good place," she indicated the wall just behind him. She was so graceful, so accommodating. He couldn't believe his good fortune having her for a wife. I'm not worthy, he thought to himself. He turned to look on with her at the inexpensively framed print of Wyeth's Christina's World. This was the only decoration Skye had brought with her when she moved in with him. "Take that down for me, and I'll make use of the same nail."

Jack removed the picture.

"In fact, hang that on the nail in the living room. We'll just switch places."

When he returned from hanging Christina's World in the living room, Skye was carefully straightening the frame of medals.

"How's that?" she stepped back.

"Good," he nodded. But it occurred to him that he would be able to see the medals from his place in bed at night. It was bad enough to lay awake into the wee hours, listening to small noises, staring at vague shadows, tossing and turning, trying not to think, because thinking involved remembering, and remembering filled those noises and shadows with extremely vivid life so they were not so small and vague anymore. "Oh, I don't know," he replied. Jack looked around himself. Maybe in the bathroom. There's an entire wall without anything on it."

"In the bathroom! Are you joking?"

Jack turned to go back to the living room. This whole thing with hanging his medals, that he didn't want anyone else to see, because 'Nam vets were baby killers and village burners, and he didn't want to brag about openly. Did anyone know, or even care that all of his larger awarded medals were for saving some other soldier's life? Who cared anyway? He didn't want the medals on display, and he didn't have to explain to anyone that he might have been a very honorable guy in service to his country, o save his comrades, not to kill the enemy unless they came after him first. He stumbled, reaching with a hand to grab the door jamb.

"You alright?" Skye gasped.

"Yeah, it's just the valium, I think…"

"Valium! The VA gave you valium?"

"Yeah. A whole bottle full."

"Praise the Lord! Pass 'em around."

4

Day of the man named Bullit

Kenny McDermott had liked to brag he was raised on an ammo dump. He said this because his youth was spent moving from one army depot to another, a result of his father being a Lifer with the Army Materiel Command. He tried a brief stint in the Army himself, didn't like the discipline, and now worked as a department store manager over the clothing section her at The White Store, owned by a millionaire bunch in Hollywood. By complete chance, small world that it is, Jack knew the daughter of the CEO there in Hollywood, his old home. The daughter and Jack had been fellow Hippies in Haight Ashbury, her zonked out on heroin, him on pot and LSD. Meanwhile, the manager insisted to his employees that he desired to be referred to affectionately by his self-proclaimed nickname *Bullet McDermott*. Aloft beyond mere mention, during breaks in the employee lunchroom, he rarely failed to take advantage of the captive audience, blabbering on about himself.In days past, those Commie soldiers would be in guard towers, machine-gun barrels keeping aim on us GIs when we walked along the west side of the Wall, he boasted. After drinking all night, we'd go over there and stand in the street right in front of them and swear loudly and flip them off. They wouldn't dare try anything, *Bullet* told his story between bites of a generously stuffed sandwich that kept falling apart from large portions of meat and BBQ sauce. In addition to an apparent strong desire for respect, Jack wondered if these tales of uniform-service bravado were not part of some larger strategy to get into the pants of Sally, the attractive teenage girl for whom McDermott could not tear his eyes from as he blabbed. He also wondered whether McDermott would be so boisterous, in the presence of Jack, about his obscene finger gesturing days in Berlin, if he knew this most quiet of his employees was a combat veteran. This was something Jack had never mentioned to anyone in his four months employment there, to anyone other than Max. The older man was a salesman in men's clothing, a likable person to whom Jack once confided the source of his limp for a blown-out knee and back injury. Max must have noticed Jack squirming in his seat at the other end of the Formica table, as McDermott went on and on about his soldier days in Germany. Recently, Max had read an article in a magazine about the real-world dangers of being an American soldier in peacetime Germany, Max remarked one day. The article reported that the greatest number of casualties incurred by our troops in Germany were not from the war-games, or incidents along the border with Russia, but rather from the danger of tipping over coke machines. It seems that our fearless soldiers over there have a reputation for beating on the machines at the US bases, and rocking them back and forth to try and get sodas when the machines broke down and kept their deposited coins. The article said that some of our soldiers, fighting for their unrequited quest for soda, periodically found themselves sandwiched between the sidewalk and an eight-hundred pound machine that had fallen on them after being rocked back and forth. "There has been several guys killed and a dozen or more injured from this above and beyond call-of-duty against the quarter thieving coke machines in Germany," Max told.

Bullet McDermott didn't like that insult. He transferred Max from floor sales to the detested duty of stock inventory. The insufferable incompetent, this old man.

One day, as his store security job required, Jack spied from behind several pieces of miniature furniture in the baby department, as a young lady stuffing silk underpants into her bra. She looked around casually, pulled her blouse neat and walked off. In minutes later, she was in the parking lot climbing into her car, home-free.

Why didn't you go after her?" came a voice behind.

Jack spun around.

I've been watching you." McDermott hovered, arms folded against his new, employee discounted polyester shirt. "You let that shoplifter get away. Friend of yours? You two got some kind of deal worked out?"

"We went to high school together. I can't bust someone who was a high school friend."

Bullet instructed, "Follow me to my office. I'm going to write you up. This is serious."

"One man's serious business is another man's dog and pony show," Jack retorted. He turned, walking towards the front of the store, knowing his days were numbered with this insult-to-injury of a job.

"What do mean by that remark?" You don't have any choice. I'm going to my office right now, and you're coming with me."

Jack stopped, turning around. Bullet pointed in the direction of his office."If you aren't right behind me, I'll be signing your last check in your absence."

"Do what you gotta goddamned do," Jack muttered.

"What! What did you say?"

"What I said was short for *fuck you!*" his calm diminishing. He stepped backwards as he spoke.

The big guy with his bad breath became red-faced. He strode forward, quickly making up the distance between them. "Why you little..." He clinched his hand at his side into a fist.

"Don't even think about it," Jack warned. He had walked backwards all of the way from the baby furniture to the hardware section. Glancing for something to even the odds with the big guy, his gaze went a row of chrome curtain rods on a display rack next to him. Before the bastard can even blink twice, I will have already smashed his head like it was a ripe cantaloupe, he thought, glancing back and forth between one of the curtain rods and his boss. They weren't lethal, but they had a lot of leverage. So there was no misunderstanding, he hovered his left hand, the closest to the display rack, like a gunslinger facing a duel.

Apparently unfazed by the obvious, like some moron who had just finished heckling a communist guard who sat behind a swivel-mounted machine-gun on lookout tower, fully loaded and ready to fire, McDermott exclaimed, "Give it your best shot!"

Jack wondered how someone with the nickname of Bullet, and *raised on an ammo dump*, could be so disconnected from the simple fact that the guy with the chrome curtain rod as weapon, commanded overwhelming advantage against the guy without a curtain rod in hand? Did he even understand that once you have the enemy locked in your sights, how simple it was just to pull the trigger? *But what else would you expect from a guy who went around depicting himself as an American hero for having once stood at the brink of that place where the entire planet was divided, entered the realm of no-mans-land, pulled his shoulders back making his best ugly face at an East German guard, drunkenly slurred a few swear words, obscenely gestured, then staggered back to his warm and safe quarters?* Jack thought, I would have squeezed the trigger if I had been that tower guard. I would have aimed right for his crotch. A bullet in the crotch for Bullet Van Hatten. No need to kill someone that dumb. Guest put him out of commission genealogy-wise, so he can't perpetuate the life of anymore retarded morons like himself.

Jack turned, walking down the aisle he had patrolled like a good soldier, in quest of shoplifters, countless times. In a world where the enemy could not so easily be identified as the guy in the black PJs carrying an AK-47, he at least knew whose side he was on when it came to choosing between the likes of Bullet McDermott and the girl stuffing under-panties in her bra. On his way out, he detoured to the candy section, grabbed a handful of his favorite chocolate bars and stuffed them into the front pockets of his jeans. As he stepped outside into the bright sunlight, despite the warmth of the day, the realization gripped him that his next paycheck would be his last - and jobs were so hard to find during this great American recession under the helm of Richard Nixon, who swore he was going to create more jobs as time permitted, and by way, he was *no crook*. Just the same, Jack had not felt this good since he quit his previous job. Before getting into the car, he took the candy bars from his pockets and tossed them to the passenger seat. He decided to stop over at his folk's house. Jack hadn't visited them in several weeks. Besides, it was still early, and Skye wouldn't be home from the restaurant until after five. As he rounded the last curve of the steep drive, the house became visible at the top of the pine tree covered hill. He parked alongside their station wagon. Granite outcroppings made a shear cliff about four feet high or more, bordering the sidewalk on one side leading to the house. Jack had strode halfway to the house when he froze to see the tip of a barefoot showing where the rock wall recessed. The absence of his M-16 in hand struck him as he steeled himself.Before him, the sight of the house where he had grown-up, quickly brought things back into perspective. Of course, I'm not over *there*. It's just the passage where the enemy could easily ambush him from overhead. His heart that had pounded all the way to his temples, returned to a regular beat. Looking straight ahead as if he did not notice, Jack resumed walking, prepared for whatever his little sister had in store for him. When she growled, leaping at him, he quickly turned, catching her by the waist. He pulled her to his side, continuing towards the house. Leslie hoisted her legs around his waist.

"Did I scare you?" she asked gleefully.

"Did you scare me? When I heard the growl, I started to say my last prayer. But I was so frightened I forgot whether I was religious or not. So, to what do I owe such a dramatic greeting?"

"Oh, I'm a cat lady. I transformed from your little sister a result of sun spots. How dare you, a mere human attempt to enter my lair without presenting me with gifts of diamonds and rubies?"

"You cat ladies are all the same," he feigned tones of despair. If could satiate your desire for precious jewels in place with mere chocolate, could I pull that off?"

"Did you say you have chocolate?" she exclaimed. "Chocolate can magically transform me back to your little sister!"

"Pheew. What a lucky break," Jack pretended to wipe sweat from his forehead."Go look in my car on the passenger seat. I've got some Hershey Bars. You can have two of them. Leave the two for me in case I get the mean munchies tonight after toking up."Leslie didn't know what the hell he was talking about when said *toking up*, and it didn't matter. Someday, when she was older, he would explain it all to her. Leslie squirmed to free herself from her brother's hold. He let her down softly. Continuing to the house, he opened the front door, suddenly finding himself surrounded by three screeching Chihuahuas. Shooing them with a foot he blurted, Get out of my way before I make canine chop-suey out of the bunch of you beneath my shoe heels."

"Is that you Jack?" he heard his father call. Stepping inside the door to the living room, he quickly pushed the door shut so the dogs couldn't follow. "I'm being attacked by a pack of bloodthirsty, mutant church mice that faintly resemble dogs," he called back to his father.

"Don't talk about my babies like that," his mother said from the dining room.

As Jack crossed the living room, he could not help but take note of the before and after of himself displayed on the fireplace mantle, despite the number of times that he had seen the pictures. To the left was a wood framed photo of him as a teenager. This was his senior year high school photo. He could not remember a smile of that quality gracing his face since returning from 'Nam. To the right, at the other end of the mantle, was a metal framed photo of him in dress uniform. This stiff upper-lip mug shot taken right after his return home was early preamble of his vanishing smile. Glancing from one picture to the next, with only two years separating them, he found it difficult to distinguish himself as the same person. Jack went on to the dining room where his parents were sitting across from each other with a half a meat loaf on a serving plate in the middle of the table. "Dining early tonight, huh," he remarked.

"I cooked the meat loaf early, planning to have it done in plenty time for our usual dinner time, but when you-know-who smelled it, he just couldn't wait." Jack's mother acted frustrated over such lack of self-control, but knew she loved the praise over her cooking.

"Sit down here and join us," his father directed to the chair between them. "Get the boy a plate, he looks famished."

His mother started to rise from her seat. "Sit down mom," he raised a hand towards her. "I'm not hungry. I'm still full from my lunch at work."

"Got you working on Sunday?" his father shook his head somberly.

"I'm not the only one. Skye had to work today too."

"What's the matter Jack?" his mother asked. "You look like something's bothering you."

She could read him like a pocket edition of pulp fiction. The sound of the front door opening distracted them. Leslie had entered from her outdoor escapades. Taking the lead came the three Chihuahuas. They ran straight to Jack barking and snipping at his feet under the table. "What's the matter with these miniature, retarded coyotes?" he exclaimed, pushing them away with one foot, and another until they left him alone.

"Don't kick at them. They're just saying hello to you," his father blurted.

"Now that we've got hello out of the way, I'm just saying *good-bye*, the only way they'll understand."

Leslie stepped up to her brother with two candy bars in hand. She hugged him." Thanks for the Hershey Bars," she said.

"I saw you out the window earlier. Don't go scaring your brother like that," their mother scolded. "God knows he's had a lifetime worth of scaring heaped on him from that war, without his own sister adding insult to injury. Did you clean your room?"

"Yes."

"You better not be fibbing. I'm going to come in and check."

"Okay, I'm going, Leslie pouted.Before you leave, I've got something for you. It's important," she assured Jack and headed towards her bedroom.

"How's that gas-guzzling hot rod of yours?" Jack's father asked. He leaned back in his chair, swirled the cubes in his glass of ice tea.

"Good. How's your gas-guzzling station wagon?" Jack knew his father was just ribbing him, but still felt put-off by the question.

"I can tell something's wrong son. What is it?Are there people out there trying to bully you around because you're a gentleman above and beyond, and an easy target for those who treat others poorly for their personal gain?" his mom persisted. She looked to her husband. "Jack is an American war hero and doesn't deserve being bullied." Her motherly insight in regard to her son's circumstances, in Jack's opinion more precise than Freudian psychotherapy in progress and ultraviolet brain scanning science combined.

"Got canned at work," he mumbled.

"You got canned, again!" his father exclaimed. "You're the only person I've ever known who makes an occupation out of getting fired."

"Leave him alone Chas. He just lost his job and he's upset. You sure you don't want something to eat Jack?"

"Ah, I'm just thirsty. I'll get myself something out of the fridge." Jack got up got up and went into the kitchen. "A gallon of beer would do the trick," he muttered to himself. "I'll just start with a can." He returned to the table with a beer.

"So, how many jobs is this in a row. Six, seven?" his father continued.

"Just four," he said, pulling the pop-top from the can with a flair.

"Four hell! Let's count 'em. Your job at the gas station just after you got out of the army." He ticked off a finger of one hand with the index finger of the other."That lasted all of two weeks.Next you got on at the hardware store, spent about a month there fighting with your boss before you got fired." He ticked off a second finger.

"Quit it now," his mother snapped."You're making Jack upset."

"I'm just trying to make a point," his father replied innocently. "Am I making you upset?"

Jack shrugged.

"See, he's upset," his mother always alongside him as public defender when his very integrity came under fire.

"I'm not upset," he insisted. "Both of you just, just quit this verbal ping pong match about my possibility of being upset, for Christ's sake."

"It's that Vietnam War," Jack's father proclaimed, a proud WWII vet. "What were we doing bombing to smithereens that little country? The boys coming home from there are mixed up."

"Did he even realize that 'Nam was not a country? He certainly must realize that Italy was not a country while his navel warship pounded the shores. It was a place for a shootout between Allied and Axis forces. The same with 'Nam.It happened to be the perfect spot in time and space for a shootout between America and Russia.Guzzling down the rest of his beer, Jack suddenly stood from his seat announcing, "Excuse me. I gotta go pee." He went to the bathroom, thinking while relieving himself how large the disconnect was between him and his father. Jack decided he wasn't going to visit his folks ever again, at least until after his father died. He stopped by his sister's room before leaving. Her door opened to his gentle knock, and he stepped into the small room that appeared to have a way to go before it passed inspection for cleanliness.

"Close the door," Leslie whispered.

Jack complied. "So, what's the big secret?" he whispered back.

She sat crossed-legged in the middle of her bed. The waded wrapping of one of the candy bars lay on her bed stand. Pulling an envelope from beneath a hardcover book that lay opened before her, she handed it to him. "It came last week. I've been waiting for you to come so I could give it to you."

He instantly recognized his handwriting to the addressed: Mia Phunan, 87 rue du Jardin, Vihn Hoa, South Vietnam. Stamped in block letters on the same surface was the familiar, *Return to Sender, Address Unknown.* Jack sat down on the edge of the bed, still holding the letter poised in one hand. He stared at it.

"How come the letter keeps coming back? You sure you got the address right?"

He exhaled. "I don't know why they keep coming back. But I know I've got the right address." This was the third time he had put a new stamp the same letter and sent it again. Given, Vietnam was not a shining example of postal expediency. Whether ineptness of the postal service or whatever, six months without having received a letter from her was too long. Meanwhile, with *his* letter being returned on the third try, Jack feared the worst. He reached and patted his sister on the shoulder."You done good," he commended her for following his directions to intercept any letters from Vietnam, since she picked up the mail at the box at the bottom of the hill when she got off the school bus. "The folks didn't see it?"

"Nope."

"You know how important it is not to mention this to anyone," he purveyed. "If it ever got back to Skye that I'm writing an old girlfriend, it could be my funeral. Remember our saying?"

"Yep. *Loose lips aren't hip.*" Leslie looked at him confused. I don't get it all. You began living with Skye, and knew you were getting married to her, and now that you're married to her, you continue to keep in touch with Mia – romantically?"

Leslie knocked Jack off-guard with her hefty question. She was no naiveté. "It's not a simple equation," he tried to come across philosophically. Actually, he wasn't confused about what he was doing.He felt certain about one thing.He loved Mia more than he did Skye, and could not let go of her in his heart and mind. "Mia is a kind of a *backup* relationship. What if things don't work out between Skye and myself? I want a relationship on *reserve*, per-se. And that's why Mia remains in the picture." Jack wondered though if it actually wasn't the converse. For instance, what if circumstances had it that he couldn't bring Mia to the United States, like he had being trying to do since returning from 'Nam?Skye was his backup. "You're a commendable *cat lady*," he assured his little sister while leaving her room.

Jack drove down the hill with the sound of yipping dogs behind. Looking in the side mirror, they were so close that all he could see was three little dust trails. The thought of slamming on his brakes and suddenly going in reverse caused him to laugh. Instead though, he accelerated, leaving them in a cloud of his dust. At the bottom of the hill, he pulled over next to the small wooden shelter at the place the school bus stopped. He took the letter out of his front pocket and opened it. There was the twenty dollar bill that he kept sending her that he might as well use for beer for himself, all things considered.He had not read the letter it since the time he originally wrote it around four month ago. He unfolded it and began reading:

Dear Mia,

I hope that you are doing well. I'm okay. I know in the the previous letter I told you that the only way I knew how to get you to the United States was for me to return to Vietnam and for us to get married. But I

54

DAY OF THE MAN NAMED BULLIT

didn't have enough money. Since then, I've found out that I can bring you here on a temporary visa, and we can get married, which will of course make you a permanent resident of the USA then. I know things are getting worse there since the Americans pulled out of your province, and I'm doing everything I can, but for now I don't even have a lot of money. However, I'm saving every penny and will send you an airline ticket when I have enough. Meanwhile, I'm sending you a little money to help with things.

Anh yeu em, Jack

It bothered Jack greatly that he could not reach Mia after these last three attempts. Things were not going well with him and Skye, and he remained in holding-pattern that one day he might bring his real love to the United States.He wondered, is this what they call a double life? He carefully returned the letter to its envelope. Folding it in half, he stashed it between his seat and the console. He stepped hard on the gas pedal. Tires spun on gravel briefly, taking bite with a loud chirp as the car went from the turnout, fishtailing onto the asphalt of the frontage road. Several hundred yards later, where the road met the freeway in an unmarked crossing, Jack sped into the slow lane. A horn blared behind him. He glanced in the rear view mirror to see that he had cut off another car. Jack quickly accelerated. He looked to see the car swerve to the fast lane where it soon was traveling alongside of him. The passenger, a woman leaned way back while the driver yelled something at Jack out the open window. He couldn't make out the manÆs words, but got the message just the same. Jack thrust his arm out his window, gesturing with his middle finger in response. The man's face went red. "You motherfucker, you motherfucker! You cut me off back there!" He yelled, his words now loud and clear. The passenger looked terrified. Bringing his left knee up to the bottom of the steering wheel, Jack began steering with his leg for several seconds so he could display the middle fingers of both hands out the window. The driver of the station wagon cringed his face ogre-like. He swerved towards Jack's car, just inches from colliding and as suddenly veered back to the middle of his own lane. Hands back on his steering wheel,

Jack retaliated by swerving within inches of the late model car. The driver was quick to avoid the parry, but overcompensated. Metal screamed and sparks flared as his front left fender scraped against the concrete of the median divider. In seconds, he had regained control and was back alongside. Like a gladiator in a chariot race, he began repeatedly veering towards Jack's car as they barreled down the freeway, with him swerving out of the way just before being sideswiped each time. The girl shrieked with each near collision.

There's only one thing for me to do, Jack considered, is to get clean out of the way of harm of this madman. He shoved his foot to the floor, the eight banger Pontiac engine with its recently rebuilt Holly four-barrel carburetor responding with a roar. Glancing to his rear view mirror as the speedometer neared one hundred and twenty, he was relieved to see the station wagon slowly shrink. Certain he had gained enough distance so the lunatic couldn't catch up, he slowed to the speed limit. The man reminded Jack so much of himself, he felt certain had just encountered another Vietnam vet - with a *mis-aligned* attitude. Of all people, Jack knew better than to mess around with a 'Nam vet.

While driving down Main Street, he glanced to see the mannequins decked out in the latest miniskirts, at the department store where his parents always took him to buy his school clothes. Several shops later was the barbershop where he got his first flap-top, and in time his last haircut before he decided to let his hair do its own thing. By the time it grew shoulder length, the Army took over responsibilities as his barber. On the next block, across the street, judging from the familiar sign on the window, the shoe store was still owned by the man who had, throughout JackÆs adolescence, profited greatly from feet that outgrew shoes faster than soles could wear thin. There his parents had once purchased him a pair of cowboy boots for his twelfth birthday. He loved these high-heeled, swirl and loop engraved, two-tone, cowhide scented footwear so much that he slept in them the first several nights. He later nailed metal taps to the heels to give a little snap to his stride. Looking back, he fancied them as the footwear version of cutting your teeth, preparing him, unwittingly, for a time when he would be wearing boots to sleep every night for months, as a matter of life and death. If we are all students of life, like someone once said, then in his case, Vietnam was certainly the graduate school of wearing your boots to bed.

While driving past the fire station, Jack had been so startled by the sudden blast of a siren that he swerved across the center line. Fortunately, there were no oncoming cars. As the siren continued to scream, Jack pressed backwards hard in his seat at brilliant flashes of exploding mortars and rockets to the eerie accompaniment of the red alert sirens of Dong Tam. Where he had come to a stop at the shoulder of the opposite side of the road, he glanced to see yellow helmeted men clambering aboard a fire truck. Even after the siren had stopped, and the fire engine went on its way, Jack sat for awhile regaining his composure.

When he arrived home, he noticed another car parked in the driveway behind Skye's Volkswagen.

"You're home early," Skye remarked when he came through the front door. Slouched in the corner of the other end of the couch with a kitten in her lap was Roma. She held a joint poised in hand.

"Hello Jack," she managed through the fog of smoke. She extended her arm high towards him. "Happy Coming Home Early." She looked like she had been in the process of getting plenty happy herself.

Jack went to the window nearest the couch and closed it before taking the joint. After his latest *unscheduled* trip to the Mekong Delta, this is just what he needed. He drew from the small cigarette, and handed it to Skye. Continuing on into the kitchen, he exhaled the smoke and called, "Anyone else want a cool one?"

"Me," both of them said at once.

"I can tell you two are sisters," he laughed, returning with three beers. After handing them around, he plopped into the beanbag chair. Taking a drink, he looked to Roma, who had never visited before this time without her husband, and inquired, "Where's Monk?"

She acted like she was going to say something, but tailed off in silence. Tears formed.

"Umm, you don't mind if Roma stays with us for a few days, do you?" Skye

57

asked.

"Of course I don't mind. As long as she pulls weeds in the backyard, and stands guard at the fort against vacuum cleaner dealers at the door, and morons on bicycles in white shirts and black ties handing out Mormon literature."

"Thanks," Roma said, wiping her eyes with the back of her hand.

"You and Monk have a disagreement?"

"Sort of…"

Jack noticed that Skye was making a face at him. She shook her head in admonishment. He understood the nonverbal queue. Getting up, he turned on the radio. In deference to what he figured must be a serious situation, he adjusted the music, that was loud when he turned on the power, to a much lower volume.

"So, how was your day?" Skye asked him just as he settled back in his seat.

"Wasn't too crazy. Quit my job. But what's new?"

Skye stared incredulous at him a moment."I thought you liked that job?"

"I did."

"Then why did you quit?"

"What else? I knew I was going to get fired, so I hurried up and quit.You've gotta be at least one step ahead of the blitzkrieg. It's trench-warfare out there."

Roma smiled; Skye glowered. She's not taking this too well, he realized. His thoughts deferred to Mia. If she were his wife, he knew how she would react to his problems, not only keeping a job, but hanging in there with life in general. She would understand everything, he had no doubt. When you return to your home from war, it'll come down upon you like bricks raining from the sky. This is not the same place I left a year ago. And I'm not the same person. Meanwhile, everyone will expect you to be stronger because of your time in combat.Actually, you're weaker. All that combat wears a guy down. It will take a while to get back to normal. Some of the guys just linger on and on in twilight.Welcome home.

* * *

"What's going on with Roma?" Jack asked when they had gone to bed.

"After teaching her elementary class for the day, she went home. It was Friday. Monk was guzzling beer. He told her that friend's were coming over to visit, being his buddy at work Lorenzo and his wife. After awhile, they showed up with a bottle of sweet wine. Roma has just a glass of it, then starts feeling real groggy. She said that she went to bed early while they were all still in the living room partying. Later, she thought she was having a nightmare that Lorenzo was screwing her. When she woke up this morning, she felt sore. That told her it wasn't a dream. He had forced himself into her while she was asleep. She figured they must have put something in her drink. She showed up here with a suitcase just after I got home from work. She said she's going to divorce Monk, that son-of-a-bitch."

Jack looked across the bedroom to his medals that were just visible in the dim light from a streetlight out the window. 'Nam had had its share of vermin like Monk and Lorenzo. But at least they had the excuse that they were involved in a war. He remembered when the platoon would go into villages, routinely searching for hidden weapons and questioning people, meanwhile, Sergeant Daisy would pick out his favorite Vietnamese woman and force her into one of the hootches. Jack could still hear the shrieking and sobbing through the thatched walls. He would look around, and the other guys were just going about their business. I don't care if it was war, I should have done something, Jack thought. "Did she call the cops?"

"I asked her that too. She said *no*. I told her to, but she wouldn't."

Jack nodded. "It's not that simple."

"Meaning?"

"Well, it's not as if Roma accepts what happened. But let's face it, no matter what she does, it's not going to change the fact. And if she does go to the cops, the whole thing gets publicized. And when she goes to court, it's her word against the three of them."

"I see what you mean. It's so fucking unfair though. The whole bunch of them should all go to jail." Skye turned with her back to Jack.

After several minutes he asked, "You still awake?"

"Yes," she whispered.

Jack cupped one of her breasts in his hand.

"Don't," she hissed. "No sex, Roma might hear us."

"The door is closed. She won't hear anything."

"How can you be so crude and insensitive?" she spat.

He withdrew his hand. The hair at the back of Skye's head looked silvery the way the moonlight coming through the window faintly illuminated it. He wondered if that's how her hair would look when she got old. I'll probably never find out, he thought. Not the way things are going. He closed his eyes. A phosphorous light flared overhead, accompanied by a popping sound. Another burning light appeared. And another. It became as bright as day, with a sky full of glimmering lights swinging from little parachutes. A village of thatch roofed structures became illuminated before him. Long and short shadows of the buildings and the surrounding palm trees danced from the sky filled with flickering lights. Fourth Platoon was conducting a search of the village. Jack heard movement inside one of the hooches. He moved cautiously alongside the building towards the entrance, the muzzle of his M-16 taking the lead. It startled him when a woman came running out. She was screaming and crying. Her breasts were exposed where the top of her black PJs had been ripped open.

Jack woke to the light of day. Since his early morning nightmare, he had slept little - at that restlessly. He stared at the ceiling for a long time, thinking about the woman in his dream who had been viciously raped by one of the American soldiers. Her face had been bruised and bloodied, and he only caught a glimpse of her. But as he dwelled on the image in his mind, he realized who the small Vietnamese woman was in his dream. It was Mia. At least it was her face.

He could have used several more hours sleep, but smelled fresh coffee and thought how much he would enjoy visiting with Roma. In the shower, he spent a long time with the steaming water, not washing himself so much as reviving from another bizarre night. It was just a dream, he thought, trying to assuage himself. He stood there until he had drained the water heater, and for several more minutes under the cold water. When he finally decided that he wasn't going to be able to simply wash away this latest nightmare, he stepped out of the shower. In fact, come to think of it, what other nightmare had he ever been able to wash from his mind the morning after? Slipping into the same blue jeans he wore everyday, and a clean tee-shirt, he shuffled into the living room.

"Hello, I'm in here," Roma called.

He followed her voice into the dining room.

"Good morning," she greeted from where she sat, a cup of coffee on the table before her. She suddenly rose, stepping over to the stove. "Don't tell me, a little cream and a heaping spoon of sugar, right?" she said, pouring from the coffee percolator into a mug.

"Yes," Jack confirmed. "Thank you." He sat down at the table.

She retrieved cream from the refrigerator, splashed a little into the coffee, added sugar, and delivered it to him.

Taking a sip of the steaming beverage, "Good coffee," he complimented across the table, where Roma had returned to her seat. "Just the way I like it!"

"Glad you like it," she smiled.

"Did you find the accommodations suitable last night?"

She looked at him uncertainly a second. "Oh, actually, it's a very comfortable couch."

"Good. I've spent a lot of time breaking it in. There's a science to it. I don't take a seat girlishly. I plop down with my full weight every time, and that eventually renders the couch cushy soft." He smiled, "You know you can stay here as long as you want."

They sipped their coffee, neither speaking for awhile. Jack rose. "I'll put on some tunes," he told her, taking his coffee with him into the living room. The speakers came to life with Eric Bergman wailing the words to his song about a combat chaplain, the war not mentioned, but presumably 'Nam. He went to the front window and looked out, careful to stand to the side of the window, as was his nature, so he could not be seen by anyone out there. He did this presumptuously to anyone who asked, to check the weather, but mostly to look over the perimeter. There were clouds overhead, and no VC below. Jack finished off his coffee. Meanwhile, the neighborhood looked deserted. Everyone's gone off to work - except for me, he thought. Fuck it, I've got better things to do with my life than work in a department store, chasing down shoplifters His gaze darted to movement in a second story window of the house across the street. Jack watched intently a moment. He could make out nothing but the obscure background of a dark room. The sound of soft steps behind him caused him to spin around. Roma looked startled. "You scared me," he uttered.

"I scared *you?*" she made an expression suggesting someone was misinformed. "I'm learning not to walk up on you too quietly. I just wondered where you had disappeared to."

"I was just looking out the window," he replied. "You know, Skye and I have been here nearly a year, and every once in a while when I look out there, I see a guy just standing at the window on the second floor of that house across the street. As soon as he notices me, he ducks out of sight."

"Sound like he doesn't want to be too sociable…"

"I guess."

"Have you done anything to him to make him want to avoid you?"

"Other than flipping him off every time he peeks out his window and we make eye contact? Just kidding. We've never even shared a *hello how are you* outside of our houses."

"You've been here this long and haven't even had a conversation with your neighbor across the street?"

"Well, I've met the guy's wife, in casual greetings. But her husband hardly ever leaves the house. I see him coming and going once in a while. But that's usually at night."

"Strange," Roma shrugged. Turning, she went back into the dining room. He followed her back to the table.

"Ready to eat?" she asked.

"Sure."

"Bacon and eggs sound good?"

"Cheerios with banana slices be damned." He went to the stove while Roma was getting things out of the refrigerator and poured himself more coffee.

"How you want your eggs?"

"Just what ever it takes, so I don't have two big yellow eyes staring at me while I eat."

"Scrambled it is."

Sitting back down at the table, he watched her as she stepped up to the stove. She cracked the eggs into the skillet. Jack cleared his throat. "Skye told me what happened, the night before last." Out of respect, he avoided looking directly at her as he spoke. Though never very good with conveying sympathy, he felt he could easily make up for that weakness with his strengths. He had already carefully laid plans to track down and beat the living hell out of Monk and Lorenzo, one at a time, or both at once. His gaze finally went to her face, and he saw Roma holding the spatula *motionless* in hand. Tears filled her eyes. She raised her head and faced him with a look that belied anger saying, "I'll never forgive him for what he did."

"I know what you're going through. Really."

After a few minutes of regrouping herself, she finished the breakfast, brought a plate to the table and set it down before Jack. "You like pork and beans, don't you?"

He nodded. "How did you know?"

"I was getting some cooking oil out of the shelf and noticed a couple of dozen cans of them stashed away for survival - in case nuclear war, I guess?"

"In 'Nam, that was my favorite meal among the C-rats. As close to home cooking you could get compared to the hammered shit in the other cans." Jack began hungrily forking down his breakfast.

Skye raised her eyebrows.

"They were popular among most of the guys, so they were in short supply. I stocked up on them as soon as I got back, some kind of homage I suppose. I don't even eat them." He flinched at the cat as it jumped on the table next to him.

"Get down Shadow," Roma hissed. "Sorry, she's a little unrefined in the table manners department."

He let down his fork and took the kitten to his lap, petting it. "It's okay. I like cats."

"You're married to someone for years, you really love that person, then…" she wiped a tear. "You know what I mean – you want some toast?"

"Yes, I know what you mean, and no thanks on the toast." Things are going to get worse before they get better he wanted to tell her.

5

Sky Pilot

I nhaling the sweet smoke, until only a tiny clump of residue encrusted ash remained in the clutches of the alligator clip, Jack did not exhale until he felt certain every single brain numbing molecule of THC had absorbed into his lungs. The heavily armed enemy forces that relentlessly unleashed volley after volley of flashbacks, in their attempt to lay siege upon the base camp that was his *sanity*, were going to have to come back some other day. Jack tossed the roach-clip into the shoe box lid on the coffee table and leaned back, his head reclining over the top of the couch. The girls were unusually quiet. He attributed that largely to the valiums he had passed around earlier. His eyes suddenly widened. Just overhead floated a fleet of purple paisleys. He blinked several times. He turned to meet her stare from where she sat by his side.

"You like it? I was stoned last night and looking up, I decided the ceiling could us the ol' Van Gogh touch."

Jack leaned his head back again, seeing for the first time the entire tapestry, the size of a single bed sheet, tacked to the ceiling in a quadrant of billows. "Wow. I thought I was hallucinating there for a second, he inhaled exaggerated relief. "Just when you think you've seen everything."

Roma laughed. "I'll be your psychedelic interior decorator anytime."

Someone knocked at the door. Jack rose and went to the side of the window, peeking out. "Well, if it isn't Born-again Jim."

"Hello! Anybody home?"

"Nope, nobody's home," Jack replied loud enough to be heard through the door.

"Come in Jim," Skye called. He friend from high school entered, pushing a bicycle.

Jack returned to his place on the couch.Looking on with resignation as Jim rolled his bike to the corner of the living room. Fucking moron, he thought. It wasn't so much the dirty tires on the carpet, or the scraping the paint on the walls, his loud voice as the way it all combined to demonstrate Jim's lack of respect for the personal space of others. The first time he had brought his bicycle into the house, several months ago, Jack told him he didn't want it in the living room. He told him to take it back out and chain it to the cedar tree out front where it would be perfectly safe. After shooting that castigating look at Jack, an uncommonly maternal Skye had told Jim that he could bring his bicycle in the house *anytime* he wanted. Upon leaning his bike against the wall, Jim sat down on the only seat available, the beanbag chair.

"You must be thirsty after that ride up the hill. You want some ice water, or a coke?" Skye asked.

"I'm cool," he replied. He pushed strands of long blond hair aside and wiped sweat from his forehead with a palm. "Merci beaucoup just the same." Looking to Roma, he said, "Haven't seen you in a Blue Moon!"

"A couple of Blue Moons," she doubled down. "You were just starting college the last time I saw you."

"Now I've found something more important than college could ever be." He interjected a moment of dramatic silence for apparently a big announcement."I found Jesus."

"Actually, I've heard," she admitted. "That's good. That's really good."

Jim smiled angelically.

"Sooo, are you still going to college?" Roma attempted conversation.

"When you find the Lord, you don't need education. All the knowledge you need comes from the Bible."

"Main thing is you're doing what makes you feel good," she summed it up.

"Praise the Lord," Jim chimed.

Jack took the upside-down shoe box lid from the coffee table and set it on his lap. From it he took a packet of rolling papers and pulled one out, fluting the tiny paper with the fingers of a single hand. He pinched up some of the ground leaves from the shoe box converted to tray, into the fingers of his other hand, expertly filling the cigarette paper.

"How's your mother doing?" Skye asked Jim, breaking the several minutes of awkward silence.

"Better, thanks. I've been praying really hard for her."

"What's wrong with her?" Roma implored.

"She had a stroke."

"Oh."

Jack expertly rolled the marijuana filled paper into a neat cylinder and licked the edge. He sealed the tiny cigarette with a quick swipe of the length of his forefinger, a task for which he had become so practiced that he often did it equally as well in the dark or even while driving.

"That must be hard on your dad too," Skye said.

"It is. If I could just get him to see the Lord, it would be much easier on him."

Jack stuck the newly rolled joint into his lips, returned the shoe box lid to the coffee table and pulled his lighter from a front pocket of his jeans. He flicked it, but there were only sparks. After about a half dozen attempts, Roma leaned forward to the coffee table, picked up a book of matches and gave him a light.

"This damned piece of shit," he grumbled at his wedding gift from Ed. He was constantly trying to refill it with butane, thinking that it had a leak, only to discover it didn't need refueling, but for some reason it wouldn't make a flame. No wonder Ed had given it to him, he decided. It didn't work anymore. He shoved the lighter back into his pocket. After taking a hit from the joint, he offered it to Jim.

"Uh, no. I don't smoke pot anymore."

"I knew you didn't *drink* anymore." Jack handed the joint to Roma. "How about a valium?" he reached and picked up the small container on the coffee table. "They're legal and everything. I've got the prescription to prove it."

"No. I don't do any drugs anymore."

"What *do* you do now, I mean besides read the Bible?" Jack inquired, returning the pill container daintily to the table.

"I share the *word* so that others might learn and find the Lord."

"How about frisbee? You used to be the king of frisbee at the park nearly every evening."

"Nope. Don't have time for that nonsense anymore."

To think, as recently as a month ago, Jim was sitting in this very spot, smoking dope, drinking booze and gushing about a Grateful Dead concert he had attended, Jack marveled. He almost envied this little nimrod, not so much for the apparent remarkable simplicity by which he had found the Lord, but mostly for the fact he had found something in which he could truly believe, *without* the aid of drugs. He wondered though, what does he and his newly found ilk really know of deliverance? God? Redemption? During that period of his life when the bullets were flying everywhere and the ground shook with one fiery explosion after another, and people were being blown to pieces right before his eyes, Jack recalled having discovered Christ; become a Buddhist; decided he was an Atheist, and rediscovered Christ - all within a span of several weeks. "I used to go to church every Sunday, in those days before I went to 'Nam," Jack informed Jim. "At the top of the list of things not to do, if you wanted to go to heaven, came under the heading of, Thou shalt not kill. I guess I'm out of the running." He tried to come off as flamboyant, but there was too much that really mattered to him in what he had said. He in fact wondered if Jim, in his newfound theological wisdom, could help him out.

"Oh, no. That's organized religion man. I don't believe in organized religion. They just want to fuel your guilt, so that you keep filling up the collection basket. If you're Born-Again, you become cleansed of all past transgressions. No collection basket in your face over and again. You ought to come to one of our meetings."

"I don't know," Jack shook his head. "Wow, I don't know." The joint appeared before him. He took it from Roma's fingers, inhaled for maximum effect, and handed it back.This down in the trenches religious discourse was weighty, stoned or not. Any attempt to contemplate God could easily have you puffing an entire joint on your own, popping a valium or two and guzzling down two or three beers in a hurry to get into crash-control. Certainly, he had serious misgivings about such drastic changes in life philosophy as Jim had made, in such a short time – what normal, down-to-earth mortal wouldn't? Leaning his head back again, Jack stared at the psychedelic cloud of purple paisleys hovering overhead. What a wondrous sight to behold. For the time being, I defer to the tapestry cloth as my personification of God. Animists saw God in the land, in the trees, in the bodies of water. Why couldn't he see God in an incredibly embellished tapestry cloth. Stoned again, he thought, the magic fingers of the drug working up the back of his head, massaging his brain, melting all offensive nerve endings into soothing hot wax, not even trying to imagine a world without marijuana, or for that matter alcohol, and all those other things that provided at least a temporary safety net from falling into the abyss the Bible referred to as Hell - the place people went when they killed another human. "We had a field chaplain. Army chaplains are nondenominational. They're mostly Christian though," he spoke to no one in particular. "We called them our *Sky Pilot's*.

6

Psycho-Vac

J ack glanced around the waiting room of the mental health clinic. Other than one middle-aged man, the rest of them were all about his age. Out of the seven guys seated amongst him, two of them wore 'Nam jungle boots. One of them wore an army field jacket to go along with his boots. Jack wondered, what is this shit? They're home now, they are what we all hoped and dreamed to be someday - comfy, safe at home civilians. He dwelled on that thought a minute and concluded, *guess that's why they're here to see a shrink*.

Considering his tendency to forget things, he felt with fingertips in the right front pocket of his jeans to find the thrice returned letter to Mia. He thought maybe the doctor could advise him on finally getting it delivered. He had all kinds of connections with the stateside Army community no doubt, and was in frequent contact with guys returning from 'Nam.

"How's the medication working out?"

"Pretty good, I guess."

"The nightmares still keeping you on your toes – so to speak?"

"Yes," Jack had to admit.

"How about the flashbacks?"

"Yes."

"Problems with hostility?" the doctor pressed on.

Jack nodded thinking, No problem. Like all else before mentioned, these things came naturally.

"Would I be correct in assuming that *"Pretty good, I guess"* is a copout?By adding *"I guess"* to your answer is glaringly tell-tell." The doctor glowered at Jack like he was a judge presiding over Jack's trial as a suspected serial killer. "You *aren't* doing well at all, and won't admit it. You're a big brave home-coming war hero, and you won't stoop to reveal any chink in your armor. I can't help you unless you're upfront with me."

Jack thought for a minute. "I like the medication. It helps me sleep. But, you know, like for an example, I still have the nightmares. But they're not as bad."

"You taking the pills regularly?"

"I was for a while. But I ran out."

"I gave you a month's supply. And that was a month ago. When did you run out?"

"Couple of weeks ago."

"What? You know, that stuff isn't candies where you all of them at once."

Jack blushed at the doctor apparently sizing-up the situation. He had indeed regarded valiums like candy.

"If you really think you really need to increase your dose, we could give it a try."

"Okay," Jack quickly accepted. In fact, that's the only reason he returned here, he thought – for more valium. His gaze went to the bronze statuette at the edge of the desk. The helmeted, ammo laden man was still stalking through enemy held jungle. Jack remembered the letter. If he could depend on anyone for help, it was another 'Nam vet, especially another infantryman. "I wanted to ask you about something else, if you could help me."

"Just name it."

He reached into his pocket and produced the letter. It was more crumpled now from being in his pocket for just a few hours, than it had been from journeying all the way across the Pacific to Vietnam and back three times. I keep sending this letter to my old girlfriend in 'Nam, and it keeps coming back. This is the third time. I'm trying to get through to her, but something's wrong. I don't know what to think. You know how it is over there."

"I would like to help, but I don't know why you're asking me?"

"You're a part of the System. You've got all of the connections. I just need help in finding out how to track someone down if their town was taken by the enemy. I don't even know where to start. This girl means a lot to me." Jack held the envelope so the doctor could clearly see it with its "return to sender, address unknown" markings.

"You still married, or what?"

Jack nodded. "But the way things are going, not for much longer."

"I really don't know what I can do. If there's anything I could do, I would."

"I was just hoping…" Jack shrugged, returning the letter to his pocket.

"I counseled a guy who was stationed with Military Assistant Command in Saigon. The reason he came to see me was because he was having problems with his Vietnamese wife. Everything was fine, until he brought her back to the States. I guess he expected her to remain, you know, subservient like she was over there. Of course, that wasn't the case. As soon as she integrated into a society where women are treated, at least more so than in her own country, equal with men, she changed."

"I wouldn't care about that," Jack replied. "I always treated Mia like a princess. What I thought was special about her, is she understood me. We understood each other. Her and I had gone through pretty much the same - that war over there. But now I don't know what's happened to her," his voice trembling to so much as imagine *what*.

"You know, if someone continues carrying around too much heavy baggage, they'll eventually breakdown. The more you wear yourself down, the less capable you are of carrying out the most routine of tasks. That goes for up here too," the doctor tapped a finger on the side of his head. "Feelings of guilt, unreasonable expectations and seeing yourself as a victim are manifestations of mental overload."

Jack struggled for words that would distance himself from this pitiful basket-case the doctor was describing, but the more he thought about it, the more the truth sank in. He visualized himself dragging a big steamer trunk behind himself labeled: *Fragile. Handle with Care. War Memories Inside.*

"So, let's go ahead and increase your medication. I'll double it. Take one in the morning, and one before you go to bed." The doctor scribbled on a prescription pad, and handed it across the desk. "I'll see you in another thirty days."

Walking towards the pharmacy with the slip of paper in hand, limping from his knee having been in one position too long, Jack imagined the prescribed, "two pills a day" as little cart wheels mounted beneath the rear of his war memories trunk. He thought, then I can roll that dude behind me instead of having to drag it.

* * *

When he pulled up to the house, Roma's car was in the driveway, but not Skye's.

"Hello," Roma greeted him from the couch as he entered the front door. She lowered a pocketbook to her lap in the manner that it would remain open where she left off.

"Hello. Skye's not home yet?" He was startled at something at his ankle. He looked down to see Roma's cat rubbing itself against him. "That's a nice, warm welcome home," he said to it.

"Skye called from the restaurant. She said the girl who was supposed to replace her called in sick. So she's going to work a double shift."

"That means she won't get in until," He counted with his fingers. "After one."

"How was the drive to Frisco?"

"Not exactly the highlight of my week," Jack replied. "Crazy fucking traffic on the way there; more crazy fucking traffic on the way back." He stepped over and took a seat at the other end of the couch from her. He removed his shoes.

"Want a beer?"

"Thought we were out."

"I bought a case." Roma let down her book to the coffee table and went into the kitchen.

"Wow, just when you get to thinking that the world is such a cruel place, voila, a case of beer appears in your refrigerator."

"Well, I didn't put the entire case in there - unless you want to drink the whole thing tonight," she said as she returned with a can in each hand.

"I'll try to restrain myself."

As she reached to give one to him, he could not help but stare at the way Roma's nipples showed through her halter-top. And he had never really noticed her legs before, not the way they looked in those tight cutoffs. He took a drink and was surprised at the flavor. Holding the can before himself to read the label, he commented, "That's about a notch and a half above the usual hooch we keep on hand."

"Glad you like it. I was going to make spaghetti for dinner. Would you like that?"

"Darn toot'n. Did you say you were going to stay with us permanently?" he half joked.

"You would get tired of me after a while."

"Why do you say that?"

"Oh, I've got lots of bad habits."

"Being?"

"You wouldn't have a single glass in the house after a month or two. I'm always breaking things by accident. And I'm hopelessly forgetful. I couldn't own houseplants like Skye." She glanced from the tall, healthy philodendron across the room from them, to the lush Boston fern that hung in the light of the front window. "I would forget to water them, and they would all die on me. Let's see, I also smoke too much; I snore, I could go on."

"Okay then, what are your strengths?"

"Now that you mention it, I know all of the United States presidents. And I give generously to local charities. Oh, and I'm good at massage therapy. How's your neck and back after that long drive?"

"Killing me," Jack slightly exaggerated at the prospects.

Roma stepped over to the radio, turning the dial until classical music began to flow out of the speakers. Returning to the couch, she said, "turn your back to me."

He set his drink on the table and turned, bringing his feet up on the couch cross-legged.

"Hey, you're good at that," she complimented.

"Had lots of practice. Wasn't much furniture out there in the jungles of the Mekong Delta."

"Take your shirt off."

Jack slipped out of his already unbuttoned plaid shirt. He promptly pulled his tee-shirt off over his head.

"You're so thin your ribs are showing. Doesn't Skye feed you?"

"That would involve cooking."

"She never was one to get familiar with the kitchen." Roma started with his shoulders and worked towards his neck.

"That feels good," his voice lowered a scale or two.

Roma's hands moved gradually down his back, fingertips finding each sore stretch of muscle, making adjustments in the pressure she applied in accordance to barely audible groans from him that went from plaintive to the pleasurable.

"I never felt any real compassion for Skye," Jack felt confessional. "Our relationship has always been more, you know superficial."

"Oh?" Her massaging rhythm broke for a second.

"I have a hard time *giving* in a relationship. After I got back from 'Nam, I discovered that I didn't have any room left inside of me for anyone else. That is if they expected a lot out of me."

"Just relax. Think about being on a white sandy beach in the South Pacific, with the gentle sound of surf. A warm breeze is blowing."

"Yeah. I'm on the beach, stretched out on a towel with the sand a soft mattress beneath me." Jack took delight in the flowing warp and woof of the classical music just at the right volume, while Roma worked her hands gracefully up his back. He became a bassoon in the orchestra, she the musician who played him.

"So then, why *did* you marry my sister, if not out of this magical bonding of hearts we call love?"

"I don't know. Us hooking up just seemed like a pretty good idea at the time. We were already living together and all. It was her idea to get married.

And I'm not good at saying 'no.' I kind of roll with the punches."

Roma found a knot in the muscles below his right shoulder and concentrated her fingers there.

"That hurts," Jack cried as she pressed hard on the place where his back was worst injured when the mortar explosion knocked him hard to the ground, the concussion a roundhouse punch, shrapnel buzzing everywhere overhead but missing him.

She continued a moment before letting up. "I don't know, I've heard worse excuses for getting married," she admitted.

"I guess I felt sorry for her. When I first met her, she was still getting over her breakup with the owner of the restaurant."

"Jerry, that manager of greasy-spoon Don Juan. I can't believe she still works there."

"I think she's still seeing him. This isn't her first 'double-shift.'"

Roma's hands became still. "You really think that?"

"I went to the restaurant one night when she said she was working a double-shift, to visit her and have a meal." He let his feet to the floor and turned around facing Roma. "When I didn't see her, I asked one of the waitresses where she was. She didn't know anything about Skye working that shift. When Skye got home late that night, I told her that I had been to the restaurant. She told me that they didn't need her to work after all, so she went and visited a girl- friend. I knew she was lying."

Through all that Jack was relating to Roma, he hoped to make her understand the world was not an innocent place. She seemed to grasp this. It might have been sobering to Roma to hear that Jack's relationship with her sister boiled down to him *rolling with the punches* romantically, but that's the way it was. His eyes went to her nipples, and back to meet her stare. Taking her by both shoulders, he gently pulled her close and kissed her.

Roma became stiff, but did not try to pull away.

Sensing a miscue on his part, he quickly released her. "I'm sorry. I thought."

"You can put your shirt back on. I'm done," she said. Getting up, she went into the kitchen.

Jack leaned back and sighed. In the swirl of detachment with all around himself, especially that all important sense of self and how we relate to the world around us, he remembered his prescription. Taking the container of valiums from his pants pocket, he unscrewed the top and shook out one of the small pills into his palm. He popped it into his mouth and washed it down with beer. Crossing the room to the stereo, he cutoff some long haired musician of the past, Mozart he believed, in search of a long haired musician of the present, who in this case turned out to be Rob Grill of the Grass Roots, not a great pianist like Mozart, but with a voice high, sweet and supple that could compete with piano strains any day of the week. My Midnight Confession summed it up well. Jack had fallen in love with another man's wife. That was only the short of it. The woman was his wife's sister. How about that? Jack returned to his seat and pulled the shoe box lid towards himself. Mia loved this American rock group, her favorite song in the world by them *Let's Live for Today*. She used to sing the words to him while strolling alongside the river in Vihn Hoa. She knew all the words to it. At the venue of their wedding reception, this would be their song to play in quadraphonic over and over. After a grace period, he brought a joint into the kitchen for Roma. She busied herself over a sizzling skillet of ground beef. He waited for her to finish pouring in a can of tomato puree, and offered it to her. She completed stirring the sauce with a wooden spoon, and set it down on the counter. "Thanks. I make some of my best spaghetti when I'm stoned."

"All yours," he said, handing it to her. He returned to his place on the couch and listened to the Grass Root's song until it ended. That band, no matter what they were singing on the radio brought his thoughts to Mia. Not since he had been with her last, two and a half years ago, had he felt her presence so strongly. He got back up and went into the bedroom, to the closet. Reaching to the shelf above the clothes rack, he took down his portfolio where it was sandwiched between boxes of his things still unpacked from when they had moved into the house. He returned to the couch.

Resting the large photo album on his lap, as yet unopened, Jack took a breath. Within were cherished memories, for starters, photos of Mia. And there were photos of his R&R in Hong Kong. In addition to the many pictures of friends and acquaintances he had made along the way, was the last group picture of the guys in Fourth Platoon, in the days prior to the ambush. He took a longer breath. They're just *pictures*! They can't jump off the page and bite you, he tried to assure himself. But he could not deny that what he had before himself, in appearance a leather-bound collection of neatly mounted pictures chronicling his war days, at core was frame by agonizing frame of picturesque testimony that his worse nightmares were very much the stuff of reality. Not only did a picture tell a thousand words, but it didn't fudge. If you had a keen eye, you could even see the emotion of the subject. They were even happy or sad, from the nuance of their expression. They were posing for a picture, or caught in the candid. You could tell with even a spark of intelligent inspection. Not only the face, but the body language told all. For instance, a stiff looking body was poised. A relaxed looking body was most natural.

Even the camera used to take these pictures was the property of a dead man. One of the guys in his platoon, Eads had taken many of the pictures of Jack. After he was killed, Jack kept his camera. He wanted to record his remaining time in Vietnam, the way Eads had been doing with such dedication. Jack steadied himself as he opened the front cover. But as soon as he set eyes on the first framed collection of images, fragments of memories exploded in his face. Vietnam was exactly as he had left it.

Roma came into the living room. "There's no way I can finish this whole doobie myself," she said, holding what was only a half smoked joint before her as evidence.

"You have my sympathies." Jack accepted the remaining herbal cigarette from her.

"What you got there?"

"My 'Nam photo album."

"Really, mind if I look?"

Actually, he *did* mind. The reason he had taken it out was to reminisce about Mia - privately.

Roma sat down so close to him that their knees were touching.

He slid the large album over until half of it rested on her lap. If recent

78

events were indication, he figured she wasn't sitting so close for any other reason.

On the first page were pictures taken around Can Tho. This was during Jack's first several weeks In-Country. Among others was a picture of himself in the middle of a muddy street in the obviously third-world country town center, surrounded by Vietnamese children, connoted the American soldier as personification of charity and compassion towards a war ravished people. He was handing out little packets of coffee and fruitcake bars that came with the C-rations.

"This was during a stand-down in a town named Can Tho," he narrated over the photos.

"These were some of our only enjoyable times out of the bush for a couple of days - hanging out with Vietnamese who weren't shooting at you." Not that the town wasn't Viet Cong controlled, he thought wryly. They just didn't want to shoot at you there, then end up having the bombers come in and level such a nice town where they too could enjoy the restaurants, bars and whorehouses during *their* stand-downs when the American's were away. He flipped the first page of his collection of photographs that within days of returning home from the war he had spent hours meticulously aligning and mounting chronologically. He had even penned captions at the bottom of the photo margins. With that, he had stored the album away, and had since referred to it infrequently.

"Who's this next to you?" Roma asked, pointing to one of the pictures taken by Eads. Ortiz and he were standing alongside each other, decked out in battle gear, M-16s in hand, posing like a couple of bad-ass motherfuckers. In the background was a huge statue of Buddha, centerpiece to one of the many temples to that deity that were scattered across Vietnam.

"Just some guy in my unit." If she wanted more information, it was right there on the bottom margin: "Ortiz and me on VC Island." Man, that son-of-a-bitch could smoke pot. Every time they went on a mission, he would go in and out of hootches from one village to the next searching not for the enemy, but for dope. And by mission's end, he always ended up with an upturned steel helmet full. One day, several months after this photo, Ortiz stepped on a booby-trap. Jack went to visit him in the field hospital in Dong Tam.

"How are you buddy?" Jack asked. The sheet on the hospital bed went flat at just below his knees.

"Let's put it this way. I'm not as tall as the last time you saw me."

Jack forced a laugh. He wondered how long it would take the implications to sink in, that Ortiz having lost both of his legs. Probably as soon as they let up on the morphine IVs. He went to the next page while Roma looked on intently. She didn't ask as many questions as he thought she might, most likely taking his hint to just read the captions. He flipped to a page of photos of him and Little John on their in-country R&R at Vung Tau.

"Look at that," Roma called attention to a picture that captured Jack standing before a giant statue of the Sitting Buddha. "Buddha. The Vietnamese are mostly Buddhists, aren't they?"

"Yes they are."

"I like Buddhists. They have a very keen nature towards personal calm and collection of thought. It's called Zen. They achieve it through meditation."

"I'm vaguely familiar with Zen philosophy," Jack replied. Mia had passed on awareness of Buddhism and Zen to him, though she was Catholic. He flipped to the next page of photos.

"What happened here?" She gazed at an entire page showing scenes of Dong Tam the day after the ammo dump explosion. The captions were brief, the pictures speaking mostly for themselves. "Crater from explosion; Airport; All flights canceled; Naval Yards - destroyed; Remains of mess hall; Radio tower - TIMBER!"

"Inside job," he replied. "Turned out that our Vietnamese janitors, maids and even the masseurs were Viet Cong in disguise of being domestics. We hired people from the villages surrounding the base camp for casual labor. They learned everything about our operations while at work, and passed that info on to sappers. They could do so much damage because they knew our every weakness. They knew when we let our guard down most, such as on Sunday's and American holidays. They knew when we liked to drink on Fridays and Saturdays, and were most off-guard when intoxicated into the evening. They discovered when we would lay down our weapons to play

80

softball after a day's work.A bunch of American soldiers, shirts off gathered in an open field – talk about a soft target for a mortar attack. They always attacked the base camp at night. Why?" Obviously, it's harder to see little men in black PJs at night, and the dark was their cover. But more-so, us Americans are one-hundred percent alert during daylight hours. When the sun goes down, in any American base camp or fire base, it's four or five guys off for the night to sleep, and one guy on guard duty for two hours at a time.If you know anything about us civilized American, the world is basically nine to five – war zone no exception."

"Well, we're civilized people," Roma proclaimed.

"Sure, eight to five are official work hours. Shave in the mirror, deodorant under your arms and off to make the world a better place.Nighttime is for sleep. But war is not civilized," Jack retorted. "The gloves are off when it comes down to survival of the fittest. When you're cast off into a jungle in the middle of nowhere, and square off with a guy with an automatic weapon in hand, and you have an automatic weapon in hand, is there going to ensue discussion about good table manners, about your daughter shouldn't date until she's seventeen, debate about whether people with round eyes and blond hair are better than people with slanted eyes and black hair, about my God is better than your God? No, it's down to the guy who pulls the trigger first – no discussion."

Several pages later appeared a picture of Mia standing on the sidewalk at the entrance to the restaurant where she worked. A natural in front of the camera. With thumb and forefinger, she daintily held large rimmed sunglasses to the end of her nose, peeking over the top of them. She looked taller and older than sixteen in her silk blouse, short skirt and high heels. Jack quickly turned the page before Roma could ask about her, the girl he cared about more than his own wife.

"Whoa, slow down, I'm missing some of the pictures," she complained.

Jack felt sweat beading on his forehead. "All these memories at once are too much," he admitted.

"I didn't realize," Roma replied. She put a hand on his wrist, patting it. "Go ahead and put the album aside. I don't want to see anymore if you don't want to."

"What's that smell?"

"Damn! I was so engrossed in your pictures, I forgot about the spaghetti sauce. It needs stirring." She jumped up and hurried to the kitchen.

Jack took the album back to the bedroom. Earlier he had desired to delight himself in looking at pictures of Mia. Now he only wanted to return the album safely to its place in the closet.

* * *

After their meal, Roma started yawning. Taking it as a hint, Jack went to bed much earlier than normal. Even with all the dope and alcohol he had ingested, the pain from his knee persisted to radiate through his leg. This was something he was beginning to accept as a part of his miserable fate. But the ambush of *images* were not something for which he had learned to accept. Such as the sudden appearance of green tracers arching from a wood line in the dim light of his bedroom. Bullets were splattering in the shallow paddy water around his position. He turned from firing at the enemy to slap another clip in his rifle, only to discover he had expended all his ammo. Artillery flares rocking back and forth on their tiny parachutes, descended from high above the jungle. These flickering lights reflected in the glassy eyes of dead platoon members lying in the paddy mud next to him. They're the lucky ones, Jack thought. He bolted upright from where he lay with his head propped against the paddy dike, not caring if this made him a better target. His only desire being escape. Looking around, he drew a breath of relief at the familiarity of his surroundings. Of course, I'm in the safety of my bedroom, he assured himself. But this did not calm his trembling. They were the lucky ones, those guys who were killed, he had no doubt. At least they don't have to be tormented by this fear and pain. It's like dying over and over again. He glanced to the clock. Skye should be home soon. The sooner the better. Covered with sweat, he kicked off the sheets. He laid back down and tried to return to sleep. It was quiet - too quiet. Turning sideways and curling up to get more comfortable did not gain him relief. He rose, fluffed his pillow and plopped his head down on it again. Finally drifting back to sleep, Jack he heard a noise, like a bump. He instantly became a one man listening-post. There were always sounds if you listened hard enough. The least audible ones were no less important than loud noises, and often more sinister in implications. Those little motherfuckers moved slowly, cautiously stepping over anything that might make the slightest snap or crunch in the quiet of the night, ducking behind tree trunks and clumps of underbrush at every step, crawling on their bellies when there was nothing to conceal them. Indefatigable in their quest to breach the perimeter, it was a rare booby-trap and razor wire fortified bream they could not penetrate. At this they were magical, warrior-magicians. Even the stealthiest of Apache could learn from these guys. The sound of a soft clump heightened his vigil. It could well be the sound of careful footsteps making a slight stumble while crossing the carpeted floor. He dared not move. Plop! Something came down hard on his stomach. Gasping, he leapt from the mattress. Jack stumbled backwards against the wall. Reaching around in the dark to find the light switch at his side, he flipped it on. In the middle of the bed sat Shadow, it's large yellow eyes fixed quizzically upon him. He shook his head, returned the cat's gaze for a second and chuckled. Grabbing his pants from where they lay on the floor, he pulled them on. Slipping through the living room where Roma was fast asleep on the couch, he went out the back door and onto the deck. Wide open space beneath the stars is what he needed. He leaned on the wood rail, taking in the brisk morning air. A breeze out of the American River Canyon caressed his face. As he inhaled, Jack detected the faint pungency of diesel, and heard the sound of a large truck straining its engine, shifting its gears along the winding canyon road. That diesel smell was one in the same with the exhaust of the riverboats that ferried the troops to battle. Just as the sense of smell is the ultimate short-circuit to our brain, even more quickly processed than the sense of touch, flashbacks of Vietnam were not complete unless they were accompanied by one or more of the many smells that thrived in the steaming hot tracts of Southeast Asia. One odor stood out above the rest. The rice paddies were the home where the water buffalo roamed. As an infantryman in the Mekong Delta, you spent a lot of time trudging through waist deep rice paddy mud. And if you became pinned-down, it was not uncommon to spend all night laying in that stinking muck behind safety of a dike. Subsequently, your platoon members and yourself carried that rice paddy mud permeated with water buffalo excrement smell around with you for days and sometimes weeks later, until a heavy rain came along, in which you stood in the open and gratefully showered fully clothed. You came to regard the smell in all of its nuances. After all, it represented the unusual and perhaps even the exotic, particular to its source. For instance, without the water buffalo, there would be sparse rice industry in the Mekong Delta. As common as farm tractors in the heartland of America, were the wooden yoked water buffaloes in Vietnam's farmland. They were a powerful beast, not unlike their American cousin. The Vietnamese farmer made good use of them. Indeed, Jack had to admit that the smell of water buffalo shit was an important part of the Vietnam experience. He would tell Skye about this sometime. Since she wanted to know more about him in relation to that war, this would be a good place to start. A sudden noise from the direction of the driveway caught his attention. He went to the side of the house to see that it was Skye's car pulling in. The engine went silent and she stepped out. He walked up to her. "You startled me," she exclaimed, slamming the car door closed. "What are you doing out here in the middle of the night?"

"Uh, actually contemplating the Zen of water buffalo defecation."

* * *

"How was your visit with the doctor?" Skye asked while taking off her clothes.

"Okay. He doubled my medication," Jack replied from bed, where he had returned preceding Skye. He sat with his back against the headboard.

"*The Valium?*" She cutoff the start of a yawn.

"Yes. You want one?"

"Bet your sweet bippy."

"Help yourself. The bottle's right there," he

indicated to the top of the dresser with a wave of his hand.

"Don't mind if I do." She reached beside herself, picking up the small container. "What'd you and Roma do tonight?" She asked. Unscrewing the bottle, she shook a pill into her palm and tossed it into her mouth.

"Oh, uh nothing. She made spaghetti."

"Yeah? She's a good cook."

"Other than being a little burned around the edges... After dinner, we looked at my photo album."

Skye crawled into bed, sitting cross-legged facing him. "Did you show her the pictures of your old girlfriends too?" She raised her eyebrows.

"What are you implying?"

"Nothing. Just teasing."

"No. You've got something to say."Jack felt it was pretty audacious, coming from one's wife who had just come home late at night from an affair with another man, to take exception to her husbands photos of his girlfriend of over two years past (If she only knew).

"Well, you have to admit, those Vietnamese girls make up a big part of your photo collection. Especially Mia."

When Jack had showed his photo album to Skye the first time, soon after they had met, (though she had gone through it herself, he didn't know how many times since), he had taken time to give verbal caption almost every picture in the album. But when he came to the section containing Mia, he only muttered, "old girlfriend," quickly moving through the several pages of her. With such pictures as the one where they were seated together behind a checker clothed table at a sidewalk cafe in Vihn Hoa, showing Mia in a snug-fitting dress going up above her knees, leaning her head affectionately on his shoulder, Jack had been concerned he might get too many questions. "I told you, she's just an old girlfriend. What do you want to know - how many times I screwed her?"

Skye became quiet. When someone becomes quiet at length in the middle of a verbal debate, it often comes down to silence is louder than words, Jack knew from experience. "Well?"

"That's not fair."

"What's not fair?"

"Why do you always have to get the last word. All of us humans have the right to recourse. Look, I've got class in the morning. I just want to go to sleep." Lying down, she stretched out and pulled the blanket over herself, turning her back to him.

Jack switched off the bedside lamp. At times like this he had learned, the best thing to do was to let her calm-down - himself too. He slid down with his head in the middle of the pillow, and stared at the ceiling. After awhile, he figured the Valium had done its job on Skye, so he wiggled up close. Reaching around her with an arm, he pulled her body close.

"I'm tired, really," she groaned.

"Just a quickie," he appealed.

She rolled to face him. "I'm not one of your Vietnamese whores," she whispered angrily. "You think you can just crawl between my legs, screw me until you're satisfied, regardless of who I am, then go to sleep?" She spun back away.

Jack shoved his hand against her back, hard enough to push her off the bed. Grabbing the blanket on the way down, she took a length of blanket with her. There was a thud as she hit the carpeted floor.

"Don't ever say that about Vietnamese women," he blurted. "Those women, even if they are prostitutes, are just trying to survive a goddamned war! They don't get the Western version of life – a working husband who supports them and comes home regular every night. There's dinner, TV and off to bed to get up early for the same routine every day.Independent of that, as single young women, they don't have the option of going to college. Even grammar school is a luxury reserved for the elite in that country."

Skye's head peeked up from the edge of the bed. "You care more about the women over there than you do for me. I've never heard you defend *me* like that," she sniffed. Her head sank back down. "You bastard. You fucking bastard," she cried.

Jack returned his gaze to the ceiling. After a minute, he asked himself, do I really care more about the women in Vietnam than Skye? In the middle of what had become full-blown memories of Mia, he though he heard sobbing.

7

Death of a Real Life Hero

Mia and Jack walked together along rue de Jardin.

"You awake?"

"Huh, what?" he weakly replied.

"You've got a call. Sounds important."

He turned to look at the alarm clock through eyes that took a second to focus. "A quarter after fucking four?" he muttered, stumbling out of bed.

Roma handed him the receiver when he arrived to the living room.

"This is Eddie's wife Raynel." Her voice was not good.

"What's wrong?"

After a pause, she sputtered, "Eddie was killed in a car accident. I got the call just a little while ago." Another pause ensued. "Sorry to wake you, but I didn't want you to have to read it in the morning paper, or hear about it secondhand."

"Are you all right?"

"I'll be okay," she replied, not so convincingly.

He waited a moment for her to continue.

"You know we were separated. I was filing for divorce."

"He told me."

"That doesn't change the fact I cared for him," she said, her tone did not sound genuine to Jack.

"A car accident?"

87

"He was driving across the tracks in Corona. A train hit his car" she exclaimed. "He was killed instantly - the police told me."

Jack could not think of anything else to say. He sensed that Ed's wife was less troubled than he was about her husband's death. "Thanks for calling me. Take care."

"I'll call you again with the date of the funeral."

"Appreciate it." He returned the receiver to its cradle. He turned to meet Roma's gaze.

"Bad news?"

"Just lost a good friend," he stammered. "We served in 'Nam together. I don't know if you met him. He was at the wedding."

"Big guy? He arrived late?"

"That's him. That was Ed."

"What happened?"

"A train and his car had a showdown. The train won." Him and I were drafted the same day. We had grown up together just across the street. We went through Advanced Infantry Training together. We took a week leave at the same time here at home, and eventually sent to 'Nam on the same day. We ended up in the Ninth Infantry Division in 'Nam together.We were in different regiments, but ran into one another in the field occasionally. We returned home on the same day – how about that? When I partied with friends here back home, I always invited Ed to join. I hosted parties at my bachelors apartment every weekend. He showed up without missing a beat, no regard to his possibly busy social calendar, Jack kidded, and we drank beer together into the night.That was my buddy by chance Ed." Jack turned and went back to the bedroom. Skye was still asleep. Laying there in the quiet of the night, he stared at the ceiling. The memories began to roll in. In high school, Jack hung out with a tight-knit crowd. Ed didn't have many friends. Even on the school bus, if Jack ended up in the same seat with Ed, he was more likely to make conversation with someone across the aisle on the bus. Graduation only several months behind them, they were drafted the same day, which resulted in them being sent to Basic Training together. Jack remembered the time some of the guys and himself in basic training conspired to *short sheet* Ed. He was such a bungling fathead that he was an easy target for such pranks. The guys just wanted something to do for a laugh. While Ed was brushing his teeth, everyone in the barracks who had been clued-in watched in secret from their bunks for the big moment. Ed soon lumbered out of the latrine, and crawled into bed. Grabbing the end of the sheet in both hands, he stretched his stout, muscular legs the length of the mattress. Instead of the expected befuddled reaction from him that his legs could only go halfway, there came a loud rip. He had shoved both feet right through the sheet. Ed looked mildly surprised, turned to his side and went right to sleep. Instead of laugher from those who had been waiting in anticipation, there were only a few incredulous murmurs. This trick had worked so beautifully every time before.Jack chuckled. It became so uncontrollable that he held the pillow over his mouth so he would not wake Skye.

"You okay?" she asked.

He took the pillow away. "Yeah. I was just... gurgling."

"Sounded like you were crying," she said sleepily.

"I was thinking about something that was funny."

"I don't know what's going on with you. It just sounded to me like you were crying."

"Where'd you get that ridiculous idea? I was laughing." He looked at Skye, only to find she had already drifted back to sleep. Jack's eyes were a little moist. He wiped them with the back of his hand.

8

Father knows Best?

They're trying to start a revolution!

"Trying? They've already started, and then some. That's because they're *trying* to stop the war," Skye retorted to Jack's father. "What's so bad about trying to stop a war?" She took a sip of beer and leaned back in her chair.

"They're tearing this country in two. That's what's so wrong."

Jack listened to the argument from the couch, his retreat in the living room. He had departed the table as soon as they had started at one another. This was a long standing dispute for which he wanted no part. He had joined in on it once, four or five months past. But when he tried to talk about such matters as the entire country being divided over Vietnam, he would start to stammer, and tremble with rage. Any position he intended to take rapidly crumbled under the weight of not only that steamer trunk full of war memories, but also another trunk full of protest days memories, and this compounded by his uncertainly about it all. How can I discuss Vietnam politics, he wondered, when I can't even deal with issues surrounding the war on a personal level? So he stood looking out the window, a can of beer clutched in hand, pondering it all. After awhile, he thought lividly, what do either of them know about 'Nam? What does *anybody* know for that matter?

"Would you rather live in a country that didn't allow their people to protest against war?" Skye proposed.

"Glad you raised that point," Jack's father retorted. "If you and your protest buddies had it your way, that little commie bastard Doctor Spock would be president of the New Socialistic United States; flag burning Jane Fonda would be Secretary of State; Instead of police departments, we would have the likes of Stokly Carmichel and his Black Panthers bunch keeping everybody in line with machine guns and brass knuckles. Is that what you want?"

"Instead of Nixon and his Nazi bunch? Might be the better of two evils."

"You're upsetting Jack," his mother intervened, just above a whisper as she came from the kitchen to take more dishes. "Change the subject," her voice raised. "And don't put your cigarette ashes in the plate. How many times do I have to tell you?"

"Couldn't find a damned ashtray anywhere," his father mumbled, the cigarette burned down almost to his leathery fingers, that section of middle and forefinger orange stained from a long life of chain-smoking.

"Let me help you," Skye offered, getting up from the table. She took the remaining dishes.

"I'll wash, you dry," his mother said.

Jack felt for his dad - an older, heavier, balding latter day image of himself. He too had fought in war, and loved his country. He loved his dogs and wife dearly. Granted, from his stories, most of his fighting was over who got dibs on what Geisha girl during his postwar days in Occupied Japan. What they really had in common, was he could not understand how such a great nation as theirs could so destructively turn on itself currently. "I'm not the only one who feels bad about this whole thing," he declared. He returned to the table with an ashtray he had fetched from the living room. Jack's father was holding a cigarette that was burning close to his fingers. "Nixon is turning things around with the war. He's got 'em over there in Paris negotiating peace. He's going to find a way to end the war so that both sides are satisfied," he said to Skye.

Jack did not agree that Nixon was doing anything that was not entirely out of desperation. But maybe the man had seen the error of his ways. He certainly had conducted himself like a crazy motherfucker with his bombing

91

campaigns when Jack was over there. He could still see the silvery five-hundred pound spindles tumbling from the underside of the jets, the fire storms instantly incinerating entire villages. Nixon knew damn well what napalm did to human flesh, and that many of those who were getting their flesh melted were women and children. Jack visualized the country the way he last saw it from his helicopter ride to the airport, the thousands of bomb craters that had transformed the vast areas of the Mekong Delta from picturesque jungle, scattered with beautiful Indo-French architecture, into moonscape. He thought about the carpet bombings, as they were called. His unit had conducted *mop up* operations afterwards. You did not have to worry about the usual ambushes and snipers as you stalked through the jungle - little jungle remained. And you did not have the always unpleasant task of storming villages and interrogating the inhabitants - no villages were left. Carpet bombings left an ugly, clean slate. At the couch, Jack finished off his drink.

"I hate to be the one to tell you the news," Skye said from the kitchen table, "But the war's been won. Not by the Americans, or the Viet Cong, but by the protesters. They are the ones who finally forced Nixon into the troop withdrawals."

Jack saw his father from the couch. He folded his arms high on his chest and glowered at Skye. The debate was over, at least for tonight. There was no use in arguing with someone so hopelessly one-sided in opinion. That went for both of them. The more he thought about it, the more he wondered who these people were, this man who was called his father, and this lady called his wife? Even his country, the place that even after being a protester himself, he loved so much that he would have given his life rather than dishonor, now seemed foreign - somebody else's country? Jack felt alarmed. Rising from the couch he found himself at the door to Leslie's room. Dylan music played within. He tapped at the door and called her name.

"Come in," a voice came faint behind the door.

Jack stepped in to find his sister sitting cross-legged in the middle her bed. "That's Highway 61 Revisited playing, isn't it?"

She nodded. A silver dollar size peace symbol hung by a chain from her neck.

"I used to have that same album."

"This *is* that album. Don't you remember? You gave it to me before you went to the army, the same day you gave me this peace symbol," she indicated, touching the medallion with a forefinger.

Jack remembered giving her his peace symbol, but did not remember the record album. This wasn't the first time that someone had recounted something that he had done before he went to 'Nam, and he could only come up with a blank. On the other hand, every single day he spent in that Southeast Asian rat-hole, hovered with clarity in his mine, admittedly with the exception of a possible battle or two he could not remember, that came with the price of apparent amnesia. Only a guy with a serious degree in psychology could figure that one out. In regard, Jack suspected his lapses in memory were out of convenience. If you're clever enough in avoiding thinking about something, it didn't happen, or at least it went into the mental cylinder file of unimportant. He took a seat at the foot of the bed. "What you reading there?" he indicated by looking to the book that lay opened between them.

"White Fang."

Jack liked Jack London. He was tempted to ask if he gave her the book as well, but afraid to ask. "That's some pretty heavy-duty reading for a twelve year old," he instead remarked. "I would expect someone your age to be cutting her teeth on Nancy Drew Mysteries, or National Velvet."

"I'll be thirteen next month," she sputtered. After a second, realizing, most likely what her brother had said was a compliment, she smiled. "What's all the racket in there?" she made a thumb toward the dining room.

"You know. The usual. Skye and dad are at each other's throat over Nixon and the war protests."

"How come you never say anything? You were a part of all that, personally. You know more than both of them, multiplied by a thousand."

Dylan was now singing something about your doctor not knowing what you've got. Jack swallowed, thinking, I can relate to that.

"You used to go on for hours about the war and the government."

Looking down, Jack shook his head. That was before he *went there*. Maybe one day when he untangled in his mind all of the 'ban the bomb' placards and being dragged to squad cars, for lobbing back the tear-gas canisters; from getting shot at in the rice paddies and the falling mortars and helicopters, *then* he would be able to talk about these things. He lifted his eyes to look at his little sister. She stared back at him with what he perceived as a look of immeasurable respect. In her protected world, she did not seem to understand that the things her brother had been through were too fantastic for even *him* to imagine.

* * *

"How was your visit?" Roma asked Jack as he entered the house.

"Great," he replied, kicking his shoes off to the side of the door. "I've been to the rodeo and back." He went into the kitchen.

"You should have come along," Skye said. "You could have helped me chop up Jack's dad and feed him to the coyotes before he gives all of his money to the Dick Nixon for king campaign."

"Boy, it sounds like I missed all the fun," Roma chuckled.

Jack returned to the living room with two beers. Handing one to Skye, he said, "Here, you need this probably as much as I do." He took a seat at the other end of the couch from Roma.

Skye took a seat on the beanbag chair in the middle of the living room.How was your day?" he asked her sister.

Nothing exciting. I lucked out. When I got home, Monk wasn't there. I got the rest of my things in time before he came home from work," Roma shrugged. "Oh, and I raided the secret cache while I was there." She leaned over the arm of the couch, getting her purse. "I want to give you guys some money for letting me stay here." She unzipped the leather bag.

"No way," Skye insisted. "You've been buying groceries, cleaning house and cooking meals since you've been here." She added, "More than some people have been doing around here."

"Hey! Just a minute there," Jack exclaimed. "I know you're not here during the day to see who's doing what, but in addition to Roma's contributions, you must notice other things are getting done - don't you?"

"As in?"

"Well, what do you think? You think the garbage just walks out to the can in the ally way by itself everyday? And, and do you think the toilet is self-cleaning?" He hesitated, thinking, "And how do you think your car keeps ending up with new spark plugs and oil in it?"

So far, Skye did not seem impressed.

His mind racing, hard pressed to find anything else to credit himself with, a wail of sirens at the front of the house came to his rescue. Headlights panned the window. Red lights began splashing across the house on the other side of the street. They all rose and went to the front window. A police car had stopped in the middle of the street. Another siren screamed out of the distance, and soon another car appeared its tires screeching at it slid to a stop behind the other police car. It too boasted a revolving red light. "Gad, hide the dope!" Skye uttered.

"Whatever is going on, has to do with the house across the street, not us," Roma remarked.

Illuminated by the swirling red lights of the two police cars was a man with a head of thick, un-kept hair seated on the front steps of the house across the street. He held a pistol at himself. They all watched out the front window.

"More specifically, it's something to do with that guy on the steps," Jack added.

"What's he doing?" Skye asked.

"Holding a pistol to his head." It looked like a forty-five. This was the guy he had been getting brief glimpses of at the second story window for the past year, Jack had no doubt.

The policemen clambered out of their cars and with pistols in hand, began advancing towards the man. A lady appeared from the back of the house. She held up her hands and walked towards the policemen. Jack opened the front door so he could hear what was going on.

"Don't hurt him," the woman cried.

He knew her. It was Judy, the lady who lived there.

"I'm the one who called. I'm his wife," she sobbed, standing between her husband and the policemen.

"Don't go out there," Roma warned Jack as he went to watch from the front steps. "Everyone has guns."

"He's not going to listen to you," Skye say to her sister. "Guns don't rate on his short-list of something to fear."

Jack went out and swung open the gate to the picket fence. He stepped into the street.

One of the policemen turned and barked, "Sir, you'll have to go back inside your house. This is a dangerous situation." To witness these pop-up target trained defenders of a usually quiet little community, brandishing pistols they did not seem to know what to do with, Jack had no doubt this was a dangerous situation. As far as his neighbor across the street was concerned, he was only dangerous to himself.

"Don't let him do it!" Judy tearfully pleaded. She turned to her husband. "Al, put the gun down. Please!"

"Go back into your homes where it's safe!" the policeman bellowed to the dozen or more people who had lined the street for several blocks.

Jack turned to go back inside. Skye and Roma hovered at the open door. "The crisis is in the competent hands of our boys in blue," he smirked.

"Ever since he got back from the war, he's been acting crazy," the lady cried.

Jack spun back around when he heard her words. He took another look at the bearded man in faded blue jeans and flannel shirt. He was leaning forward, his head bowed, holding the pistol with the end of its barrel resting on his temple. "That crazy son-of-a-bitch is a 'Nam vet," Jack muttered. He glanced to see one of the cops leading the lady to a squad car. Pulling the back door open, the starched and tight-fitting uniformed man helped her into the seat. "You're going to have to just sit tight right here out of our way until we get this situation is under control," he assured.

Another cop stood outside of his car with a handset pulled to the limit of its coiled cord out the driver's window. "Looks like we've got a serious problem out here. Just found out from his wife that this guy with the gun to his head is a Vietnam veteran, fresh outta the jungle."

"Excuse me," Jack said, approaching the cop nearest himself.

The man turned, looking surprised. "I thought I told you to get inside."

"I just want to see if I can help. I'd like to try and talk him out of it. I'm also a 'Nam vet."

A skeptical gaze gradually softened to a hint of regard, and he said, "Wait here." He went over to the second squad car and spoke to the other officer a minute. When he returned, he said, "Okay. We don't have much else we can do. Meanwhile, we've got you covered. If he starts waving that gun around, hit the ground."

Don't have to tell me - I know all about that shit, he thought. He walked over to within several yards of the steps and cleared his throat loudly, not wanting any surprises. His neighbor, more importantly the fellow 'Nam vet looked up. From the appearance of his weary, red eyes, Jack guessed he had not had much sleep. Such eyes were a too familiar sight in his bathroom mirror.

"Hello there neighbor. What brings you to my side of the street?" he said, his jaw taunt.

Jack made a nervous laugh. He held both arms out a little. "You know, I just found out that we're not just neighbors. I also served in 'Nam."

The tightness in his jaw went away. He blinked several times. But he continued to hold the pistol pointed at his head.

"My name's Jack. I was in the Ninth Division in the Delta in '68."

The man now relaxed his grip on the pistol, his finger appeared to be easing up on the trigger.

"I've met your wife, but never had the chance to meet you."

"Oh. I'm Albert," he said like he had just remembered his manners. His head bobbed a little. "I was in the Fourth Division, out of Pleiku."

Another siren wailed in the night. Tires skidded at the arrival of another set of splashing red lights. "Either you're some very brave, or some very dumb motherfucker, because there's a whole bunch of guys with guns, just waiting for me to make the wrong move. And you're standing right in their line of fire."

"You're not going to make the wrong move, are you?"

Albert looked as if he was uncertain on that point, but the barrel of the pistol began to slip from its aim at his temple.

"I don't know very many 'Nam vets in the area. Nice to know I have one for a neighbor. It's mighty good of you to come out here and risk your life for me."

"That's what we did for each other over there. As far as I'm concerned, nothing has changed." Jack meant what he said. "What'd you say you let that gun down real slow. This bunch surrounding us would love nothing better than to be able to brag back at the precinct that they blew your brains out to keep you from blowing your own brains out."

Albert broke into a smile. "I'm going to take your advice on this - because I like you." He let the pistol down, laying it on the steps at his side. He put both hands behind his head like you were taught to do if you were taken prisoner of war.

The sound of scrambling footsteps announced the arrival of five policemen. Two of them grabbed Albert, spun him around and slammed him face down against the stairs. They handcuffed him.

Jack watched as the police took his neighbor away, now a brother-in-arms. He looked down the street to see at least twice as many people as before standing on their lawns and in the street. He was tempted to yell, telling them that they could go back inside - no bloodshed this time.

* * *

Jack was alone at the house when he got a call from Ed's wife. She told him that the funeral would be Saturday. He thanked her, not bothering to mention that he would not be attending. He had his own way of paying last respects to his friend. He went to the closet and dug out his jungle boots. Finding the can of black polish, he spent a half an hour shining the old boots to a high gloss. It would be the kind of service the combat chaplain and company commander gave in the field after a mission where they endured

KIAs. For every man killed, there was an empty pair of boots neatly placed in a ghost formation. Stuck in the ground upside-down, by virtue of a fixed bayonet was an M-16 between each pair of boots. Of course, Jack did not have an M-16, or a bayonet. His shotgun would have to fill in. In the middle of the backyard, out of view of the neighbors and the road, he neatly positioned the boots, and shoved the muzzle of his shotgun into the soil between them, adjusting it until it was perfectly upright. It would be nice to have a steel helmet to complete the ad-lib memorial, he thought. He stepped back and stood at attention. "I'm going to miss you buddy. I didn't know you from Adam before. But now you're my brother for all eternity." He reached into his pocket and with his fingertips, felt the cold. He lowered his head. His vision was blurred so badly there were only blotched shapes where his gaze had settled. He wiped his eyes with fingers. A sharp pain assaulted his stomach, and his left knee gave out. He crumpled to the ground, landing softly to his back. He took a deep breath. "We thought we were coming home to the land of the Giant PX," he muttered. "And we were going to live happily fucking ever after." He lay there a long time, looking at the dark sky. He wondered at the void, and where are you during all of this?

9

The VC in Aisle Five

How are you doing?

"Kind of up and down. Mostly the latter," Jack admitted with a shrug.

"Could you elaborate?"

"Well, I still get put off a lot."

"As in?" the doctor pressed.

"You know, with everybody and his uncle. His brother and sister too."

"I see. Anything else been bothering you in addition to the feelings of hostility towards *everyone?*"

"Yeah. For instance, I'll be in a place where you would least expect it. You know, like the supermarket and VC will be waiting for me you know, in one of the aisles in ambush."

"Viet Cong - just standing there in the middle of the supermarket aisle?" The doctor made an expression like he had been surprisingly ambushed by a lair of VC.

"Not just standing there. They wouldn't do that. You don't know the VC very well if you think they'd be standing there in plain sight. You can't *see* them. You just know they're there. You can sense their presence. They're behind the rows of canned food, or in the bakery behind the tall aluminum cart of bread rolls. They're very good at choosing ambush sites."

"Do you actually believe that Viet Cong are waiting in ambush for you in the supermarket?"

"No! Of course not. It's just what I think, you know."

"This is something we will need to come back to, but today, let's keep our focus on the anger. Describe your feeling just before you get angry."

He stared at the brass infantryman on the desk a minute before glancing to meet the doctor's gaze. "I get worked-up over fairly common things. Like someone following my car too close on the freeway. I'll slam down on my brakes to get the son-of-a-bitch off my ass. If that doesn't do the trick, if he's still tailgating me, I'll lock the brakes, coming to a stop, even if it's in the middle of the freeway. Hopefully the other guy will get the hint."

"That's your actions," the doctor said. "What I want to know is, what are you feeling when such an incident occurs?"

"I don't know," Jack shrugged. "I see red."

"You *feel* the color red?"

He thought for a minute. "I *feel* angry, because someone is fucking with me."

"You're getting there. Look at it this way. Words are mere symbols of our true feelings. Visualize the period of time between you discovering the car tailgating you, and you bringing your car to a complete stop on the freeway. A very dangerous measure just to show your irritation at another driver, I hope you're aware."

"What I'm aware of is, someone is risking my life, and has to be dealt with." His stare returned to the little infantryman as he strained to make sense of the ease at which he changed from just another motorist putting down the road, to one very dangerous dude. As he stared, Jack felt his finger resting on the trigger. He scanned the surrounding jungle, fully prepared for whatever hell might break loose. Calculating every step, knowing it could be his last, he carefully moved among the shadows of the triple canopy foliage. A throat was being cleared. He turned his attention from the statue to the doctor.

"That's your feeling?"

"It happens like this. I'm somewhere in the Mekong Delta, stalking along a jungle trail, almost enjoying the beauty of the tropical scenery. The scenery erupts into a burst of machinegun fire. Without even a thought, I'm mowing down every leaf and branch and anything behind it with my M-16. That's the same thing as when I'm driving down the freeway minding my own business, and I encounter some asshole who is risking my fucking life by following too close at a high speed. It's kill or be killed."

"Now we're getting somewhere," the doctor nodded. "The consequences of your anger and subsequent aggression are not what I want to spend a lot of time on; but rather the source of it. You've just given me one such significant example. What we want to do is explore that source, and the accompanying feeling."

"You mean in back there in the bush, or now?"

"You cannot separate the two. That eighteen year old had some terrible things happen to him. Those things translate to what we call traumas. That eighteen year old is still inside of you with those unresolved traumas, still fighting for his life."

That makes sense, Jack thought. But a lot to digest. Too much in fact. "I don't think I can go on like this," he muttered. His throat became constricted and he began to tremble. His sight became blurred.

The doctor produced a box of tissues from one of his desk drawers offering them. Taking two of the tissues he said, "Thanks," wiping his eyes.

"This is a good place to conclude the session. Try to look at it this way. You survived all of that. You're a survivor."

That had more of the ring of a verdict, than a note of encouragement. He replied, "A *survivor* - Whoopee." His thoughts, fuck a survivor in the big survivor pussy.

* * *

On his way from his car to the mailbox, Jack heard someone call, "Hey there, Ninth Infantry!"

He turned around to see Albert coming down the same stairs that had been center stage of all of the excitement last week. "Hello brother!" he replied, waiting as Albert crossed the street, ambling up to him.

"I want to thank you for the other night man," he extended a hand. Jack grasped it firmly. Albert slapped the palm of his other hand over the top of their handshake and held it like that for a minute.

"Come on in. Got some cold-ones in the fridge," he offered, forgetting about the mail. "You drink beer don't you?"

"Any kind, any time." Albert followed.

"That you Jack?" Roma's voice came from the kitchen.

"Yep." He continued into the dining room. We've got special company," he told her. Roma was standing before the stove. "Smells good. What'cha got cooking?"

"Four cheese lasagna. If you liked my spaghetti, you'll love my lasagna. Who's the company?"

He went the rest of the way into the kitchen and said in a low voice, "It's the guy who lives across the street, Albert."

Roma looked concerned. She whispered, "Unarmed, I hope."

"He comes in peace. I think… At least I'm pretty sure." Jack went to the refrigerator to fetch the beers. "Hasn't Skye got home yet?"

"Oh, she called. Jim invited her to some deal with his church group. An 'open house' or something like that. She didn't know how long it was going to last."

"I can't even imagine Skye going to a church meeting," he laughed. "Jim must have finally wore down her resistance." He headed back to the living room. "When you can break away there, come on in and meet our guest." Stepping into the living room, he found Albert seated on the beanbag chair. "Sorry to take so long. My sister-in-law was just telling me that my ol' lady is probably going to be home late tonight." He handed a beer to Albert, and took a seat on the couch. Ripping the tab off his can with flare, Jack started to drink with his newfound friend. Mindful of this being something of an occasion, he raised his can and said, "To brothers-in-arms and next-door neighbors."

"To us," Albert said, raising his can in response.

Jack guzzled his beer.

"Where'd you get the cool couch?" Albert asked, looking over the piece of furniture that sat at a right angle just several feet from him.

"I was driving down the street one day and saw it there leaning against a dumpster in the ally. It looked back at me and said 'Take me home.' Since I didn't have a couch at that time, I replied, 'OK, this could go on to evolve in a cushy relationship.'" Jack affectionately patted the cushion at his left. "I took the legs off so it sits nice and low. It was missing one leg anyway. The Madras tapestry is nuevo art expression. Paisley shapes defined the pattern in blue field. My sister-in-law is the interior decorator. She did that too," he pointed up to the billows of psychedelic clothe.

Albert glanced overhead at the soft colorful East Indian tapestry hanging from the ceiling in a quadrant of billows. "I was admiring that earlier. Matches the couch, huh? So your sister-in-law an *interior decorator?*"

"Not officially. A housewife. Or ex-housewife I guess you'd call her. She split the sheets with her ol' man. That's her in the kitchen. She's making dinner. She'll come in and visit us in a little while."

Albert nodded. He took a drink.

"So, how you doing?"

"Better than the last time we met. I thought they were going to take me to jail. Instead they took me to the booby-hatch."

"County Hospital, huh."

"That's the place," he nodded. If you ever feel like you're going crazy, pay a visit to that place. They've got some fruit-loops in there that'll make you feel like the most normal person in the world."

What *was* that all about?" Jack asked. "If you don't want to talk about it," he quickly added.

First taking a drink, Albert replied, "Things had been getting kind of crazy. I ripped off the grocery money from Judy's purse and bought a lid. She went off her rocker when she found out." He paused, his eyes fixed on the upturned shoe box lid on the surface of the coffee table. "Man, I gotta have pot. I'll go over the cliff if I don't have at least a couple of doobies a day." He inhaled deeply and went on. "After getting fired from my job last March, with everybody and his brother chasing my ass for overdue bills, and with Judy giving me hell night and day, I guess I just snapped."

Jack looked to see Roma entering the room with a drink in hand. "Hey, there she is. This is my sister-in-law. Roma, this is Albert my brother-in-arms."

"Hi," she smiled, taking a seat on the couch.

"Hi."

"We were just discussing the merits of marijuana in regard to human life form," Jack said. He leaned forward to the coffee table and plucked one of the pre-rolled joints from the shoe box lid.

"That's one of my favorite topics," Roma replied. Before he could find the matches, she came up with a book from her end of the table, struck one and offered a flame. In correlation to the joint making its hand-to-hand orbit around the group, conversation had fallen victim to those properties of the cannabis that play hell on the brain's motor functions. Jack did not want to be the first to interrupt this shared moment, and wondered just how well his tongue would serve him even if he attempted to speak. He leaned back, legs crossed atop the couch cushion, basking in the undulating harmony of The Marmalade musically blubbering about their sorrows and sad tomorrows, the words drifting from the large speakers painstakingly positioned, so his usual place on the couch would benefit from the greatest stereophonic effects. The front door opened. Skye appeared fanning a palm before herself. "Somebody call the fire department, the house is burning down," she exclaimed as she closed the door.

"Fire?" Albert sat up from where he had been slumped in the beanbag chair. He glanced back and forth.

"Relax," Jack hoped to console. "Skye's an environmentalist. That kind have a tendency to panic when there's a little smoke in the room."

"Little? You can't even see across the room for the smoke. Hi there." She acknowledged Albert with a curious glace.

"Hi. I'm Albert, your next-door neighbor, and new family friend."

She glared at him for a moment and said, "I knew about the first part. Excuse me while I get into something more comfortable." She went into the bedroom and pushed the door closed.

"She likes you. I can tell. She likes you very much," Jack kicked back, hands behind his head and grinned.

"I think she had a tough day," Roma said. "I'll get dinner ready."

In several minutes, the bedroom door opened. Skye entered the room wearing shorts and a sleeveless blouse. "Don't you want to open some windows? It's too warm. And I don't see how you can breath with all the smoke."

"If you open any windows," Jack said to her as she walked into the kitchen, "the smoke gets out, some 'law abiding citizen walks by, smells that we're smoking pot and calls the cops. Then what? We're being hauled away from our nice smoke filled house in handcuffs."

"I know all about that," Albert said. "I mean the part about the being hauled away in handcuffs."

Skye returned with a glass of beer. Every once in a while she got fancy, pouring her beer in a glass - at least an inch of foam on top and all, Jack took note. "So, did you get Born-Again?" Jack confronted Skye.

She seated herself at the other end of the couch. "Actually, I enjoyed the meeting. I was kind of wary at first, but there's a lot of upright people among them. I don't think I could buy into their Born-again thing though. One of the first things that happens is you quit smoking dope. Kinda spooky."

Albert clumsily rose from his seat. "I guess I'll be getting along," he excused himself, wavering slightly. His eyes were red, and his shirttail hung out of his pants on one side. "Nice meeting you," he said to Skye.

"Come over any time," Jack said.

"You fish?"

"Sure do. Haven't gone in quite a while though."

"I'm going salmon fishing tomorrow. You want'a join me? I got a boat."

"Sure."

"You got a license?"

"To fish?" Jack laughed.

"The game wardens will confiscate your pole and give you a fine if they catch your ass."

"That's never been a problem with me. If I see a game warden coming, I just toss my pole into the water, but hang onto the line secretly. When he's gone, I pull it back out of the river by the line."

"He loses more fishing poles that way," Skye remarked. "I can think of at least two times that you've had to dive into the river to salvage your pole after the line broke when it snagged on something," she said.

"Wouldn't it be easier just to buy a license?" Albert asked.

"That'd ruin all the fun of it. Besides, nothing tastes better than an illegal fish."

Albert lifted his eyebrows with interest, as if for the first time hearing such an irrefutable truth. "Meet me in front of my place at five," he said turning. When he pulled the door, it came only slightly open before making a "clunk." Albert looked down, stepped back a little and pulled the door the rest of the way open. He looked back. "I get it now. You move your foot out of the way, *then* you open the door," at which point he successfully exited the house.

"Good thing he doesn't have to *drive* home." Skye rolled her eyes.

* * *

Jack woke to a banging. "What the?" he muttered.

The bedroom door opened. Roma was in her nightgown. "Albert's here," she said and disappeared.

He turned to see the lighted numbers on his clock-radio. It was just a little after five. He had not fallen asleep until around three. "What's he doing here at this hour?"

"You sure you want to go through with this?" came a muffled voice from the pillow where Skye's head was buried.

"Not really."

"Tell him to go away then."

"Good idea. "Just tell him to go away," he called to Roma.

"I don't think she heard you. I think she fell back to sleep," Skye said after a minute.

By the time it took him to wrestle with his conscious that made a big issue out of camaraderie, get dressed and finally stumble out the front door into the cool morning air, it was nearly six.

"You Vietnam vets *are* all fucked up in the head," was Skye's way of saying *have fun*. Visible only as a dark form slumped down behind the steering wheel of his old pickup truck, it appeared Albert had fallen asleep while waiting. Atop the truck roof, an upside down turned, shallow draft aluminum boat was strapped by rope, extending at a steep angle from midway over the hood downward to several feet beyond the tailgate. Albert perked up at the metallic creak of the passenger door opening. Jack climbed in, slamming the heavy door behind himself. "Goddamned roosters aren't even awake yet," Jack complained.

"Good morning to you too," Albert replied. He sat up and reached to the steering column turning the key. In seeming defiance to the rickety and rusting hulk for which it was contained, the engine instantly roared to life. Adeptly working his feet on the pedals, one hand on the steering wheel and the other jerking the floor shift into gear, the truck lurched forward. "Want some coffee?" He indicated with his thumb to a stainless steel thermos on the seat between them.

"Thanks, but I think I'll just catch some shuteye while we're in route." He slid down in the seat, propping his knees against the dashboard. He woke abruptly. Undulating tree branches were passing overhead.

"Sorry about that," Albert muttered. "You really need a fucking jeep to navigate this road."

Jack sat up to discover they were bouncing down a rugged dirt road flanked by heavy foliage. An occasional branch slapped the windshield screeching against the metal side of the truck. In a moment, the foliage ended, and a river appeared.

"Ready to catch dinner?" Albert asked, bringing the truck to a sudden halt. As they shoved off from the muddy shore, the sun peaked through trees at the east side of the Yuba River. Albert began pulling the rope of the small outboard engine. It roared briefly, sputtered, spit and bellowed black smoke. He made repeated attempts, with the same lack of success. Meanwhile, the boat began moving rapidly, turning sideways result of the strong river current.

Jack grabbed the oars, directing the boat until the bow faced down river. "Did we want to go to Sacramento?" he called to Albert who now leaned over the engine fiddling with the spark plug wire.

"Motherfucking son of a motherfucking son-of-a-bitch," he cried. He glanced over his shoulder. "Sacto isn't for another five miles. Just keep us away from the shore and any other boats until I get this piece of shit motor going."

"Why don't we just anchor here?" Jack suggested. "Looks like a good place as any. After we catch some fish, we can row right back to shore and don't have to worry about starting the engine."

Albert backed away from the outboard motor and sat down. "Good plan. Watch out," he cautioned, picking up the small anchor from the hull. He tossed it overboard. The coil of rope in the center of the boat quickly began to unfurl, and snapped taut at its mooring on an eye ring at the bow. The boat shuddered to a stop midway in the river. "This one's yours." Albert handed over one of his fishing poles.

Jack accepted it by the handle where a heavy duty reel was mounted. It looked to be loaded with what must have been at least forty pound test filament line. "I didn't know we were fishing for whale," Jack kidded.

"Hey, I've had big-ass salmon break my line more than once. I'm not taking any chances."

They each baited their hooks with pieces of sardine Albert kept in a metal ice chest atop cans of beer and what appeared to be sandwiches wrapped in tinfoil. They cast on separate sides of the boat. A warm breeze moved up the river gently rippling the water. Jack began watching his line, reeling in any slack the moment it occurred. The fog of last nights drugs, compounded by too little sleep was clearing some with the invigorating morning air. There was a time when he went fishing nearly every weekend - before 'Nam. Now he only fished when the mood struck him, which wasn't very often. He loved the peace of the water and the open sky. Even if he did not catch any fish, he always felt good after a day of just being with nature and away from everything. He smiled to himself that when all else about his past had been shattered, at least there was this simple pleasure. I need to get back into my old fishing routine, he thought. Looking around the place for the first time, Jack noticed the nearest shore, about twenty meters away was lined with trees and dense undergrowth. In the morning when you awoke in wonder to a canopy of coconut fronds overhead, looked around from your makeshift bed on the ground and saw you were surrounded by jungle, the very first thing you did was feel around at your side. You instantly felt good when your fingers set down upon that familiar shape of stock, or trigger housing, or barrel of your most valued possession, your M-16. Jack tightly gripped the handle of his fishing pole, a palpable reminder of those days before the war when a machine gun was the farthest thought from his mind. But what he actually felt was how similar the handle of the pole felt to that part of his M-16 where the stock met the trigger housing. His gaze shot to movement in the screen of foliage nearest him. Probably a bird or a squirrel, but still he watched. He knew that if he had his M-16, he would be taking aim on that spot, ready to spray bullets at the slightest cue.

"This is the life," Albert declared, the tip of his pole flexing with the motion of him reeling in his line.

"Uh, you bet," Jack muttered.

"Leave all your troubles on shore," Albert worked his fishing pole as if he had a bite. After a minute he said, "Got beer in the cooler, and some sandwiches."

"Wow, you think of everything. I feel kind of bad. I didn't bring anything." He reached into his shirt pocket and plucked out a fat joint, displaying it. "Except this."

"That makes us even friend," Albert grinned. "Save it. We'll have it to celebrate after we catch something. I got one!" he exclaimed, jerking his pole.

As Albert carefully reeled in his catch, Jack watched the line making zigzagged slices across the river surface. With the sun lifting over the treetops, the morning mist quickly evaporated to reveal a river alive with brilliant sparkles dancing upon rippling waves.

"Motherfuck! I lost it," Albert cried after a minute.

A light tug alerted Jack to his pole. he worked his reel to keep the line taut. After awhile, it became evident the fish had lost interest in his bait. He began looking around again. In the starkness of full daylight, the degree of their isolation sank in. The only other boat was so far away, the two men aboard were no more than faceless silhouettes. "You sure know where to get away from it all," he said.

"Yep. It took a lot of reconnaissance to find this stretch of river," Albert bragged. "To tell you the truth, I don't like to be around other people. Even the old lady gets to be too much company after a while."

"I hope I'm not taking up room in your personal space."

"Hey man, you aren't another person," he replied. "You're a 'Nam vet."

Jack grinned at the endorsement. "So, how you doing? Things getting back together there on the home front?"

Albert looked pensive, shook his head slowly and said, "Judy won't let up on me. It's, 'Why can't you keep a job? You drink too much. You smoke too much dope, nag, nag, nag, nag.'"

"Just another day in the life of… I'm always telling Skye not to the sweat the small stuff. I mean, for instance losing a job or two isn't the end of the world. You can always find another one."

"And Judy keeps hiding my guns on me. I have to look all over the damn place to find them again. A man's gotta have his protection, right?"

Jack nodded. But in Albert's case, he felt relatively certain that if he needed protection, it was from his own self.

"You ready for a cool-one?"

"Beer? I haven't even had my coffee yet." He glanced to the thermos sitting between them, alongside the tackle box.

Albert had already fetched two cans from the ice chest.

"Well, if you're going to force it on me." He leaned forward to take the offered can. Jack did not realize how thirsty he was until he took a drink. He guzzled down the contents in a minute. Crumbling the empty can, he tossed it into the river, watching as it slowly drifted with the current. *So, it isn't just in my head,* he thought. *Us 'Nam vets* are *different - we've got our own club. And everyone else is a Rear Echelon Mother Fucker.* There was not even the remotest possibility of club membership for that bunch. But then, in a private club, he wondered, isn't there supposed to be organized events, or commemorative occasions, or even just a designated time and place to get together? The only thing that ever happened when Jack got together with any of his war buddies, was they drank and smoked dope and complained about everything. "I guess it takes time to get over. I mean I thought I would get over that fucking war after a few months. Then a year went by; and another year." Jack said. "I don't feel like I thought you were supposed to feel when you come home from war." He watched the can as it continued its journey down river, gradually taking on water until it sank.

"I know what you mean. I've got this little door-gunner in a little chopper flying around inside my head," Albert said. "He's there everyday, searching the jungle below for a clearing to land, wondering if this ride is ever going to end." He watched his line where it entered the water as he spoke.

Jack broke his stare from the place where the can

disappeared to look at his friend. "What happens if he finds a place to land? I mean, he hasn't arrived home. He's just landing in the jungle."

"Home! That's not even on the map," Albert laughed. "You keep talking about home. You must have a bigger map than me. I've still dealing with a couple hundred square kilometers of jungle in the middle of fucking nowhere."

"No. I'm with you," Jack conceded. "I've got this little rice paddy humper inside my head. He's not even important enough to carry a map. He just wants to somehow get beyond enemy lines and back to camp."

"The shrink at the hospital told me that I need to 'come down to earth,' after I told him about the little door- gunner. He told me to come down to earth, then gave me a bottle of pills to stay up in the clouds with," Albert laughed. He picked up the beer that had been sitting on the seat next to him. Finishing it off, he crumbled the can in his fist. "To tell you the truth man, I'd rather be back there in 'Nam. At least there, when you came in from a mission, you felt really good at just being alive another day. You could goddamn smell and taste being alive. Those were the worst days of my life; and they were the best days of my life."

"Speak of the devil," Jack started. "Sometimes I'm

at home by myself, and I can't deal with any company. When you come over, I'll call, 'What's the password?' I mean, I can see anybody that comes to the house from where I sit on the couch. I'll know it's you. But, I mean don't be offended if you know I'm home and I don't say anything. I mean, you know, sometimes I just can't deal with company."

"Hey man. You don't have to explain. I'm the same way. I go for days sometimes, hiding out in the spare bedroom upstairs from the ol' lady, from everyone. Sometimes you need to hunker-down." Albert tossed his crumbled can into the river.

Jack watched as it bobbed down river, taking on water, sinking when it got about as far as the other can had traveled. His gaze settled on the smooth surface of the water. Mix a little more mud in there and it could be confused for a stretch of the Vam Co Dong river. And it was quiet. But too quiet. He envisioned a row of AK-47s behind that emerald screen on shore, muzzles following the movement of the boat as it journeyed down river, trigger-finger anticipation growing as the boat neared the kill zone. "Hey, you want to get outta here?" He hoped Albert did not detect the tremble in his voice.

"What? We just got here."

"I'm getting a headache or something," he replied.

"Relax, it'll go away. The sun is shining, we're away from it all, we still got a cooler full of suds and sandwiches."

"No, I mean I've really got to get out of here. This place is getting to me."

"You're not serious? This is the most relaxed I've been in months."

He wondered, do I really need to explain this? But then, Albert *was* the one who wanted to land his imaginary copter in the jungle, with no plans beyond that. Jack began reeling in his line.

10

Bodycount

The two American companies had been pinned-down all afternoon beneath the roar of Chicom rifles and fifty-one caliber fire. Mortar rounds erupting into tall geysers of rice paddy water, throwing mud and shrapnel everywhere. Behind the earthen dike-turned-rampart, keeping their heads down was about all the American troops could do, as the battalion of NVA showed-off their stuff. Field-radios busily crackled and modulated under the strain of repeated cries for more air-strikes, more artillery - and how about some fucking reinforcements in here?

By popular request, barrage after barrage of American artillery screamed overhead, leveling groves of coconut trees, setting large portions of that emerald screen ablaze. Any lull between salvos of artillery instantly filled in with resurrections of heavy enemy fire. The sound of rotor blades announcing the arrival of a formation of slicks carrying fresh troops and supplies, greeted from earthen bunkers in the wood line with gunfire turned skywards. As hundreds of bullets smashed through the thin metal of the crafts, wounding numerous men before they could even set foot on ground to fight, forcing the helicopters to make a quick retreat, most without unloading. Alpha Company was running low on ammo. Charlie Company had taken a lot of casualties. Eerily, all fire from the wood line ceased at once. Jack watched, openmouthed as dozens, then hundreds of uniformed North Vietnamese soldiers began filing out of their jungle redoubt. They each held their rifle at arms length, overhead in surrender. "What in the name of?" The guy next to Jack uttered. "They *really* giving up? They don't have to. They've got us outgunned."

The battalion of enemy soldiers began lining up on a paddy dike that extended from one end of the network of rice paddies to the other. They evenly spaced themselves on the dike.

"Hold your fire," the captain of Alpha Company cried. "I don't know why, but I think they're surrendering." The command was repeated down the line of Americans who lay prone in the mud, rifles barrels resting across the foot high dike.

The enemy soldiers began kicking their legs high in synchronization, swinging their AK-47s like batons, performing a military rendition of a chorus line dance. All that was missing was an orchestra in the pit.

"They're Cancan dancing. I think," Jack gasped. In collective wonder, the hundred or so American troops peered over top of their section of dike. As he marveled at this extemporaneous performance, a bizarre demonstration, apparently of goodwill, put on by the enemy troops, Jack knew that even if the order were given, he could no more be capable of opening fire on these guys than he would the Bob Hope Christmas Show. He wondered if this was a Southeast Asian version of the old Trojan Horse trick. As he watched the toothy smiling North Vietnamese troops continue their rice paddy venue floor show, Jack blinked hard. This is not happening, he told himself. Blinking again, a flat white surface came into focus. As he gazed uncertainly for a moment, a faint piebald spot from rain seepage, gave away that it was the ceiling he was staring at. His head ached and his heart beat rapidly. He tried to swallow, but his mouth was too parched. All that aside, he felt greatly relieved that he had only been dreaming. Beneath that levity, however, he shuddered at how far he had gone over the edge in his sleep. A nightmare jam-packed with rattling machine guns, exploding mortars and people dropping dead in droves was scary - but at least it contained the rock bottom foundation of reality. These bizarre, downright psychedelic nightmares had him concerned about his sanity. A nearby noise startled him. His gaze shot in that direction. Through the wide open bathroom door, he saw Roma. She was putting things into her overnight bag. Jack sat up.

"Do I hear a sign of life?" she said from where she stood at the sink.

"If I appear alive, it's only that my hair and fingernails are still growing," Jack groaned. He thought to look at the clock, but decided he didn't even want to know the time. The bright light coming through the window was evidence enough that he had squeaked through another night. As he watched, it occurred to him that Roma was packing. "You going somewhere?"

She stepped out of the bathroom, her small piece of luggage shouldered by a long strap. Pushing a length of hair from her face, she announced, "I'm getting my own apartment. I called around this morning and found a place in Sacramento. That'll be far enough from here to decrease my chances of running into Monk in a store or on the street. And I need to find a job."

"Yeah, I've got that one at the top of my list of 'Things to do.'"

"We've got to work."

"We've got to make money to live on, you mean. Beyond that, it's all going through the motions. Doesn't matter if you're the CEO of a big company and make five million a year. You have to get up morning, get dressed and go off to the drudgery of being a slave, likely of someone else's version of what is important in life. We're just going through the motions."

"Ah, life is but a stage, and we are all but actors."

Jack nodded. "You got it." Feelings of self-condemnation over his behavior last night began to sink in. Undoubtedly, *he* was the reason behind her leaving in a huff. He plundered his nightmare ravished, morning-after numbed brain for the right words, but figured anything he had to say, would most likely not change her mind. It was like she said, *life is a stage and we are all its actors.* And he knew that she knew, he was the villain in this particular play. With so much practice, a role for which he seemed to be getting more comfortable – at least mummified.

"I really appreciate you and Skye taking me in," Roma said.

"Anytime. You know that. Can I help you carry your bags out?" He started to get out of bed.

"I've got everything already loaded into the car, except for this." Roma slapped the side of her bag. "Oh, one more thing." She stepped into the living room a moment, and returned with the cat in her arms. "The apartment doesn't take pets. Until I get back on my feet, I don't have any place for her. Do you mind?"

"I'll take care of her for as long as you want."

She set the cat down gently on the bed. "It might be a while."

"No problem."

"She just needs food and water, and a little company between long naps. I left a five pound bag of cat food in the kitchen."

"Perfect. Food water and sleep are my general area of expertise."

"Thanks. See ya," she said, then turned and went out the bedroom door.

"Your mama says you're going to be low-maintenance. You better not disappoint me," Jack warned. Shadow curled up at his feet, returning a reassuring gaze with its large amber eyes. Waiting until he heard the front door close, he jumped out of bed, slipped into his jeans and went to the window. He saw Roma's car just as it turned onto the street. She glanced towards him, swerved a little and tooted her horn. He waved as she accelerated down the hill in the direction of another shot at putting it all behind herself. He noticed that the usually dry ditch alongside the road had become a stream of turbulent muddy water. Though the sky was cloudless now, he figured that it must have been a pretty good rain while he was asleep. The quick moving stream easily captivated him. A particular stretch of roiling waters drew him in as it turned into itself. The water gurgled crazily beneath his legs that dangled over the stern of the riverboat. Now that the mission was over, this was his first chance to spend time by himself for repose. In the past two days since the ambush, he had been buoyed at his good fortune. It had even crossed his mind that perhaps he was invincible. Look at everything I've survived so far, he thought. Contrary to the rush of elation, the weariness that invariably comes at the end of a long, arduous mission began to sink in. For instance, he began to realize how wrong it was to feel good about surviving while others had died. Jack leaned forward so he could see into the water better. As for the guys who where killed, at least they no longer had to suffer that repeated shock of witnessing others being killed, or to endure that gnawing inside that never went away, fearing in near panic if you would be next. The water that churned and tumbled and rolled within itself transfixed him. I should be with them, he had decided. He leaned forward even more until he was teetering on the edge of the metal riverboat's surface. He could even see his boots now. They were just above the roiling prop-turbulence, pieces of paddy mud gradually washing from them in the splashing water. It surprised him how inviting the river water looked. Letting himself fall all the way forward, the awful world departed forever behind him. He flinched. Stepping warily away from the window, as if that really were the beckoning waters of the Rach Ba Rai river outside his bedroom window, Jack hurried into the bathroom. He turned on the cold water tap all the way, and splashed his face repeatedly. Feeling only marginally better, he went to the kitchen. As he had hoped, Roma had left him a pot of fresh coffee. He poured himself a cup and went to the living room. Staring out the much safer front window where instead of broiling waters, there was only a very pastoral looking front yard with a large cedar tree. He wondered if there would ever be a time when he could look deeply into a stretch of muddy water, and not become swept up into the shores of the fucking 'Nam. He glanced at movement beyond the red truck of the tree in his yard to see Albert crossing the street. Jack did not feel like company. He considered ducking back into the bedroom and hiding out. But how could he deny the company of a fellow combatant? He sat at his usual place on the couch, just as there came tapping at the door.

"What's the secret password?" he called.

"Fuck you in the left ear."

"Step forward and be recognized."

Once he had settled into the bean bag chair, Albert remarked, "Saw Roma putting her things in her car."

"She got herself an apartment in Sacto.She wants to moderate into low profile mode." Distracted by the radio Jack exclaimed, "I like that song." He jumped up, stepped over to the stereo and turned up the volume. He returned to his seat and began singing along with Glen Campbell's song, *Lineman For The County.*

When the song came to the part with the lineman lamenting about his need for a vacation, Albert remarked, "I could use one of those too. Just can't afford it. At least I have the mental vacation option."

"We're all linemen for the county.Our entire lives are about trying to keep up with repairs of communication circuits. Does anyone get that song?" Linemen were paid well, Jack had no doubt. They were respectable members of the community. He reached and took a joint from the shoe box lid.Someone was trying to get to him on the line, but foul weather took down the line, and now Jack could not be reached by that person who wanted to warn him about the worse snow storm in a half century, black ice on the road in forecast, descending upon his very abode.

"I was going through the want-ads this morning. Couldn't find anything that I qualify for. Except a gas station job," Albert grumbled. He scratched his beard thoughtfully. "I can recite the phonetic alphabet forward and backward; strip down an M-60 right down to the firing pin, clean and oil it and put it back together before you can say, 'Jack be nimble, Jack be quick,' ten times fast; call in artillery from two miles away and land the very first round right on a dime." He took a breath. "But who cares?"

"I do. You're my goddamn hero," Jack said. He lit the cigarette.

"Kiss my ass."

"Guess I should start getting serious about looking for a job myself. I'd give my left nut to get a job at the sawmill." Jack took a deep drag from the joint and handed it to his war buddy.

They listened to the music, passing the small cigarette back and forth until it had burned down to nothing. The hourly news came on at the radio station. Among the top stories was the usual Vietnam update, which always concluded with the latest *body count*. It was several minutes after the news ended when Albert muttered, "When's that shit ever going to end over there?"

Gonna get worse before it gets better," Jack vowed.

11

A Gemini in the House

J ack leaned back with the chair resting on two legs held upright by virtue of his knees resting against the edge of the dining table. In one hand, he held a mug of steaming coffee. The newspaper, opened to the comics, lay on his lap. "What's so funny about some asshole sergeant beating one of his troops to a pulp," he mumbled, this in regard to the comic strip *Beetle Baily*.

"Read my horoscope," Skye asked from across the table. A college textbook lay open before her.

"Let's see. Leo, right?"

"You know damn well I'm a Gemini."

"Yeah, but you behave like a Leo.Oh. Okay. Here it is. 'A capricious, fun-loving side of your character is trying to emerge. Today is the time to prove to your detractors that you are not a stuffed-shirt. Do something scandalous, like robbing a convenience store in the nude. Or perhaps call the FBI and tell them you are going to blowup the White House. When they ask who you are, give the name of a good friend instead.'"

"Thanks. I guess I asked for it," she rolled her eyes. Give me the paper and I'll read my own horoscope." Skye reached across the table, taking it from him.

"You don't really believe this shit. Do you?"

"I *don't*. But I've heard that even if you don't believe in it, that there's something to it." She straightened the paper, holding it so he could no longer see her face. "Don't you have your doctor's appointment soon, Mr. Skeptical?"

He glanced to the wall clock in the kitchen. He had two hours before the appointment, and could normally make the trip door-to-door in an hour and a half. But when you factor in the unpredictable beast of Bay Area traffic, he decided he should be leaving right away. Getting up from the table, he reached into his pocket to make sure his keys where there. "I don't know. I just can't believe you fall for that crap."

"Well I can't believe that you're still driving around on four bald tires."

"Three. I had a flat with one of them yesterday and replaced it with the spare. The spare has tread on it." He started towards the door.

"I stand corrected. Three bald tires and no spare. You do believe in something, I'm beginning to discover."

He hurried for the door, not wanting to hear it.

"Your death wish. It's your religion, your outlook on life."

"I'd really like to talk about this some more, but I gotta go." Three bald tires, four bald tires. What's it matter anyway? She's always sweating the small stuff, he thought as he went out the door.

* * *

The doctor greeted him with a smile like they were old friends, indicating to take a seat with his eyes, and promptly returned his attention to the file folder on his lap. Jack tapped his fingers on the arms of the wooden chair he was beginning to think of as the *hot seat*. He quickly began reviewing in his mind the past month since his last visit - panic attacks, jumpiness, flashbacks, the problems sleeping to include nightmares, ad infinitum. He wondered how long it would take for these problems to die a natural death. The MD who was treating him for his knee, had broken the news that Jack's injury would not necessarily improve with time. This could not be true with nonphysical problems, Jack hoped. All of those hand grenade tossing, mortar firing, machine gun shooting little men running around inside his head would die a natural death by dent of sinking deeper into memory with the passage of time, he felt certain. He could not even imagine continuing to dive for cover at the sound of a car backfiring when he reached his seventies. But then, there was always the chance it would just keep getting worse, like his leg - the skepticism for which he was developing a solid reputation, rearing its ugly head.

"How are you?" The doctor looked up from the folder.

"I'm alive."

"The medication starting to help any?"

"Helps me sleep better. I still get the nightmares."

"The Vietnam stuff huh?"

Jack nodded. "I had a dream the other night where the NVA came out of the wood line and started doing a Cancan dance with their AK-47s for batons. It was like they were putting on a USO show. I've never had a dream like that before. I dream about being in battle all of the time. But it's always the way things really happened over there. Not something like that. Am I losing my mind?"

"Was it a nightmare though?"

"Guess you would call it that. I didn't wake up screaming or anything like that. I did wake up and couldn't get back to sleep."

"Well, I wouldn't worry too much about the NVA doing a Cancan dance for you. It's got to be better than them shooting at you in your dreams, or otherwise. Main thing is we need to get you where you're sleeping better. You notice any decrease in those kinds of nightmares since you started your medication - the ones where you wake up abruptly?"

"No. But now that you mention it, a little." God, the nightmares. They were so powerful in dimension, that it was a wonder the four walls of his bedroom were strong enough to contain them. Yes, the medication helped. But as badly as he needed sleep, even just a couple of nights worth in a row, what scared him is if the medication might prevent him from waking when the nightmares started getting rough. At least when you wake up crying out, the nightmare is over at that point. He wondered, was that NVA cancan dancing dream any indication the medication was turning his dreams to some kind of psychodrama? His reason for taking the medication wasn't just to feel better. He had hoped that it might provide a safety-net, to some extent, from this goddamned free-fall into the hot LZ of his war ravaged mind.

"You ever entertain the notion of suicide?"

Jack recoiled at the question. "Now that you mention it," he felt more defensive at this question than any other the doctor had asked. "Every morning when I wake up after a night of poor sleep and a hangover."

"You have anyone you can talk to about Vietnam. You know, someone close?"

"No."

"You must have someone you can talk to, another veteran, your wife, a parent."

Jack shook his head. "Not really. My wife is always asking me to tell her things about the war. Actually, I try to talk to her about 'Nam, but the words can't seem to do it any justice. I just freeze up."

"How does she respond to your outbursts and such?"

"She's the one who insisted I seek 'professional help.'"

"She is right about that. You need to get these things off of your chest," the doctor confirmed. "This keeping everything inside is making you a, a..."

"A walking time-bomb?" he dared utter the popular label placed on 'Nam vets, parlance for which the doctor seemed to be politely sidestepping.

"Well, now that you mention it. Yes. You've heard the stories, seen the news, might even know a couple of guys who fit the bill. You certainly don't want to be one of those characters, do you?"

"Course not," he replied, "Who in their right mind would want to be a 'Nam vet if they could prevent it?" He watched the news, knew the rap. Only difference, he had not shot anyone yet in a rage - at least not stateside. The way things were going, it was just a matter of time. When they sent him to 'Nam, as powerful as the fear of death, was the fear that he would cross the line his religion had warned him, above all else, in reference to Commandments, not to cross. But as soon as you become witness to several of your buddies getting killed, it's pretty easy to cross that line, and start seeing the world as a place where it's either kill or be killed, religious upbringing aside. Damn, here back Stateside, when, say you're on the highway and some asshole comes up behind you tailgating, and alongside of you staring at you like they have an issue that you're only doing eighty and they want to do a hundred, and aggressively pull over right in front of you. This is intentional. It comes down to chariot racing. My chariot is going to run your chariot off the road, get the fuck out of my way. Aren't they the enemy? Doesn't it make sense that you get angry at them?

"Why don't you tell me some more stuff you keep locked up inside? Think of me as the guy who knows how to defuse those time-bombs."

He thought for a minute. The scene of an incident in Ken Hoa Province conjured itself.

"We were coming into a hot LZ. Bullets were making holes in the copter skin. Several whizzed right past my ear. We're about twenty feet from landing. 'Close enough,' I thought, and jumped." Jack's palms were becoming sweaty. He wiped them on the lap of his pants. After hitting the rice paddy boots first, he had dropped to the prone. Something crashed onto his back. In a second he realized someone had jumped with him, and in all of the excitement did not even consider where and how he would land. "Get off of me," Jack cried. It had to be the new guy, Drake who followed him everywhere. He had been sitting right next to him at the open copter door. "You've got a rice paddy the size of a football field and you had to land right on my fucking back," he admonished. Lifting his head out of the mud, he looked over his shoulder. He noticed that the guy who was laying crossways on top of him was covered with blood. Pulling himself out from underneath the guy, he discovered it *was* Drake, and that he had been shot to death somewhere between the copter and where he had landed. "I was in charge of this new guy. I had been teaching him the ropes." Jack tried to get it out, but a lump rose in his throat. There was a lot that he wanted to tell the doctor. But with the war memories steamer trunk finally pried open, he trembled to realize he was peeking into a Pandora's Box full of bullet and shrapnel mutilated battlefield ghosts.

"You really need to find someone to talk to," the doctor went at length to stress. "There's nothing like someone close for whom to confide. Meanwhile, you want to avoid people who are negative.I have to tell you right now, in a case like yours with so much stuff to sort out, you need to understand, it's likely going to get worse before it gets better."

There! Confirmed by an official. I knew it all along, he thought.

12

Stash

As he descended the stairs, the pain in Jack's knee increasingly flared with each step. Images of red-orange explosions and swirling volleys of shrapnel accompanied each burst of pain. He could only dream of the day that his claustrophobic fear of elevators would become less a terror than the pain that came with walking down a flight of stairs. When he reached the lobby, Jack took a chair for a minute to let the pain subside. Watching the other vets around him in the crowded lobby, he thought about the doctor's advice. He did have someone to confide in, but that person Albert had his own special problems. Jack did not want to burden someone who could hardly bear the weight of his own trunk full of war memories. He used to be able to talk about most anything with Ed. A train engine had cut short that conversation. Someone who had survived the same war certainly had the potential of being a confidant. There were not a whole bunch of those guys left, especially within convenient visiting distance. There is somebody who fits the bill, it occurred to him. Jack was standing at the edge of a rice paddy in the soggy Delta heat waving to the homebound Stash who looked like a kid on a carnival ride, his feet dangling out the side of a skyward straining helicopter. As the craft leveled off over the tree tops, Stash flashed a peace symbol with fingers. That was the last time he saw his old buddy. He had told Jack he lived in the Bay Area.

Taking his wallet out, Jack searched through it, soon finding the little piece of paper with Stash's phone number. He had been carrying it around since that day, always planning in the back of his mind to call his old friend.

"Is, ah Stash home?" he asked from a pay-phone in the hospital lobby.

"There's no one here by that name," a lady replied.

"Wait. Dan I mean," Jack finally remembered beyond the nickname.

"Danny? This is his mother. He doesn't live at home anymore. I don't know when you saw him last, but he's married now." She gave his current phone number.

At that number, he got Stash's wife, introduced himself and told her he would like to drop by to visit. She told him Danny would be home soon, and gave directions to their home in Martinez.

Afternoon commute traffic snaked over the Bay Bridge, finally slowing to a stop just south of Berkeley. A short distance ahead, he noticed the highway narrowed to a single lane. To the left, a row of flimsy rubber pylons separated him from a long stretch of recently completed thoroughfare. The new pavement looked dry enough. Work crews or road equipment were nowhere in sight. For someone who had once ignored orders from the company commander to machete a path through several hundred yards of thick bamboo to reach their objective, instead requisitioning three wobbly sampans from a nearby hamlet to swiftly ferry his squad by way of a provincial canal around the bamboo forest, his actions alone proved he was no poster-child for patience. In regard, only idiots sat in traffic. Cranking the steering wheel hard left, he squeezed his long sedan through the space between the orange and white striped construction cones. Once under way, as he breezed atop the virgin pavement, the bumper to bumper procession of frowning motorists melted to a bamboo thicket-like blur. Soon, Jack reached Richmond, where a large heap of asphalt in the middle of the new stretch of road marked the end of his do-it-yourself express lane. No sweat. The traffic jam was behind him now. Bouncing a rubber pylon out of the way with his right front fender, he swerved back into the lane of fast moving cars to the reception of a wailing horn from a car he nearly took off the guy's left headlight he came so close. Though he had never been to Martinez before, with the exception of being born there twenty-two years past, he managed to drive straight to the address among the row of drearily homogenous, single storied clapboard homes. He pulled into the cement drive behind a mid-Sixties Ford sedan. The neatly mowed lawn and manicured shrubs leading to the house entrance did not strike him as the work of a combat veteran. You hid from the enemy behind bushes, or they used it to hide from you. You slashed your machete through it, or hacked an opening in it for the helicopters to land. Either you did that when it hindered your headway, or you trusted your life to its quality of providing cover. He could not imagine the Stash he knew spending his evening and weekend hours working hedge-clippers, pruning shears and edgers. But on second thought, it could be a therapeutic form of taming the ol' beast. We all have our own way. "Hi, I just called," he said to the attractive girl who answered the doorbell.

"Hello." She held the door only slightly open. "I wasn't expecting you so soon." She gave him a once over, seeming only half convinced that he was not a dictionary or vacuum-cleaner salesman, or maybe even a cunning rapist who had called ahead, posing as a long lost friend of the away-at-work-husband, just to get inside. "I don't expect Danny to be home for another twenty minutes or so. Didn't you say you were in San Francisco when you called?"

"Yep."

"I heard on local radio just a little while ago that traffic was backed up for miles."

He knew firsthand. "Still is. I took my secret shortcut."

"You'll have to share your secret with Danny." She acted impressed. "He's been spending an hour or more on the stretch between here and Berkeley on his way home, ever since they started that construction. Come in." She stepped back, pulling the door wide open.

Jack followed her into a sunlight flooded living room. The large window framed a hilltop view of a section of the North Bay. She turned to face him. "I'm sorry," she said. "You know who I am, but you don't know my name. I'm Vicki." She smiled, offering a lissome hand.

Clasping with his car repair calloused hand, complete with oil besmirched knuckles, he gave her wilting fingers with long polished nails a hardy shake.

"My name's Jack."

"Yes, you told me on the phone." She withdrew her hand. "Can I get you a drink? I have fresh squeezed lemonade."

"Sounds good," he cordially accepted, though he craved a cold beer. He started to sit on the couch.

"Just a minute!" she gasped. Striding into the kitchen, she instantly returned with a dish towel. "Can you put this down where you're going to sit?" She grinned, handing it across the coffee table to him. "White couches are so hard to keep clean."

He obediently spread the small towel at the place on the spotless cushion where he intended to sit, dirty jeans and all. Vicki soon returned with a glass of lemonade in each hand. After neatly placing his drink on a coaster, she sat in a armchair that faced the couch from the other side of the marble surfaced coffee table.

"I thought about getting one of those plastic covers for the couch, but decided it would be too tacky." She leaned back casually taking a sip of her drink. "So you and Danny were good buddies over there?"

"We knew each other pretty well," he nodded. Picking up the glass she had placed on the coffee table, he took a thirsty drink. "We were in the same company, but different platoons. When you find out that there's someone else from California in your company, you go out of your way to get together."

"Why is that?"

"Well, maybe you haven't been in that situation. If *you* were stuck in a strange country for a year, and you had the choice to hang out with someone from California or say Alabama, and you're from California, what would be your choice?" He could not believe he was having to explain this.

"That's easy. California. I would make that choice even if I wasn't from California. I see what you mean."

"Anyway, we hung out together every time we got a chance."

"Funny, he's never mentioned your name. Not that I can remember."

"In 'Nam, the guys called me Tinman."

"You're Tinman?" She showed genuine surprise.

"That's me.

"Yes, he has mentioned you. He wanted to get in touch with you when he got back, but he didn't remember your last name. He knew you lived in the area, but how do you find someone in the phone book with *Tinman* as the only name to go by?"

"Really. Humm, we traded phone numbers."

"He lost it. He loses everything. He forgets everything," Vicki shook her head hopelessly. "He's lucky he has me. I make him put everything in the proper place. So how did you get a nickname like The Tinman?"

"Every time we came out of the rice paddies, onto dry land, I would say 'Squeak, squeak.' I would extend my arm like it was stiff and go, 'Squeak.' I extended a leg like it was stiff, 'Squeak. Damn! Anybody got a can of oil, I'm all rusted up again!' you know, like the Tinman in the Wizard of Oz. So the guys in my platoon gave me the nickname 'The Tinman.' That's how we got our nickname, like with Danny. We gave him the name 'Stash' because he had a big mustache."

Vicki glanced to the wall clock. He noticed her gaze going to another part of the wall. "That's his medals there."

Jack looked to see a deep-framed collection of six decorations. The display looked impressive. These were the same campaign and service medals as his. But he would never display his medals in plain sight. Everybody who came into the house, whether they knew you well or not, would be asking questions about each medal, one in agonizing account after the next. Anyway, they were not some ornament, or art piece with which you filled an empty space on the wall, or something that you hung to give balance to compliment or offset the decor of the room. When he moved slightly, reflected sunlight sparked off the glass of the frame. He started at a sniper's muzzle flash against the darkness of a jungle wood line. Caught in a Sniper's Sun, he cursed, knowing that the game was up. Jack's heart began to race. He wiped palms on his lap that had become clammy. At the corner of his eye, he could see that Vicki's gaze now settled on him. The lady, he suspected, awaited some form of compliment of her husband's decorations, or at the least, enlightening testimony coming from someone in the know. Perhaps he would point to one of the medals, cite the military campaign for which it represented, and seize that opening to launch an anecdote about how Stash and himself had celebrated victory, after raiding an enemy headquarters during a particular campaign, by sharing a bottle of captured rice wine. Turning to meet Vicki's gaze, he started to say something, if for no other reason than to make her happy. However, that part of him, the only part of him capable of telling such stories, was still trapped somewhere behind enemy lines.

"I suppose those medals represent a lot."

"Got that right," he uttered. They in fact represented the *ultimate*. When you sacrifice your life for a cause for your country, is there any greater commitment for anything? When you wear a medal Springfield rifle in wreath on your lapel"

Vicki softly smiled, possibly understanding the ease at which he was overwhelmed by anything to do with the war. After all, she *was* the wife of a 'Nam vet. But how much did she understand? Does she know, for instance, that many of us are so grubby because we became used to marching in waist deep mud, crapping in the woods, sleeping in muddy trenches and wearing the same dirty clothes for weeks on-end during a mission. Does she understand that after the war, many of us would rather live in such vagrancy, than take jobs in gas stations and restaurants waiting on a bunch of dickheads who got out of the war with college deferments, and now drove around in expensive cars and ate in nice restaurants because they got all of the good jobs while we were in the jungle fighting a war? Jack picked up the glass of lemonade before him. He took a long drink. Vicki shifted the position of her legs as if trying to get comfortable and said, "Could you do me a favor and set your glass on the coaster, instead of the table surface? Do you need more sugar?"

He was beginning to wonder if she washed the sheets and deodorized the bedroom every time she and Stash had sex.

"No. It's fine." He moved his glass to its proper place on the cork coaster. "So what does Stash do for work?"

"He teaches gym at a high school in Berkeley." She took a sip of her lemonade. "He goes by his original name 'Danny' now that he's back from the war." She replaced the glass to its proper place on the coaster. "What did you and Danny do when you weren't throwing hand grenades at enemy bunkers?"

"Well, when we got leave to the base camp, we would go to the mess halls where they served hot meals. And there was a library and PX. They even had a swimming pool there. It was one of those above ground types. But it was pretty big." For this perfumed and powdered goddess of propriety, he would refrain from telling her stories about the whorehouses, beer swilling, pot and opium parties that defined their every moment away from the fighting.

"That sounds nice. Danny told me that you guys did a lot of drugs and went to whorehouses in your spare time."

"Oh, yeah. That too."

"I probably know a lot more than you think I do about what he did over there," she said smartly. "Danny doesn't like to talk about the war, but I get bits and pieces out of him. In fact he told me that one night you and him remained in the base camp bar during an artillery attack, getting drunk while the base camp was getting blown up all around you."

Jack grinned to himself at the memory. "It was actually a rocket attack. 122 mm Chinese rockets," he corrected. The sirens started screaming and everyone took off running for the nearest bunker. But no rocket attack was going to ruin their night of drinking. They did not get many opportunities to party, being in the field most of the time. As he remembered, they had also smoked several pipes of opium before going to the Enlisted Club. After the place emptied-out to the sound of exploding rockets, they found themselves heir to a dozen or more tables full of unfinished beers. Outside, fire trucks and ambulances were racing back and forth. Helicopters were taking off to clear the airfield. An occasional rocket hit so close, the ground shook the building's foundation, with shrapnel pelting the side of the wooden structure. Meanwhile, Stash and Jack took full advantage of the situation, going around from one table to the next gulping down all of the free beer they could swell, before the others returned when the all-clear siren sounded.

"I'm sure he told me *artillery* - that it was an artillery attack."

Jack stared at her a second. "Hell, I don't know for sure," he retorted.

132

"There might've been some artillery mixed in there. It isn't as if the VC commander says, 'Okay comrades, tonight is Thursday, so remember, Thursday is Artillery Day. Tomorrow is Friday, and as you all should know by now, Friday is Rocket Day, and so on, according to the outgoing armament itinerary for the week. If I catch anyone mixing in artillery with rockets on any given day, or the other way around, there's going to be hell to pay.'"

Vicki flushed. "Well, no need to get all sensitive about it." She glanced to the wall clock, then back to him. "You know Danny was drafted and sent to Vietnam against his will," she said like she had some bad news for him.

"That speaks for about half the guys sent over there, including myself," he shrugged.

"Danny comes from a very respectable family. He never even *considered* the alternative of going to Canada to avoid the draft. That wouldn't have been patriotic. I respect him for that. But I still don't agree with his decision."

Jack spun in the direction of the front door at the sound of a metallic click. He continued to watch as the door swung open. A heavier, but instantly recognizable Stash entered. It might have been yesterday that Jack stood on the edge of that rice paddy and yelled above the roar of rotor blades, "don't use up all the pussy or drink all of the beer before I get back," the most relevant words he could think of for the occasion of his friend's farewell. Sitting with his legs hanging out the side of the copter that was taking him away for good, Stash grinned like that was exactly what he had in mind.

"Whose car is..?" Stash stopped mid step, staring at Jack for a minute. Familiarity crossed his face. "Tinman!" he blurted, letting a nylon sports bag drop to the floor.

"Stash!" Jack stood.

"I can't believe my eyes. How'd you find me?"

"Just made a few phone calls. Got your grid coordinates, struck an azimuth or two. 'Course your mom's phone number you gave me, that I still carry around in my wallet helped." They met halfway, clumsily hugging and slapping each other on the back.

"You haven't changed a bit. Except that you're not wearing jungle fatigues," Stash laughed. He turned to look to his wife. "Can you believe this?"

133

Vicki squinted the hint of a vicarious smile.

"Sit down man. Get us a couple of brews would you sweetheart," he told her. "Wow. It's going to take me a few minutes to get over the shock!" He rubbed a thumb and forefinger over his eyes, making an exaggerated double-take at his old friend.

Returning to the couch, Jack remained acquiescent in sitting on the dish towel.

"He arrived about a half an hour ago," Vicki said. She got up and walked into the kitchen. "He called from San Francisco earlier and I gave him directions. Oh, Jack has a shortcut to tell you about," she said over the kitchen counter.

Stash sat down in Vicki's place. "I just can't believe you're sitting here in front of me," he exclaimed. "What, are you living in the city now?"

"No. I'm still in the boondocks. I was visiting our friendly, neighborhood VA hospital."

"Boy, that's a classic example of insult to injury. I was still having problems with Immersion Foot when I got back. The VA doctor I went to gave me some antibacterial cream, a bottle of pain pills, told me it was incurable and wished me luck."

"That sounds like *my* doctor."

"They're all the same at that place. Swear to God." Stash shook his head, his expression remaining incredulous.

The phone rang. Handing Stash and Jack tall glasses of beer, then plopping down extra coasters on the table, Vicki turned to the end table where the phone sat. "That'll be your mother," she said, picking up the receiver. "Hello," she chimed. "Fine, how are you? Just a minute." She glanced to her husband, holding the receiver towards him.

Stash took a quick drink. He set his glass down on the coaster before him and said, "Excuse me a minute." Getting up, he stepped around the coffee table, taking the receiver from his wife. "Hi mom," he picked up the base of the phone and went as far as the line would allow to the end of the room.

Vicki took a seat at the opposite side of the couch.

Guzzling down some of his beer, Jack glanced to see Vicki staring straight ahead with arms folded. "You've got good taste in furniture." He spoke to her mainly because she made him feel nervous. In truth, he considered the Greek style furniture gaudy, pretentious and ill-suited to such a small, simple home - or anywhere for that matter.

She unfolded her arms and turned to meet his gaze. "You and Danny might be good war buddies, but I could never become your friend." She kept her voice low, trimmed and stenciled eyebrows arching with her every carefully pronounced word. "Here years later, he still hasn't got over what happened to him over there. He can't watch movies with shooting, he's always waking up in the middle of the night from nightmares, he jumps from loud noises."

"Hey lady, don't blame *me* for that."

Stash returned the phone to the place on the end table. "That was my mom. She calls me every day after I get off work." He sat back down in the chair and took a drink from his glass. Looking at Jack like he had something important on his mind, he finally said, "You know, I remember your first name, and your nickname, but that's all."

"Jack."

"I could have told you that," Vicki muttered.

"That's right. Now that you mention it. I would have tracked you down a long time ago if I'd remembered."

"Vicki told me you couldn't find 'Tinman' anywhere in the phone book. I'm the one who still has a phone number. I should have got in touch with you sooner," Jack confessed. "It's just that things have been such a blur for me ever since I got back."

"I know what you mean. All I've been doing is going to school and working."

"Teaching gym, huh?"

"Yeah – a high school couch. Part time," he nodded. "I take classes at the university in the morning, and teach in the afternoon. How about you - what've you been up to?"

"Thinking about getting a job as a dog-catcher, but found out you need experience first."

Stash chuckled. "You keep in touch with any of the other guys?"

135

"I got together with Ortiz a couple of times after I got back. After that we lost touch. Did you know he got hit?"

"No!"

"Happened a few weeks after you left. I was right behind him on the trail," Jack recalled. "He stepped on a Bouncing Betty. Lost both legs."

Stash looked shocked. He stared a minute without speaking.

"What's a 'Bouncing Betty?'" Vicki asked.

"It's a booby-trap that pops out of the ground when you step on it," Stash said. "It's designed to detonate several feet above the ground, where it can get a guy about crouch level."

Appropriate that they give it a female name, Jack thought, still smarting from Vicki's Bouncing Betty style of hospitality. "Did you know that I came home a month early 'cause I was wounded?" he asked Stash.

"No."

"Got some shrapnel in the knee. A mortar round blew me right out of this fucking coconut tree I was coming down from." He looked to Vicki, apologizing, "Excuse my French."

She made a crossed look, asking, "What where you doing in a 'fucking coconut tree' in the first place?"

"I was conducting treetop reconnaissance." From her expression, he could tell she did not know what in the hell he was talking about. He explained, "We got lost. I climbed a tree to see where we were."

"How you doing now?" Stash glanced to Jack's knee, returning eye-contact after a second, his gaze filled with the compassion only known between guys in the same outfit.

"It still gives me a little trouble. Got a limp out of it. All things considered, I got off pretty light." He knew as he returned the gaze, he did not have to explain to Stash how a possibly lifelong limp could be so easily shrugged off. He was witness along with Jack, for instance, of the fairly routine sight of guys getting limbs blown off. "You remember Ed in 3rd Platoon?"

"Sure. The big guy. He's from your neck of the woods isn't he?"

Jack nodded. "He was killed in a car accident."

"When was that?"

"Just last month." That stuff he carried around inside, the memory of all those lost buddies, the sense of being cursed because they died in your presence, and now you were doomed to live with their ghosts, to say nothing of the sorrow, the weight too much to carry around anymore; all this in motion, with that lump in your throat only being the tip of the iceberg - this coupled with Jack's most recent loss. That Ed had survived the war, only to come home and get killed in a car accident, was some kind of cruel and twisted turn of events, even beyond which he had come to expect in 'Nam. This was the second time today that his vision had became clouded because of his inability to maintain a grip on himself. "A train hit his car."

"He saved my ass once," Stash said. "I don't know if you remember one night, we got hit by a company of NVA just after we set up for the night on the edge of a hamlet in Kien Giang Province. I had just gone off into the bushes to take a crap, when suddenly hell broke loose. I had left my rifle back at the perimeter. The gooks were real close. I thought, if they see me running, it'll be a duck shoot. But I knew I couldn't stay where I was, because if they closed in, there I was without a rifle. Then, just as I'm zipping my pants back up, wondering how much longer I had to live, Gibson comes crashing through the bush with a rifle in each hand. He tossed me mine. We kept low until the shooting stopped, then ran back to the perimeter. Hell of a guy."

They picked up their glasses almost at once and drank. After a minute, Stash asked, "Did you keep in touch with Tom Russell?"

"Yeah, in fact, I visited him about six or seven months after I got back. He's a jazz musician in the Seattle area now. He's doing okay for himself."

"That's great. I remember once we set up for a few days next to a bamboo grove. He cut one of the stalks with his K-bar, screwed around with it for a few hours, then came up with a flute. That son-of-a-bitch sat there and played 'Stars and Stripes Forever' with the damned thing. It sounded good too."

"You think that's something - him and I were laying behind a paddy dike one day during an air-strike, and he starts telling me the musical keys of everything from the scream of the jets to the sound of the bombs hitting the jungle."

"Wow. You still have his address?"

"Yeah. Unfortunately I don't carry around everyone's address in my wallet like I do your phone number. I'll track it down and get it to you. It's been awhile."

He smiled. "Hey, can you stay for dinner?"

Vicki shot a look at him. "I only defrosted enough meat for two."

"Well, I can go down to the store and pick up another steak."

"Hey, appreciate the invite, but I gotta split," Jack assured his war buddy. "I've had a long day and still have a bit of a drive home."

"Wish you didn't have to go so soon," Stash acted like something was caught in his throat. His eyes filled with moisture.

Jack felt that way too, but tried his best to conceal it. "I'll call you soon."

"Yeah. Thanks for all the news about the other guys."

"Hope I didn't bum you out or anything."

"I can take it. Let me know when you can visit again, and we'll have a barbecue or something."

* * *

Returning to his car, Jack noticed his tires were coated with tar. Bits of fresh asphalt had splattered all over the fender. "Damn, guess the pavement wasn't so dry after all," he swore. While driving back to the freeway, it started sinking in just how lousy he felt from the encounter with Stash's wife. Not quite what the doctor recommended, he thought, now speeding down the overpass ramp to Interstate 80. True, his reunion with Stash more than made up for the generous helpings of bitter lemonade and tidbits of affronts, compliments of the Countess of dis-reception. Jack remembered how in 'Nam, Stash was always going on about his preference for women with big tits. Well, he got that with Vicki. However, those tits were minuscule in comparison with the size of her attitude.

A light rain greeted him as he sped past the Vacaville city limits sign. He saw a hitchhiker at the exit of an overpass ramp. Taking pity, he pulled over.

The guitar case carrying man ran up to the passenger side of the car where Jack had the door open for him. "Going in the direction of Sacramento?" he asked.

"Hop in. I'm going right through the middle of it."

The man negotiated his bulky guitar case over the high headrest, letting it down easy onto the back seat and jumped in. "Nice wheels," the long haired man complimented.

"Thanks," Jack said as he zoomed back onto the freeway.

"You live in Sacto?"

"No. I'm from 'Frisco. I'm going to a party there." His hair and coat were soaking wet.

Jack turned the heater on to high. Just as he reached a comfortable speed, he came upon two cars, side-by-side blocking the freeway. He began tailgating the car in the fast lane. "Look at that. She's going exactly sixty-five and has no intentions of moving out of the way for anyone who wants to go faster." He started blinking his headlights. The car held its course. "I don't care if the speed limit is sixty-five," he groaned. "The reason I bought a GTO is so I could travel like a bat-out-of-hell. Now get the fuck out of my way before I run your ass off the road."

"Just mellow out. Take it easy man," the hitchhiker advised.

"That's your typical woman driver," Jack complained, goosing the gas pedal until he was within several feet of the car's bumper. He could see her glancing into her rear view mirror. She slowly speeded up. In a minute, she cleared the car in the slow lane, gave a turn-signal and gradually began to merge into the other lane. Jack stomped on it, speeding past the car that was still taking up half of the fast lane. He came so close to her car that she blared her horn at him. "Stupid fucking bitch," he said into his rear view mirror, continuing to accelerate until his gas pedal was nearly to the floor.

"Watch out!" The passenger yelled.

Returning his attention to the road ahead, Jack saw the semi swinging into his lane to pass another tractor-trailer. A two lane wide wall of slow moving aluminum and steel now loomed before him. He hit his brakes. The rear sections of the two trailers began sliding away from him until they both disappeared out the right side of his windshield. He released his foot from the brake, meanwhile turning his steering wheel in the direction of the spin. It was too late. A sweeping, headlights illuminated view of the rolling, wildflower covered hills across the southbound lane now appeared. He thought to step on the accelerator to come out of the skid, but his car had turned backwards. In his windshield, the car he had just passed appeared. Her car started fishtailing when she hit her brakes. As the cars closed in on one another, his headlights caught the lady open mouthed and wide-eyed. Short of crashing head-on, the lady's car slid sideways to a stop. The scene of her car slipped away out the right of his windshield as his threadbare, tar slicked tires continued their death defying pirouette atop wet asphalt. He felt the rear tires suddenly drop. The front tires were next to exit the pavement. Gravel and debris pummeled the underside of the car as its full weight set down into the median. Jack was okay with the out of control slide as long as it didn't involve hitting anything along the way. His passenger did not appear as cool-headed. He braced himself with arms extended forward and fingertips dug into the dash. Jack glanced to notice his eyes were squeezed shut. The car continued in its thirty or maybe forty mile and hour backward slide across the arroyo that separated the freeway traffic, and launched onto asphalt again. Fortunately, the section of Interstate 80 was clear of traffic as the car tobogganed at a right angle across the two westbound lanes. Jack kept an eye out in the rear view mirror for anything coming. It was not as if he could do much about it, except to hang on tight in case of impact with something. He felt the car gradually losing its momentum. It settled to a gentle stop on the highway shoulder, several feet short of going over a small embankment. "That could have been worse," Jack let out the breath he'd been holding since they had crossed to the wrong side of the freeway. He shifted to neutral and cranked the ignition. The engine that had died with the car traveling backwards a quarter of a mile or more while in fifth gear, instantly roared back to life. "Probably should start thinking about getting myself some new tires on this beast." He waited for a car to go by and when the coast became clear, stomped on the gas, crossing to the median. The traffic on the east bound lane was heavy. While waiting for an opening, he heard the car door open and looked to see his passenger getting out. "Hey, what are you doing? We're right in the middle of the freeway," Jack exclaimed.

"I'm outta here man."

"I thought you were going to Sacto?"

"I'll find another ride." His eyes looked wild. "If I didn't owe you for giving me a ride, I'd knock your head off. You nearly got both of us killed."

It's the adrenaline talking, Jack knew the signs and did not take much offense. It came with something like dropping into a hot LZ with bullets flying everywhere, while the copter was taking forever to land. By the time your feet made contact with the ground, and you stood there facing the enemy who had been throwing everything they had at you, when you were at your most vulnerable, you became so whipped up from the adrenaline rush, you were ready to take on the whole North Vietnamese Army, with or without the help of your platoon.

The rain was coming down steady and it was turning dark. The chances of the guy getting a ride at night, especially in the rotten visibility of a rain storm, were slim. "Come on. Get in. I promise I'll keep it under eighty."

"You gotta be crazy if you think I'm getting back into that car with you."

Son-of-a-bitch doesn't know a minor incident from a hole in the ground, Jack thought in a change of heart over feeling sympathy for the guy. He's obviously never been in a hot LZ or a mortar attack, or he wouldn't be taking this so seriously.

"Suit yourself." When it became apparent he wasn't going to get back into the car, or close the door, Jack glanced to the freeway, saw a clearing and jammed his foot into the accelerator, knowing the sudden movement forward would slam the door shut. He heard a yell. "Wait, stop!"

Too late to change your mind now buddy, he thought. He was back in the flow of traffic and not about to stop. When the car reached ninety-five, he eased up.

* * *

Jack did not arrive home until way after dark. As he stepped out of the car,

141

Skye came out of the house. "Where have you been?" She sounded upset.

"Oh, I stopped and visited a war buddy - Stash. I told you about him before. I don't know if you remember."

Skye nodded. She had been crying. He could tell.

"Sorry I'm so late. What's wrong?"

"I was fired. 'Laid off' was the term Jerry used." Her lower lip quivered as she spoke, tears welled.

He was about to remind her not to sweat the small stuff, but *this*, he realized, was no small stuff. For instance, how were they going to pay the rent? "Why? You're a good waitress."

"He said business is slow. And since I'm going to college and not working full-time, I'm not an 'essential employee.'"

"That motherfucker. You want me to do anything?"

"Do *anything* like what?"

"Punch-him-out for you."

"And that's going to get me my job back?"

"No. But it'll teach him a lesson."

"Maybe that wouldn't be such a bad idea," she smirked.

"What you got there?" She looked past him, towards the back seat of his car.

Jack turned around. He was surprised to see the guitar case. "Holy cow! The guy I picked up hitchhiking must have forgotten it."

"You gotta be trying pretty hard to forget something as obvious as that."

"Well, now that I think about it, he probably didn't forget it. The guy left in a huff," he laughed.

"Didn't like your driving, I bet."

"He's going to have to wait in line. I feel kinda bad. There's no way to get it back to him. I didn't get his name or anything. Well, looks like I inherited a guitar. You know, when I was a kid, I always wanted to learn how to play guitar."

"You might get your crack at Carnegie Hall after all," Skye looked on with Jack at the expensive looking case. "Are you sure it's a guitar?"

"It's a guitar case. What else could it be?"

"I don't know. Al Capone carried a machine gun in a guitar case."

All the better, he thought, considering my past accomplishments, and manner in which I best make an impression on people, I would have a much better chance at getting a crack at Carnegie Hall with a machine gun than a guitar.

13

The Bridge

Jack used to take Skye to park at Robbers Roost, a scenic promontory high above the American River. With sufficient moonlight, you could see broken sections of the river glittering in its wayward course deep in the canyon. On a clear night, pine covered mountains made a panoramic display of craggy silhouettes against a star filled sky. They would spend hours in the front seat of his GTO drinking, smoking pot and necking. He could not imagine a greater way to spend an evening. Now, with all these problems in their life, he thought perhaps by revisiting this carefree phase of their relationship, they could salvage some of that lost magic. The car came to the end of the dirt road. When the headlights revealed a pine needle covered clearing, untainted by the likes of beer cans, fast food containers or even tire tracks, his spirit lifted. After parking the car on the level hilltop, he looked around, marveling that after all this time, apparently no one had discovered his spot. Jack turned to look at Skye. She was still frowning over him having dragged her away from the comfort of her couch. "Just like when we were dating. Huh?"

"Except that we have a house now."

He took pause at how attractive she looked tonight with the silver tassel earrings that gleamed against her long hair in the moonlight coming through the windshield. "But there's something magical about this place. Don't you think?"

"Sure. Let's really bring out the magic." She produced a joint from her purse.

The stars glowed brightly this warm Spring night. It reminded him of the very night they had left it over a year ago. His arm resting on the door frame, Jack listened to the canyon breeze blowing through the pines. Leaning his head out the window a little to look around a tree to catch a glimpse of the river gorge, something jolted him out of his reverie. A bridge! Its construction had been completed since their last visit. "They ruined it. They've ruined my view, and my sense of being at one with nature with putting up that fucking bridge," Jack cried.

"Here. Smoke massive amounts of this and you won't even notice," Skye offered him the joint.

After passing the tiny cigarette back and forth until it was almost finished, he remarked. "I can remember the first time we parked here."

"Me too. You tried to screw me right here in the passenger seat."

"I didn't have any choice. You wouldn't get in the back seat with me."

"I used to have this thing about screwing in the back seat on my first date."

"That's why I tried to screw you in the passenger seat." Taking his alligator clip from the ashtray, Jack carefully mounted the remainder of the joint. He handed it to Skye. "Go ahead. Finish it off," he said and leaned back in the partially reclined bucket seat for a minute. "It's not working."

What?"

"The bridge is still there. The curare didn't make it go away."

"Maybe I should take it back to the guy I bought it from and insist on a refund," she joked. "But then he'll probably make me fill out a little form: 'Reason for return.' I'd write on there, 'Smoked entire joint, and the bridge did not go away."

Jack smiled. "You start talking like that, next time the guy will charge you twice as much for a lid." He returned his attention to the view, but no matter where he looked, the bridge remained in the periphery of his vision. He found himself staring straight at the intrusive trestle. It spanned nearly a quarter mile of rugged ravine over nine-hundred feet above the river bed. Jack thought about the only suicide from the bridge which he was aware. A friend told him about it several months ago. She said the guy who jumped had financial problems, and his wife had left him. She also told him that the man was a 'Nam vet. Hearing someone whom he did not know had jumped from the bridge was back-page news for Jack. That the jumper was a 'Nam vet was huge, block lettered headlines, whether he knew him or not. It took Jack days to get over this stranger's death. Now, thinking about his reaction to that news, he began to understand it more. .In those days, when guys next to you were getting blown away on a fairly regular basis, and were ever in line to be next, you changed in many ways. For one, you came to grips with the natural fear of death. This was how you kept from going crazy. It only follows, if you were miserable enough with life, and there was no foreseeable way of improving your situation, jumping off a bridge just might be the way to go. I wouldn't do anything so crazy, he thought. Besides, it would be a waste to kill myself after going to all that trouble of staying alive in Vietnam. He wondered about Ed Gibson - if his death were really an accident. He swallowed at the ease at which he imagined himself in Ed's place, stopping the car at that railroad crossing, and watching the monolithic chunk of steel with its single, illuminated eye bearing down on him. All things considered in this miserable fucking life thinking, fuck it. I just found a way out. With the brakes of the huge train engine locked, steel wheels screaming as the tons of machinery slid towards him, only seconds from impact, a guy like Ed would be thinking, *I really appreciate that they would go to so much trouble to try and stop the train for me. But I've made up my mind. I want to put an end to this pain.*

Jack saw himself leaning over the railing at the center of the bridge towards that ribbon of water nine-hundred feet below. There were the serious financial problems, and things were not going well with the ol' lady. Death did not frighten him. He lets his hands slip from the railing. His shirt suddenly inflates like a wind sock; pant legs snap and air rushes at his face. Jack flinched at his place in the driver's seat.

"You okay?"

"Pheew. Good dope." His heart raced.

Skye leaned against his shoulder affectionately. After a minute, she sat upright, giving him a once-over. "Your tee-shirt's inside out. Do you even know that?"

Yeah. I put it on that way intentionally. It's an old trick I learned in 'Nam. After it gets dirty on one side, your turn it inside out. Presto! Clean shirt, at least in all appearances."

"That's quit a trick. Get twice the mileage out of it before you have to clean it huh?" She went along with him.

"You know us Ninth Division guys in the Mekong Delta were called River Rats."

"Really? That doesn't sound like a very lofty choice of a motto."

"What do you want for a bunch of guys who lived in the rotten, stinking swamps and jungle for weeks on end, like so much vermin. Actually, river rats commanded a lot of respect over there. We found a VC once who had been badly wounded in a fire fight. He'd probably been laying there on the edge on the canal about a half and hour before we found him. His nose and ears had been completely chewed off by river rats. He was still alive! Not in very good form though."

"Gad!"

"Once, were on a mission, and I woke up one morning there on my poncho liner next to a canal, and there's one of those suckers, big as a fat cat, twitching it's nose about two inches from my face. I froze. It turned and sauntered off after seeing my eyes open. I guess he figured I would put up too much of a fight while I was awake."

"Remind me not to go camping next to any jungle canals." She made an exaggerated shiver. "Do you know that the only two human-interest type stories you've told me about Vietnam, had critters for the main character? The first one was a frog; and now a river rat?"

"They're living beings too."

Skye shook her head pitifully. "So, what are your plans?"

"Plans?"

"You know, *future*. What are going to do with your life?"

"I don't even know what I'm going to do in about five minutes from now, much less with my life."

147

"This is important stuff. Are you going to get a job? Are you going to go to college? Do you have prospects of inventing a perpetual motion machine that will make you rich and famous? I never hear you talk about what you're going to do with your life. I get kinda curious."

Now that she's getting me to talk about the war, guess she figures she's got a foot in the door for picking my brain, he thought. "To start with, it's not my fault I can't find a goddamned decent job. Try going into that employment office downtown, and have them explain why your skills in plotting and directing artillery fire, leading a squad through enemy held territory, defending a fire base without sleep for three days and occasionally saving the life of a buddy or two doesn't even qualify you for a job as a lousy janitor."

"I detect that I hit a chord..."

"What they tell you is, 'First you need the *experience*.' Experience? I can tell you all you want to know about *experience*. If you served in an infantry platoon in the jungles of Southeast Asia, you've got a PHD in *experience*, general in nature that it might be."

"Sonya's husband Mike just got on at the sawmill. She says they're hiring for the season. Anyone can get a job there - *experience* or not."

"That's bullshit. Mike's uncle is a foreman there. That's how you get a job at the sawmill."

They looked out their separate windows for several quiet minutes. Skye finally said, "You never say you love me. Even when we were dating you never told me that you love me."

"What the...? I don't know what you're laying on me. Please help me Jesus!"

"You can defend a fire base with your life, but you can't even express your feelings to your own wife."

"I love you. There!"

Skye looked devastated.

If I'm going to start passing out feelings, Jack thought, does she have any idea how she rates in my book over those guys who got their arms and legs blown off right in front of me? And all those guys that were killed. "Ready to go?" he said, starting the car.

"No."

He turned off the ignition. "You just want to sit here?"

"You're the one who made such a big deal about coming here. You know, 'magical place.'"

"It's rapidly losing its magic. I gotta pee." Jack got out of the car. Walking to one of the tall pines, he stepped close and pissed on its trunk. When he was done, he looked up at a branch several feet overhead. Reaching with both arms, he grabbed hold of it, pulling himself up. The last time he had climbed a tree, he remembered well, was along that jungle trail leading to the Vam Co Dong River. He got himself blown out of that tree. Straddling himself awkwardly over the thick branch, he sat up and looked around. He wanted to go higher, but his knee was already painfully throbbing. A steady breeze rocking the tree, and the scent of pine needles stirred powerful memories of those times spent in the treetops of his youth, staring from high above at that puzzling and sometimes troubling world he lived in. From his lookout, he would always have things figured out before he descended back into that world. Now, reaching up and grabbing the next higher branch, Jack swore to himself that his knee injury was not going to come between him and his carefree, tree climbing childhood. But he was unable to continue upward, or even downward, not until the all-out assault of pain on his knee subsided. Tears filled his eyes. He grinded his teeth angrily wondering what was worse - the pain, or the *reality* that he could no longer climb trees. "What are you doing up there?"

He looked down to see Skye with her hands on her hips, gazing at him. *Just trying to get high enough to have a look around, so I can figure out where I took a wrong turn*, he felt tempted to reply.

14

Sortie's

S kye was sitting on the cement steps at the front of the house when Jack returned from his latest trip to the employment office. She watched as he strode up the sidewalk. He figured something was amiss right away. For starters, her car was heaped in every available space - leaving only enough space for the driver - crammed to the limit with a disarray of what appeared to be everything she owned. Apparently, she was in such a hurry she did not even bother to get boxes. As soon as he was close enough to see her face clearly, he recognized that look. This same expression had eventually manifested itself upon the faces of other girls who caught the last UH-1 out of his personal firebase, before the place got overrun by nefarious forces – result of his own inability to defend the camp. He noticed she held her car keys in a fist. She was not even going to stick around long enough to share a last beer with him. Jack stood silently before her, watching her rub the ignition key with her thumb and forefinger. Not very far in the back of his mind, he heard the thud, thud, thud sound of the medi-vac dropping out of the sky, coming to take away the wounded. "Pop green," someone yelled. Jack watched from where he stood at the edge of the rice paddy. This sense of desperation was more than he could continue to carry around. He was down to his last smoke canister. Gripping it tightly, the pull-ring clutched in the index finger of his other hand, he hesitated, realizing he had used up all the greens. All he had left was a red. Why, he wondered, was everyone else catching sortie's, but not me? At this rate, I'm going to be the only one left. He looked back to meet Skye's gaze. Shading tear filled eyes from the overhead sun, she uttered, "I, I just can't live with you anymore."

Jack tried to swallow the lump that had formed in his throat.

She came to her feet. "I was going to leave you a note, but I know how you feel about those lily-livered, wimps of the world - 'noncombatants' as you call them. So instead, I decided to wait for you to get home."

"Where are you going?"

"I'll stay with my sister in Sacto until I find a place of my own." She walked to her car and got in. Jack realized that this was his last chance to ask her not to leave. He took a step towards the car. Stopping, he wondered, want am I going to say? The little air cooled engine clattered noisily as she started it. Black smoke puffed from the tailpipe.

I could tell her I'm going to change. But who am I fooling?

Skye revved the engine several times then shifted into gear.

Jack lifted his hand to wave good-bye. She didn't even turn her head to acknowledge him as she drove away.

"Go ahead, ditty maw, ditty fucking maw," he swore at the rear of his wife's car. You *are* a noncombatant! As she disappeared down the road, and out of his life, he wiped away the clouding in his eyes with a swipe of the back of his hand.

* * *

Someone knocked at the front door. "What's the password?" Jack called when he saw out the window it was Albert.

"Fuck you in the left ear."

"Step forward and be recognized."

Albert was grinning as he stepped into the room. Reaching into his shirt pocket, he proudly displayed a roll-your-own between thumb and forefinger. "You know what this is?"

"From here it looks like a joint that was rolled by someone who was already

151

stoned."

His grin widened. "Fucken' Acapulco Gold. A dude I know at the shoe store in town turned me on to it."

"Have a seat," Jack invited, pulling out his lighter from the left front pocket of his pants. As usual, it was all sparks and no flame. He returned the lighter to his front pocket and found a good old reliable book of matches suitable to the task.

* * *

"Didn't she say why she was leaving?" Albert asked.

They were eating peanuts and drinking beer after Jack had told him everything. "That kind of goes without saying," he shrugged. "If I were her, I would have left me a long time ago."

"I see what you mean," Albert scratched his beard.

Jack's cavalier assessment of the situation did not at all reflect his ability to deal with it, the results of which he surveyed as they spoke, a tipped over bookshelf, coffee table sitting on edge with its heaping mess spilled across the carpet, a broken lamp with its shade crushed, a wooden crate of record albums thrown to the corner of the room, one of his expensive speakers gashed open in front. But at least the stereo still worked. Jack listened to the music. It was beginning to grate him though that the speaker that had taken a direct hit from the box of record albums, that once resonated concert hall quality bass sounds, now only emitted the raspy, discordant semblance of a drum beat.

He grabbed the arm of the couch as the delayed effects of the premium grade dope climbed up the back of his head and swept through his brain. He gasped at the vestige of jets screaming out of the sky. White-phosphorus canisters began exploding around him. Fountains of the glowing chemical rained everywhere, disintegrating stretches of jungle and entire hamlets. Villagers with clothing and hair on fire ran towards him. He gazed at the scene in horror for a moment, turned and joined the fleeing women and children. Jack sprang to his feet.

152

Albert, who was sprawled on the beanbag chair, looked at him through bloodshot eyes and said, "Get me a brew while you're up."

"I'm going out on the deck," Jack wheezed. He stumbled quickly through the dining area and out the back door. A crescent moon shining just above the mountain range to the west provided light enough for him to see his way across the plank surface of the deck. He tried to grasp, What's with the white phosphoresce canisters? He heard footsteps approach from behind. Jack inhaled the fresh night air. "You get the flashbacks very much, you know, of the war?" He asked Albert, who joined him at the railing.

"Sometimes. I'm thinking about the 'Nam all the time anyway. The choppers drop you off in a rice paddy. Why does it always have to be a hot LZ? Why can't we just drop off in a cool LZ? We trudge across the rice paddy in knee deep mud, come up to dry land, enter a village and have rice with fish eyes and rice wine. Does it get any better? Part of the reason I drink and do drugs, is so I can take a break from thinking about it all." He looked up at the star filled sky. Hot LZ's are fucked." Jack wondered how people could believe in such a thing as God in such a mean world as this.

"I've been at the lock-and-load end of some of that shit," Albert replied. Neither of them spoke for a minute, then he said, "We were flying reinforcements into an area out of DaNang during some heavy fighting. One of the door gunner's in my squad lost it and started shooting everything in sight. There was a platoon of our guys right below us. He thought they were the gooks. But the VC were actually in another part of the jungle. Before someone, I think it was the pilot, started yelling that we were shooting our own guys, he had killed three of them and wounded seven others. Afterwards, there was an official inquiry. I, uh *he* thought he was going to get court-martialed, but nothing came of it, except that the brass took the trigger happy moron off the front line and put him in a typing job in Saigon for the rest of his Tour."

"That's more like winning the lottery," Jack remarked.

"Really, I mean I can't believe he got off so easy. He should have been hanged by his balls."

"I knew guys that got away with stuff like that. I just feel sorry for them. They have to go through life living with those ghosts."

153

Albert smirked. "You know that little door-gunner I told you about?"

"Yes."

"You know that cartoon where the guy has an angel on one shoulder and the devil on the other for his conscience?"

Jack nodded.

"Well, I just got this evil motherfucker on one shoulder, and no one on the other."

Jack looked at Albert. In his eyes, he saw the image of that little door-gunner with his swivel-mounted M-60 pointed straight down, rattling loudly, shell casings flying everywhere. He had lost himself in his enthusiasm for the battle, and was inadvertently firing into a platoon of our own troops. They were screaming and dropping to the ground as bullet mowed them down.

"So, what you gonna do now?" Albert asked.

"I don't know." He had taken his medication, the usual self-prescribed double-dose, smoked some powerful dope and drank three or four beers since Skye had walked out on him only hours earlier. He was in no condition to speculate upon what he was going to do next, other than perhaps blow his own brains out. Beyond which, his only concern was why all the attempts at numbing himself had achieved so little results. A slight rustling of bushes at the far end of the yard brought Jack out of his musing. He stared for a long time, looking for shapes in the dark, straining to hear anything else that might harshen his buzz. Come to your senses, the enemy is on the other side of the planet; you're safe in your backyard now, he tried to assure himself. However, the imagined enemy did not flee the area of operation at his well-aimed rationale. The truth of it is, he realized, he was not going to exorcise that rice paddy humper inside of himself with drugs alone, in fact, probably not with anything less than a frontal lobotomy. So he decided that he might as well go with the flow.

"How would you like to raid an enemy headquarters'?" Jack asked. "That seems to be the only kind of employment we're qualified for."

"You're joking. I'm not going back there for anything."

"I mean an enemy headquarters right here in the good ol' USA."

"I don't get you."

"This is another war zone we're in now. The opposing forces are the haves and the have-nots."

"I know all about that shit. I'm on the have-not side."

"We're on the same side partner. So, how would you like to raid enemy headquarters'?"

"Count me in." Albert grinned with sudden understanding. "Gas station or something?"

"No. That's just an outpost. I mean a *headquarters'*. A bank."

Albert raised his eyebrows. "That's some high risk operation you're talking."

"Come on. We risked our lives everyday for less than a hundred bucks a month Army pay," Jack scoffed. How about risking your life for just a few minutes for a couple of grand?"

"Hell, I don't even care that much about getting killed. I just don't want to go to prison."

"Okay. Don't get caught. You know how not to get caught from all that combat experience. Don't you?"

"Where would this enemy headquarters happen to be?"

"The B of A in downtown Sacto. Nobody would recognize us there. And that bank has a lot of moola on hand."

"You've already thought this out, haven't you?"

Jack nodded. "Right down to setting off fire alarms in other business's around the area."

"Diversionary tactics."

"Right. Keep the confusion level up - cops and fire trucks headed in every direction. Pych-warfare," he smiled.

"When?"

"Very soon. With Skye, er my monthly paycheck gone, I'm not even going to be able to make next month's rent. We'll need to stakeout the place. Also, get familiar with fire alarms in the area around the bank."

"The AO - *the area of operation*," Albert nodded. It was obvious he was in his element with this kind of talk.

Jack felt the same way. It was times like this the normally disconcerting lack of any sense of time and space between him and the war now assumed a reassuring feel about it. At least in 'Nam, if you were in trouble, you could always count on a buddy to come to your rescue, no matter what the risk.

The moon began to drop behind the mountain range. Even though it was early morning, air moving up the river canyon felt warm. Jack thought he detected something familiar in the breeze, like the lingering residue of smoldering thatch somewhere in the distance, suggestive of a village burned during the previous night of battle. Against the orange glow of the setting moon lingered stratifications of smoke - evidently all that remained of a recently extinguished forest fire. Invigorated by the night air, and this beautifully glowing specter of pine-covered mountains, he inhaled deeply. With the air he took in was the hint of smoke from that spent forest fire. Or was it the smoke of a smoldering village?

15

A Remf!

How are you? How's that increased dosage working out for you? The doctor asked while looking at a folder.

"I don't know." Jack slouched in his seat. "I still get the nightmares beating me up in my sleep. Tell you the truth, I don't know what's wrong with me. Nothing's really improved with me. In fact, it seems to only to get worse."

Closing the folder, the doctor dropped it on the desk. He stared expressionless at Jack a minute before speaking. "I'm doing all I can for you. I don't pretend to have all the answers. It would help if you were at least a little motivated about your own recovery."

Glancing to his hands, Jack discovered they were engaged in some kind of wringing showdown. He pushed one flat to his lap with the weight of the other.

"All I know is that you guys returning from Vietnam are *different* from veterans of previous wars. We've made a lot of progress with shell-shock cases, and use that knowledge on you guys. But it doesn't seem to apply."

"Wow, I feel better already."

"I don't mean to imply that your condition is not treatable. Let's say, you have some *special* problems."

"Well, you know some stuff from personal experience don't you? I mean being a 'Nam vet too." Jack glanced to the statue of the M-16 toting soldier at the edge of the desk.

"*Me*, a Vietnam veteran! Oh, that?" The doctor chuckled. "That's just ornamental. I got that at a craft fair. I've never even been in the military, much less in a combat zone."

Jack looked incredulously at the doctor. "And you're treating me for things that happened to me in combat in 'Nam?"

"What's the difference anyway? I also treat people who have had nervous breakdowns. You're not suggesting I would be more qualified to treat that person if *I* had experienced a nervous breakdown."

Jack shrugged at the question. Maybe so, he thought, the man before him rapidly shrinking in stature. A fucking *noncombatant*. He felt angry with himself over having revealed so much to one of *them*.

The doctor looked at his watch. "Damn. Here I am going on, and I've got an important meeting several minutes," he exclaimed, quickly closing the folder on his desk.

Jack glanced to the statue of the infantryman, as the doctor hurried to replace the folder into its zip-and-lock courier pouch. Maybe that's the difference between them and us, he thought. You might be fourteen or fifteen hours into a mission without even a wink of rest, but you cannot afford a single second of mental lapse. In one second the whistle of **incoming**, translates into five meters of kill zone for a 122mm Chicom rocket. In one second you can direct the automatic fire of your M-16 on a sudden movement in the bush and kill him before he kills you. In one second you could sidestep a booby-trap, avoid falling into a punji pit, drop to the relative safety of the prone position upon springing an ambush. What would a noncombatant know or understand of that?

"So, I'll see you next month?"

"Sure," Jack said as he rose from his chair, not wanting to let-on he would not return next month, or any other month, ever. He wasn't going to tell one more damned personal thing about himself to a noncombatant. If need be, he would rather continue with the nightmares, flashbacks and whatever else the enemy-held territory of his mind could throw at him, even if he had to continue in that beleaguered state for the rest of his life.

* * *

It was nearly five O'clock, and the bridges out of town were undoubtedly starting to bottleneck with commuter traffic. Jack decided to let rush hour do its own thing, while he was enjoying a visit to nearby Golden Gate Park, his favorite hang-out in the days he lived in Haight Ashbury that year before he was drafted. He walked around the park for awhile, when what must have been two bus loads of Japanese business men crowded the paved walkway before him. They were standing in one place, pointing and taking pictures of everything. They don't seem like such bad people, the 'Nips' as dad calls them, he thought. They've certainly come a long ways from making kamikaze attacks on American warships, to taking pictures of each other with American trees and flowers for backdrop. Kind of benign looking little guys in fact, smiling and laughing, extra polite to one another, having the time of their life in such simple pleasure. They, in fact, looked like plump Vietnamese. Rather than weaving through the herd of suit and tie bedecked Orientals, or going off the trail to get around them and coming between them and their picture taking, he turned off on a dirt trail that led away at a right angle. Soon he found himself on a densely forested rise. The low sun made shadows long. A sense of urgency came over him. He stopped for a minute and looked around, relying mostly on his instincts. It was *too* quiet. Jack stepped to the side of the trail. Here you could more easily take cover behind a tree if *all hell broke loose*. He was careful to sidestep dried twigs and anything else that would give him away. Hesitating before a cluster of bushes, he checked out the possible ambush site before proceeding, noticing the trees were mostly eucalyptus and oak. Through a small opening in the dense foliage, you could see a row of Victorian buildings in the distance. He realized it was not his surroundings he need fear, but rather *himself* - his out of control, jungle-patrol disposed thoughts. He spun around, hurrying back down the dirt trail to his car.

As he drove homeward, the sign for Martinez reminded him that his old friend Stash was just a heartbeat away. When he came to the freeway exit, he automatically pulled his steering wheel towards it. Vicki's face loomed in his mind before him like a huge *Wrong Way, Do Not Enter* sign. The bitch. If she weren't a woman, and if it weren't for Stash being such a good buddy, I would punch her lights out the next time she said something offensive to me. He visualized that beautiful, meticulously rouged and stenciled face with a swollen black eye. Jack felt requited at such an image alone. He pulled up and parked on the curb in front of the house. Crossing the yard, he noticed the lawn was just as manicured as he had left it. Vicki answered the door. "We weren't expecting you." She stared for a moment, as if perhaps he would go away. "I'll get Danny." She left him on the steps.

"Hey, Tinman!" Stash greeted. He was holding a section of newspaper in hand. "Come on in." He pulled the door wide open.

"I'm on my way home from a VA appointment. Thought I'd drop by and see if you wanted to go out for a drink."

He glanced over his shoulder, and back to Jack. "We were getting ready to eat. Uh, well sure. I can go out for a quick one. Let me tell Vicki to keep my plate hot."

"I don't want to interrupt your meal," Jack blushed. "We can make it another time."

"You sure?"

"Sure I'm sure."

"You all right? You look like something's wrong."

"I'm fine. Really," Jack lied.

"Bullshit. I know you better. Something's bothering you."

* * *

At a bar in the old town center of Martinez, the war buddies were each on their second beer. "So, how's that knee of yours?"

"Feels like someone's sticking a branding iron to it most of the time. Other than that, it feels great."

Stash took a drink, glanced at a bar napkin that had jokes on it, turned again and asked, "Well, other than *that* how are you?"

Jack looked at his nearly empty mug and smirked. "Let's see. I lost my job. My ol' lady left me. The landlord is getting ready to kick me out of my house because I can't pay the rent. Other than that, all's well on the Western Front."

Stash chuckled. "Sorry. It's just that you make it sound funny."

"Had worse things happen to me. Remember when I discovered that huge leach on the head of my cock that night when we were pinned down in the rice paddy?"

"How can I forget? That was pretty bad. Especially when you tried to get it off with a match."

"God, I don't know what was worse, the bite or the burn."

"You really should've been dusted off."

"Shit, then everybody would have found out about it. That's why I declined the lieutenant's insistence that I should get a dust-off. The incident probably would have ended up in the 'Strange and interesting news from the field' section of the Stars and Stripes. What a legacy that would be to live down. You ready for another one?"

"Naw. I got to get home. Vicki's already pissed because I left just before dinner."

"Whatever happened to my old drinking buddy?" Jack muttered, tempted to tell Stash that he should bitch slap Vicki, and tell her that she's going to have to learn some simple good manners if she's going to be such a model of propriety, like she puts on.

"Come on man. Don't do this to me."

"By the way, I've been trying to get in touch with my old flame in Vihn Hoa. Mia. You remember her, don't you?"

"Sure. Man, you were big time in lovvve," he puckered his lips and grinned at Jack. "Why are you trying to get in touch with her after all this time?"

"Now that I'm free from any other commitments, I want to bring her to the United States. Problem is, I can't reach her by mail. My letters keep coming back."

"Really." Stash drew a breath that sounded deep. "You remember *Casanova* in 'B' Company?"

"Bettendorf?"

Stash nodded. "I got a call from him several months ago. We've stayed in touch since 'Nam. He's a drill sergeant at Fort Ord now. Sucker's making a career out of it. He even did a second Tour."

"He always was kind of a crazy motherfucker."

"We got together four or five months ago. He was telling me then, that after the Ninth pulled out, you know, we were turning over all of our stuff to the ARVNs, that they needed some of the infantry guys to work with the transition. If you volunteered, you got a cash bonus, officer grade quarters at Dong Tam and an extra R&R. Casanova took them up on it. He didn't know what he was getting into. As soon as most of the Americans were gone, the gooks proceeded to level Dong Tam. They did the same to all of the surrounding towns that had been friendly with the Americans. They didn't show any mercy."

It did not take long for him to figure out that Stash, as gently as he knew how, was breaking bad news to him. He felt weak to his stomach. "Did he say which towns? I mean, he didn't mention Vihn Hoa specifically, did he?"

"Actually, he did. I didn't know if you had heard or not."

Jack stared into his empty glass for a moment.

"Let's get refills." Stash got the attention of the bartender by waving a five dollar bill. "I'm sure most everyone was forewarned, and got the hell out of Dodge in time."

"God, I loved that village. I can close my eyes right now and see it, just like I'm there now. And if it wasn't for Mia, I don't think I could have made it through the war. You know what I mean?" Jack saw in his mind what was left of the French Colonial structures crumbling to the ground. To the backdrop of exploding rockets were the silhouettes of people running for their lives. "I seriously wanted to bring her back here. Then I met Skye." He had seen what happened to a village that sides with the Americans. The women were raped, and the men killed if they refused to convert to Viet Cong. His unit had come upon such scenes afterwards - more than once.

"Listen man, I need to tell you something."

Two fresh beers came. Stash gave up his five dollar bill.

"Fire."

"Uh, the ol' lady, you know, doesn't like me hanging around with other 'Nam vets. She thinks it reminds me of the war too much..."

"What are you saying? No, never mind - don't tell me. I know what you're saying."

"You understand - don't you?"

"No, I don't understand." Here they were – war buddies who once sat across a table together in the Mekong Delta, in a small restaurant the other side of the world in the middle of a war having warm beers together. Flash to now.

"That's just the way it is man. I'm sorry." Stash shrugged his shoulders with finality.

That's right, just shrug me off you motherfucker, he thought bitterly. Jack stared at what they had done - the smoldering foundations of hootches were the only remains of the village. Bodies were everywhere. Children had crawled out of the bunkers where they had been stashed at the sound of approaching jets, crying as they wandered amongst the devastation that was once their home. They did not even know yet that they were orphans - and things were just going get worse before they got better.

* * *

After Jack dropped off Stash, his war buddy, he decided to stop and see the folks.

"...battle stations. I was running in the direction of the gun turret when the first one came out of the blue." Jack's father was in the middle of one of his war story. "Bullets were ricocheting everywhere. The nips were attacking."

His voice began fading in the distance as Jack sank deeper into thought. So *this* was the difference between them. In Jack's war, he did not hate the enemy. He did not even dislike them. In battle, he rarely returned fire in anger.

"... crew member. I yelled, 'get down on the deck.'"

Jack wondered, how can I be this man's son? How can we both be war veterans and be so different? There was something even more screwed-up that troubled him, but he could not figure it out. He swigged down the rest of his beer and rose from the dinner table where his father and he had been visiting for the past hour. He went into the bathroom. Closing the door, his hand trembled as he set the latch. Jack stood before the mirror. He saw someone with sunken cheeks and dark, deep-set eyes - eyes filled with self-loathing. "I didn't hate the soldiers of the other army, but I hate my own friends and family members? Who *are* you?" he cried. "I'm not me anymore," Jack raised his hand in a fist, and slammed it against the mirror. Chunks of glass fell, crashing into the sink. Startled, he stepping back looking at the shattered remains of the mirror on the wall, where beneath a splatter of blood, exploded pieces of his face returned the stare. He looked into the sink to find more fragments of his face. Mortar rounds began exploding around him. Men were screaming as shrapnel tore into flesh.

"You all right in there?" his father's voice came through the door. When Jack did not answer, his dad tried to open the locked door. After a minute, he began jerking the door back and forth. "Jack! You okay in there?"

"What's going on?" he heard his mother exclaim.

"I don't know. He got up from the table, went into the bathroom, then I heard glass breaking. Are you okay Jack?"

"No," he whispered.

"Can you hear me. Are you all right?" his mother called.

Jack took a deep breath. "I'll be out in a minute." He examined the back of his hand. Several knuckles were bleeding. A sliver of glass suck out of one of them. He pulled it out and it bled worse. Taking the shards of glass out of the sink, he tossed them in the plastic container beside the wash cabinet, turned on the spigot and rinsed the blood from his hand with cold water. He wrapped his hand in toilet paper and opened the door. His mother gasped at what she saw, blood already soaking through the tissue paper. His father looked at him and to the mirror. "What did you do in there?" he exclaimed.

"I'm not like you. I didn't want to go to war!" Jack cried.

His father made a baffled expression and lifted his chin high.

"Besides, how can *anyone* feel good about killing another human? Or is it because they're Oriental, they're less than human?" He did not look to see his father's reaction to those words, but rather brushed past him and rushed out the front door. When he returned home, Shadow greeted him as he stepped inside, weaving between his legs, rubbing itself against him at each pass through. "Don't *even* ask how my day went," Jack said to the cat as he went to the kitchen for a beer, Shadow running alongside. "I'd rather be back in 'Nam than have to put up with the shit I get thrown at me everyday around here. At least in 'Nam I could shoot anybody that fucked with me, *and* maybe even get a medal for it." Looking to the food dish on the floor, he exclaimed, "Damn, you ate all that food I left you. What'd you have, an all-you-can-eat party while I was gone?" He stepped over to the cabinet and took out the bag of dry cat food, refilling the dish. "Is that what you want?" Shadow quickly began eating from the heap of tiny nuggets. Jack looked to ensure there was plenty of water in the other bowl. Finished with taking care of the cat, he got himself a beer and went to the living room. Plopping down on the couch, he kicked his shoes off. He looked around the room. Even though he had put everything back in place, and fixed everything that was broken, he was still down to one stereo speaker, and the place did not look warm and homey like before. Jack wondered if he watered the plants that were going from green, to yellow and brown on the tips, and developing black spots all over, if that might brighten the dingy room, over time. He returned to the kitchen and got a glass of water, going from one plant after the other, pouring a quarter of a glass each. He went into the pantry and found Skye's atomizer. Filling it with fresh water, he returned to his task. "You little motherfuckers. You know, you're kind was responsible for aiding and abetting the enemy. Take twenty or thirty of you guys fully grown, and you're all jungle to me. I don't know why I'm looking out for you."

Someone tapped on the door.

He glanced out the window to see it was Albert. "What's the password?"

"Fuck you in the left ear."

"Step forward and be recognized."

His good buddy came into the house. "What's happening?"

"Just spraying the plants."

Albert looked around from one plant to the other. "With what, Agent

Orange?"

"I haven't been taking care of them too well since Skye left. I was hoping maybe I could revive them."

"How often you water?"

"This is the first time since she left."

"That's been, what, over two weeks?"

"Yeah, I overheard them calling their ilk to send out vines with murder in their heart in conspiracy to strangle me in my sleep if I didn't water them soon. I'm going to have to move out anyway, I don't know why I even bother."

"When you moving?"

"Soon as the rent runs out at the end of the month. I don't have any dough."

"When we do the beer warehouse job, that'll take care of you for awhile."

"Even if we hit the jackpot, I don't plan to stay here anymore. It depresses me too much. It reminds me of Skye too much."

"Where you gonna go?"

"I don't know. Let's see how much dough is in that safe, and I'll know what I can afford."

"You know my basement has a cooking area and a bathroom."

"You really want to rent it out?"

"Just cover your gas and electric and it's yours for as long as you want."

"You think Judy will go for it?"

"Sure. She likes you."

A knock on the door intervened.

Albert was still standing just inside. He reached and pulled the door open. "Jack home?"

"Yes."

"Mind if I get past?"

Albert stepped back, pulling the door wide open. As soon as the front tire of a bicycle appeared, Jack knew with whose company he was about to be honored. Jim rolled his ten-speed the rest of the way into the living room and carefully propped it against the wall. He looked around to find Jack, still standing before the hanging plant, atomizer poised in hand. "Hi Jack!" He said, smiling.

"Hey there Jimbo. Skye's not living here anymore you know?"

"I know. Actually, I came to see you."

"Oh. Well sit down," he indicated the couch with the muzzle of the atomizer. He stepped over to the philodendron at the end of the couch opposite Jim and started spraying the leaves. "You can sit down too," he said to Albert.

"I'm going to head back home shortly. Just came by to see how you're doing.

"Skye asked me to stop by and see how you're doing," Jim said.

"You've seen her?" he stopped spraying, now turning his full attention to the retarded nimrod.

"Yeah. She was at last week's prayer meeting. We all prayed for you."

"Are you kidding?" Jack exclaimed.

"About us praying for you?"

"About Skye attending your prayer meeting."

"She's become a regular."

He stared at Jim for a minute. "You're kidding me. She's turned holy rolly?"

"If you want to call it that. She's accepted the Lord."

He would have laughed if he had not been so shocked. "I can't believe this. She left me for what the... for Jesus?"

"That's not for me to say," Jim shrugged. "I'll just say that she's a lot happier now."

"Get out of here," Jack said.

"I just came here to visit you!" he protested.

"You remember the way you came in? Go back out that way."

Jim rose from the couch. He pushed a length of his long curly hair out of his face dramatically and stared back at Jack. "You know that's part of the reason she left you, your proclivity towards being hostile."

"You want to see hostile? I'll show you hostile," he cried. He went over and picked up the expensive bicycle by its mid-frame.

"Hey, what are doing! Where are you going with my bike," Jim uttered.

Swinging the door open with his free hand, Jack looked to ensure the way was clear.

Jim came up and grabbed the rear wheel with a hand. "Stop! That's an expensive bike!"

He jerked it loose from Jim's grasp, and flung the bike as hard as he could, surprised at the ease at which it launched into air. It hit the sidewalk on its rear tire, bounced three or four feet in the air, turned upside down in mid-flight and crash-landed, aluminum alloy smashing into cement at the end of the sidewalk. It flipped once to its side, finally coming to rest on the lawn. Jim gasped, running out the door.

Jack slammed the door behind him. "That felt *good*," he muttered to himself. Crossing the room, he picked up the atomizer where he had left it on the arm of the couch, and went to the asparagus fern that hung by macramé strands at the corner window. Since Albert had mentioned it, the plant did look like an Agent Orange casualty. He doused the plant all the more, until its puny remains dripped water like the plants in the jungles of the Mekong Delta would after a monsoon rain. He had his doubts if this plant, or any of them in the house would ever pull out of it. He turned from the dying plant and gazed upon the couch from which he had just expelled Jim, the place that had once doubled as a bed for Roma, and the comfort of which he once shared daily with Skye. Its emptiness glared back at him. He looked to the wall where his medals had once been displayed so briefly, to be replaced by Skye's reprint of Christina's World. Now it was just a bare, lonely looking wall with a nail sticking out of it. On the other side of the wall is where they had relocated his medals. There too was only a nail, having removed the plaque of medals just several days ago, returning them in safe harbor to the closet. The frequent nightmares were bad enough without the insult to injury of his place of sleep increasingly being ambushed by that little flashback factory. I can't wait to move, he thought. Staying in this place any longer, the way the plants look is the way I'm beginning to feel.

16

Lady in Silk

J ack turned the ceramic coffee cup upright in the saucer. Resting his hands on the counter, he twiddled his thumbs until a waitress appeared. "Hi Jack," Janet greeted. "Long time no see." She reached to the coffee machine and took out the nearly full pot.

"Howdy. Ten cupfuls please. If you can give it to me intravenously, that would be better."

"You always say that," she scoffed, filling his cup. "How's everything?"

"A Mardi Gras. Every day's a Mardi Gras." He poured cream into the coffee from the stainless steel dispenser.

"Skye came in and gave her notice a couple of weeks ago, but didn't tell anyone why. But then there were the rumors."

"Rumors of?"

"Among other things, people are saying that she left you, uh, for someone else. Hope you don't mind me saying."

"Doesn't bother me." If you wanted to count Jesus Christ as the other man, he thought. Replacing the creamer, he used the handle of his fork as a stirrer. "Any other rumors?" He knew Janet well. She was like a slot-machine. When you pulled the handle on this one, you usually got rumors, or gossip, or other forms of miscellaneous bullshit. But every once in a while, you got a big juicy piece of news.

"Someone said, well you know... abusing her."

Great! The stereotype about 'Nam vets beating their wives and drinking up the grocery money – loaded guns in every room. He shook his head.

"I didn't believe that one for a minute though. I never saw a scratch on her the whole time I knew her. And she was pretty outspoken. She would have said something if that was true."

"Anything else?" Actually, he was afraid to ask.

"Just that I heard that you were messing around with Skye's sister when she was staying at your house."

Jackpot! Jack thought. That was too close to home to be free-floating gossip. And Skye would not have mentioned it to someone merely based on suspicion. Roma must have complained to her. That's why Roma left the next day after he made the advances on her. He wondered, is that also why Skye "got-religion," and finally left him? Knowing her, it made sense. By nature, Skye was not confrontational. But she sure took her vengeance seriously.

Janet put a hand on her hip, looking at him a minute before speaking, and said, "It's none of my business, but you can do better than her. You know I worked the same shift with her for over a year. Personally, I think she's too stuck-up. Who wants a wife like that?"

"Hey Jack, how's it going there?" the cook called from the kitchen. Ready for your paddy melt and fries?"

"Yeah. Feed me!"

"How's that goat running?"

"Still running. Got it up for sale. Know anyone who might be interested?"

"A lot of people. I just might be one of them. How much you asking?"

"Excuse me," Janet said. She disappeared to the back of the restaurant.

"Seven-hundred."

"Pheew! I don't have that kind of cash. I mean, not that it isn't a good price. I'll pass the word around. Haven't seen you coming around in a while."

"I said 'rare.' Does anybody here know what rare means? Is there anybody here that speaks English?" someone raised his voice from a table.

Jack turned in his stool to see what was going on. A young waitress who someone might mistaken for Asian, but he suspected was American Indian, stood by the table looking like she did not know quite what to do.

"This is the third time I've sent you back with *still* another overcooked slab of meat. I want my plate to be full of blood. I want the cow to go 'moo' when I bite into it. I'll throw this plate with this pathetic, burned piece of meat right though that front window if I don't get the kind of steak I ordered!"

Jack got up and slowly walked over to the table. He glared at the man.

"And who in the hell are you?"

"You don't need to know that. You just better apologize to this young lady and shut the fuck up."

"That's right. Apologize to her," the lady seated across from him said. She turned to Jack. "He's drunk. He gets this way when he drinks too much."

"Shut up!" the man said to the overweight girl who wore too much make-up. Standing, the large man looked down at Jack. "Who do you do you think you are you anyway?"

"I'm the guy who's going to kick your knee caps out from under you."

"Good for you," his companion said.

"Now, apologize to the waitress," Jack insisted.

He stared hard at the moron.

"I'm not bluffing. You don't know what I'm capable of. Just apologize to her right now and I won't have to hurt you."

"Good for you. He needs to be taught a lesson," the lady smiled.

The man grabbed Jack's shirt at the chest, pulling him close with such force, the top button of his plaid shirt popped off. He held the fist of his other hand poised at eye level.

Jack pushed the man back hard with a straight-arm to the abdomen.

"Stop this - both of you!" the waitress cried. "If you two keep it up, I've not above coming up from behind one of you at a time while you're fighting, and kicking you in the balls!"

"Good for you lady," the lady at the table cheered.

The man let go of Jack, turned to look at the waitress, and after a moment said, "I'm sorry. I get this way sometimes."

In response, Jack released his handful of the man's shirt and turned, going back to his seat. His favorite dish, a paddy melt was sitting next to his coffee.

171

"Who the hell *was* that?" he heard the man ask the waitress.

"I don't know," she replied.

Janet leaned against the opposite side of the counter. "We can use someone with your charm and persuasion around here more often."

"Way to go man," the cook called from behind his portal.

"If you would give him what he wanted, that probably wouldn't have happened," Jack said.

"He's been in here before man. He's a troublemaker. It doesn't matter what you do for him."

In a minute, the other waitress came over and stood before Jack, across the counter. "You didn't have to, to go ballistic like that," she said. "I had everything under control."

"You told 'em hon," Janet remarked.

"Thanks," the girl replied. Her dark eyes reminded Jack of Mia, her brown skin and black hair reinforcing the image. Her white blouse was silk. He could tell by the way it delicately draped over her shoulders and down her upper body.

"You new here?"

"Yes."

"I like your style. Let's run off together."

She looked at him with squinted eyes.

"Okay. That's a little too fast isn't it. How about a date?"

"Listen, just because you *came to my rescue* doesn't mean I feel obligated to go out with you. Besides, I don't date my customers."

Jack made an exaggerated pout. Glancing to her name tag, he said, "'Shannon.' Got a phone number to go along with that name?"

She made an expression like something was on her mind, picked up a canister of sugar and went back to the dining area. When she returned a few minutes later, Jack had finished his meal, and sipped his coffee. "Now that you've got all those sugar dispensers refilled, you going to go around and fill all of the salt and pepper shakers - or can you visit a minutes?"

"Sure. I only have one table left, and the guy there has suddenly become a model citizen."

"You know what you said about not dating your customers. I've done some serious soul-searching. This is difficult for me, but I've decided not to be a common *customer* anymore. I going to try and be just a normal human. Will you give me a chance to prove that to you?"

A glint in her eyes, and a slight blush betrayed possibilities. She pulled a pack of cigarettes from the pocket of her silk blouse. Taking one out, she put it in her mouth. He did a quick-draw of his lighter. But, in spite of his efforts at repeatedly flicking it beneath the tip of her cigarette, it would not light. "Damn. I refilled this sucker with butane just this morning."

"You're trying too hard," she told him. "Here, let me try." She took it from him. At her first attempt, a flame leapt high. Holding the lighter daintily, she allowed the cigarette to glow with a bright amber before returning the lighter to him.

"I'll be ," he remarked. As she had advised, he *gently* flicked the little wheel. A flame leapt instantly. "You've got magic in your fingertips," he chuckled. He returned the misanthrope lighter to his front pocket. Jack watched as Shannon inhaled, her nicely rounded breasts expanding. She turned her head high, blowing out the smoke. There was something special about this moment. He did not know why he felt this way. The *way* he felt was all that mattered. One thing he knew for certain, he had to get his hands and lips on those breasts.

"Tell you what. If you don't mind giving me a ride home, you can save me calling my dad for a ride. I get off at six."

"My pleasure," he said and glanced to the wall clock to see it was just a little after five. "I'll wait."

"I'll clean up if you want to get out of here early," Janet called with her back turned from where she was taking out an insert from the juice dispenser.

"I still have the table with Mr. Bloody Meat."

"He's not going to be a problem anymore. You kids go ahead and get out of here."

"Thanks Janet." She turned to Jack. "Just got to call my dad and tell him I got a ride, and I'll be with you."

"Thanks," Jack too said to Janet. He slapped down a five dollar bill on the counter, which would make the tip just about equal the price of the meal.

* * *

"You don't have to be home right away do you?" he asked.

"No. I'm a big girl. I keep my own hours."

"How about we just drive around?"

"Sure."

He thought about taking her to the promontory, but the bridge would probably bum him out. "What's your tribe - Piute?"

"Everybody asks me that because they think I'm from around here. I'm Sioux. My dad met my mom in South Dakota."

"Shannon didn't sound like a Piute name to me."

"Actually, that's not my name. I put it on my name tag because I don't want strangers to know my real name."

"Being...?"

"Audrey."

He took the joint from her that she had fashioned on an alligator clip. "I'm glad you told me that. This could only mean you no longer regard me as a customer."

"I'm going out with you, aren't I?"

"I feel like a new man."

"This is some powerful dope. vI don't see how you can drive."

Jack took a final hit and dropped the alligator clip into the ashtray. He rounded a curve. Accelerating up a hill, another sharp curve came at him fast. Now that she mentioned it, he had been thinking the steering wheel had too much play. And for that matter, the tires were not handling the road well. It was like one of them was under-inflated. Or maybe the alignment was off. Or is it just me, he wondered? In fact, his head felt a little rubbery and under-inflated. Then the road started playing games with him, throwing the curves faster than he could respond to them. An oncoming car appeared out of nowhere. He yanked his steering wheel hard. They slid into loose gravel, to what sounded like bullets pelting the underside of the copter. Once fully onto the shoulder, the car began fishtailing.

"The tree!" Audrey cried.

He jerked the steering wheel again. The car continued to fishtail, but his quick response cleared them of the tree by several feet. All four tires nicely came back onto the pavement. He stepped on the gas and began steering down the country road like nothing had happened. "I wasn't going to hit that tree," Jack assured calmly. "Besides, they shouldn't put trees so close to the damn road. No wonder cars are running into them all of the time."

Audrey looked at him and laughed.

"You know, I was doing fine there until you asked me how I could drive, after smoking that joint," he admitted.

She slumped down in her seat holding her stomach with both hands laughing harder.

"Maybe we should park it for a while. You want to go to my place?" he suggested.

"What are we going to do there?" she asked, pulling herself back upright.Do you want to fuck me?"

"I haven't planned that far ahead. Can we just get there, then figure out what we're going to do?" Gad, she's got my number and everything, he thought. Is that all us guys think about, getting drunk and fucking?

"Okay. Got anything to drink there?" Audrey's face was flushed from laughing so much.

"Got a couple of beers in the fridge."

"I like wine. Stop at a liquor store on the way."

* * *

Jack pulled up behind Albert's truck and turned off the engine.

"I see this place from the main road every day on my way to work. You lived here long?"

"A little over a week. I used to live over there," he pointed to his old place across the street. "Things got bad, and things got worse, and I departed.Meanwhile, this house belongs to a good friend. He and his wife are letting me stay in their basement." When he got out of the car, he noticed Albert in the shadows of his usual second story window. Jack waved. Albert waved back. "That's him now," he said to Audrey, who had also just stepped out the passenger side of the car. She raised a palm and waggled her fingers to wave. Albert grinned, and moved away from the window.

"Come on. The entrance is around back." He led the way, with Audrey close behind. "Watch yourself. That last step is a doozy." He let her in front of him at the step going to the door. "It's not locked," he told her when she stopped. As soon as they were inside, he pulled her close, gently joining his lips to hers. Audrey was unyielding as his kiss became more passionate. He squeezed her closer.

After a moment, she pulled away. "You don't waste any time do you?" she smiled. Her eyes were red from the pot.

"Allow me," he said, taking the bottle of wine she held in one hand. He went to the pantry converted to kitchen, setting the bottle on top of the washing machine, and started looking for a corkscrew. He noticed the bottle had a screw top. Jack looked at the bottle closely for the first time. Turning the label to the back, he pretended to read the ingredients. "Let's see, 'Sugar, water, Red Dye number one, two and three, monosodium glutamate, lighter fluid, rat urine, rat poison, chemical coloration for appearance.'" Didn't know you were a wine connoisseur," he feigned veneration.

"Quit making fun of my wine," she said.

Opening the shelf, he found only two glasses among numerous cans of pork and beans. He took one and filled it nearly to the brim with the beverage. "I'll leave the cork, er, bottle cap off your wine so it can breathe."

Audrey did respond to his ongoing teasing.

He turned to hand the drink to her, noticing she stood before his plaque of medals, where he had hung them on the alcove section of wall facing the kitchen sink. He stepped to her back and reached around, holding the glass before her. She took it after a second. "Thanks. You were in Vietnam?"

"Unfortunately."

"So that's why you weren't afraid of that guy who was about twice your size – you were in war, in combat?"

"He was drunk. I could have handled him with one hand tied behind my back, blindfolded."

"Well, I was about to show him my batting average with a family-size bottle of ketchup."

Gad, she's like Mia, Jack thought.

"What's that one there?" she pointed.

He put an arm around her waist from behind and brought his head alongside hers to see which of the glass encased decorations she was referring to. He took pause at the specter of his eyes hovering, superimposed over the bronze emblem boasting a diving eagle with lightening bolts clutched in its talons. V "That's an Air Medal. We were given those for helicopter missions over enemy territory. Those little brass things pinned on the ribbon are called 'oak leaf clusters.' Each one represents another of the same medal."

"You were a pilot?" she asked, and took a drink.

"No. Infantry. But we traveled all over the place in the helicopters. Son-of-a-bitches were tin-ducks. Us ground troops were the bulls-eye."

"Tin ducks?"

"Like at a shooting gallery," he replied in confirmation. "What we did was called 'hedgehopping.' If we didn't come across the enemy on patrols, then our battalion commander would want to speed things up by having the choppers haul us around, all day if necessary, landing and taking-off until we found the enemy, where they were usually dug-in and waiting, and all hell would break loose," he stuttered the last several words. Despite his attempt at casual treatment of the subject, the zinging of **incoming** bullets from a hot LZ, and deafening roar of return fire from the door-gunner's M-60s was drowning out his words. "Then we would jump from the copters and..." he trailed off. Jack straightened himself and stood back a little away from her.

She turned and looked at him. "You don't like talking about it, do you?"

It was all he could do just to concentrate on his breathing for a moment. He felt attracted to this girl, and did not want her to discover his problems so soon, and flee like all of the others. "I'm okay," he said after a few seconds.

"You seem kind of tense. Maybe if we smoke another one."

"Better yet, I've got some rum I've been saving for a special occasion."

"I've never had rum."

"Finish that sugar-flavored kerosene you're drinking and I'll make you a rum and coke."

Audrey went and sat on the edge of the bed - the only place to sit in the tiny apartment. When he moved here, Jack had quickly recovered from the sentimental attachment he had developed for his couch, since there was no room for it anyway. With Albert's help, he took it to the city dump where he as well had jettisoned Skye's dying plants.

Shadow appeared from under the bed, looked around with sleepy eyes, and jumped on top the mattress. "And who would this be?" Audrey asked, taking the cat into her lap.

"Oh, that's our resident expert on napping before and after meals. Her name's Shadow."

"What a nice kitty. And pretty." She stroked with a forefinger beneath Shadow's chin.

Jack went to the kitchen and made the drinks. When he returned, he handed the one mixed with coke to Audrey. His drink was straight. "Here, drape this over your tonsils. Sorry, I don't have any ice."

"No ice!"

He sat down beside her. "I went without it for a year when I was in 'Nam. At first you think you're going to lose your mind if you don't have something cold. Then you start developing a taste for things without ice."

"Like what, coffee and hot chocolate?" She took a sip, pursed her lips and blinked marginal approval.

"Cheers," he said, clinking his glass against hers. "Oh, I forgot to mention. An additional attribute. You'll grow hair on your chest if you don't use ice."

"Just what I've always wanted," she grimaced.

The siren at the nearby fire station began to howl.

"What's that?" she asked, eyes alert.

"Fire station. You must not live in town."

"No. We're about three miles out of town. I've heard the siren before when I was in town, but never this close. It's eerie."

He nodded. If she only knew just *how* eerie. Finishing off his drink, he looked to see Audrey had hardly touched hers. "What do you think?"

"It's strong. You're not trying to get me drunk are you?"

He blinked culpability.

"Well, forget it. I can hold my liquor better than you think." She drank more. Glancing over her glass with a soft look, she said, "I've never been with a married man before."

"I was going to tell you. Really." Janet, that big mouthed bitch, he thought. I'll know not to ever trust her again.

"What, as soon as you get me drunk and finish seducing me?"

"What? Me? I wouldn't dream," he gasped theatrically.

Audrey sipped her drink while petting the cat. "Why did she leave you?"

"I'm not sure if it was because I lost my job and she had problems with supporting me, or what." The *'what'* he failed to mention included frequent nightmares that probably scared her as much as they did him, where he would wake screaming, often jumping out of bed, tripping and falling over furniture or running into walls; the angry outbursts over the smallest things; the too frequent traffic mishaps and the drugs and booze he increasingly relied upon in proportion to the futility that fed on inner-turmoil, and inner-turmoil that fed on futility. He noticed Audrey had finished her drink. "Ready for another one?"

"Sure." She handed over the glass.

He went to the kitchen and refilled their glasses, nearly doubling the rum to coke ratio for her this time. Even though he felt like a real asshole, when Audrey had so accurately presumed he intended to get her drunk and screw her, this did not preclude following through with such aspirations. He returned with the drinks. Jack stood before her as he swigged his down. After she drank some of her's, he expected a remark on the even stronger mix - but she said nothing. He sat down beside her and put his glass on the floor and leaned over and planted a long kiss. The cat jumped to the floor as they pulled close to each other.

"Your lips are sweeter than rum," he said.

"That the Jamaican form of 'kisses sweeter than wine?'" Audrey asked. She finished off her drink and set the empty glass to the floor. Leaning back, she let her head down into the pillow at the head of the bed. Jack pushed his shoes off with one foot, and the other. He scooted himself onto the mattress alongside her. As they kissed, he did not waste any time in slipping a hand under her silken blouse, finally groping one of those breasts he had been unable to get out of his mind since seeing Audrey for the first time. He moved his free hand down her backside. She pulled out from under him, bringing her feet to the floor. "I'm dizzy," she announced. Her face seemed to be losing its color. "Where's your rest room?"

"Right there," he pointed.

Audrey stumbled to her feet, hurrying to the bathroom.

He sat on the edge of the bed, picked up the guitar that leaned against the wall, and started playing Dylan's *Don't Think Twice, It's Alright*. The music stopped as one finger jammed between strings, and another failed in its attempt to stretch far enough to form the chord. "Goddamned 'F' chord," he swore. He continued working on it, his tongue sticking out the corner of his mouth, straining along with his forefinger that had once proven itself as a highly accomplished trigger-finger, but now could barely conform to the seemingly simple process of making the strings twang to various notes. The sound of Audrey retching distracted him from his latest attempt at music. Might have poured that last one a tad too strong, he suspected. He returned to the recalcitrant finger, wondering if he wasn't wasting his time trying to teach himself to play guitar. He was good with four or five chords, but there were many more if he wanted to learn to play even a few of his favorite songs. The mere thought made his head hurt. He heard the toilet flush, and the sound of water running in the sink. If I hurry up and get this chord right, I can be singing to Audrey as she steps out of the bathroom, he envisioned himself the serenading troubadour. Beneath the sound of a loud thump, most likely that of a body hitting the floor, the image he had conjured, crumbled. Jack flung his guitar beside himself on the bed, and rushed to the bathroom. He tried the door. It only moved several inches. "Hello. You okay in there?" No answer came. He tried to push the door open again, but it only budged another inch or two. He entertained no doubt at this point that she was out-cold on the floor. Running out the door of the basement, he rushed into the back door of the house that led into the kitchen. Judy stood at the stove, he exclaimed, "Where's Albert?"

Spinning around, she made a startled look. "He's upstairs," she pointed in that direction with a large wooden spoon.

Jack ran into the living room. He stopped at the foot of the stairs and called, "Albert! Albert!"

In seconds his friend was coming down the stairs. "What's up?"

"Got a situation in progress. Come on. Quick!" He turned, racing back out of the house and to the basement.

Albert followed. When they reached the door that was slightly ajar, Jack said, "She passed-out, I think. She might have drank too much, too fast."

"She's in there now?"

"Yes. I tried to open the door, but her body's blocking it. I was concerned I might hurt her if I pushed too hard."

"What did you do, give her some of that 151 proof rum?"

Jack nodded admission.

"We gotta do something," Albert contended. "Let's just push real easy, and maybe she'll slide across the floor a little until there's enough of an opening to get in." He leaned with his shoulder against the door gently pushing.

Jack assisted with a single extended arm. When the door opened enough, he turned sideways and slipped through the opening. Audrey was laying on the floor sideways to the door. He sighed relief to the sound of her breathing. "She's okay," he called.

"Pull her out of the way so I can come in."

Lifting Audrey slightly with his hand under her arms, Jack pulled her into the center of the bathroom until she was clear of the door.

Her eyes opened briefly. She moaned.

Albert stepped in.

"What in the hell is going on?"

Jack looked through the now wide open door to see Judy with her hands on her hips.

"Will someone please tell me what is going on?" the heavyset woman raised her voice.

Albert turned towards her, then looked back to Jack.

"She told me she has a highly contagious virus. Tropical Mononucleosis. It's incurable and highly contagious. Better clear out," he warned.

Judy looked at him suspiciously for a moment, turned, and exited the door.

"If you need anything else, just give me a holler," Albert said.

"Thanks," Jack waved. He watched until they were gone.

"I want him out of here," he overheard Judy say as they walked past the window. "I mean it!"

Wetting a wash cloth with cold water, he gently wiped Audrey's face. After a minute, she began to stir. "How you doing?"

She opened her eyes and looked up at him. "What happened?" she said weakly.

"You apparently passed out." Jack had despaired that she had fallen to the cement floor and busted her head.

"My head started spinning."

"Come on," he said, lifting her until she was standing with his support. He walked her out of the bathroom, and to the bed where she reclined the length of the mattress. "Lie down here for a while until you feel better. You didn't hit your head when you fell, did you?"

She felt around with a hand. "I guess not. There isn't a bump or anything. I think I'm all right now."

"Just take it easy. You're still a little weak."

"You did get me drunk, didn't you?"

"You drank too fast," he replied defensively. "Also, I might have put a little too much rum in your drink," he permitted.

"I had your number all along, didn't I?" She reached up and put a hand on his cheek.

Stroking his fingers through her soft hair, he whispered, "You brought the animal out of me. I couldn't help myself." He let himself down on the bed beside her. She soon drifted off to sleep. Strange, Jack thought, he felt perfectly content just laying by her side, listening to the rhythm of her breathing, running his fingers through her hair.

17

A Courthouse for San Refeal

Gazing at the display of stars scattered across the black sky, Jack wondered, with all that incredible panorama floating around up there, doesn't there have to be a *creator* - some kind of higher being? A crinkling of his empty beer can, from an unconscious contraction of his grip, brought him back down to Earth. In addition to the sky, Albert and himself also had a commanding view of the enemy outpost, represented among other things, the 'Haves' - those guilty of prospering from the drinking habits of people like them - the 'Have-nots'. Soon they would turn that all around. Jack had specifically picked this spot, not only for the clear view of the warehouse and entrance, but also for the fallen tree that gave them a place to comfortably recline as they conducted their reconnaissance.

"Only a grunt would know how to turn a patch of forest with a half rotted log into a living room," Albert yawned, stretching his legs and arms at the same time.

"You can count on me there. My talent for converting any ol' stretch of jungle or not too flooded rice paddy from the South China Sea to the Cambodian border into a living room would have brought even Frank Lloyd Wright to tears of inadequacy," Jack replied, as opposed to his ingenuity, not renowned for his modesty.

"Who's that?"

Frank Lloyd Wright? Sometimes I wonder if my witty remarks aren't wasted on your ass. He's an architect that builds *around* the trees instead of cutting them down. He likes trees and designed fancy looking buildings to rise from blasé landscape."

"Well, did he consider that you have to cut down trees to get the wood to build the house?"

"Actually, he built with stone, cement and glass."

"How come you know all this?"

"My dad was a building contractor before he retired."

"How come you don't follow in your old man's footsteps?"

"I'm not *that* smart."

"Look, there's a car going into the parking lot," Albert pointed.

They watched as the sedan with an official looking seal on the door came to a stop in front of the building. A man got out and shined a flashlight through the front window. After a minute, he returned to the car, and drove off. "That's it? We've been here nearly four hours and some asshole comes by and shines a flashlight in the office window and drives off. This is going to be a piece of cake," Jack said.

"So, should we wait to see when he comes again?"

"Sure. Let's wait another four hours. Are you kidding? Even if he comes hourly, we've got plenty of time to pull the job between visits. What we'll do is wait until he comes and goes, then do our thing. It shouldn't take over fifteen minutes for the whole job."

"What if a cop comes by while we're there with the truck sticking out of the window?"

"I thought you had this all figured out in advance?"

"I was leaving the *field* operation stuff for you."

"Thanks. Well, if a cop comes by and sees us, that's exactly what it'll be - a *field* day. Unfortunately, for them, not us. Both of us are going to need to keep a watch out for headlights. The first sign of anything, we jump back into the truck. If the car turns into the parking lot, we drive into the woods where we can ditch the truck and make a run for it."

"But the truck license can be traced to me."

"Take off your license plate. And take everything out of the glove box, and clean everything out until it's just like you got it off the dealer's lot."

"I guess you're right. I really like that truck though. I hope we don't have to abandon it."

"Now that the security guy won't be back for a while, let's go down there and do a walk-through to see where we're going to cut the line, and find a good escape route."

"Got one full one left."

"I'll split it with you."

After they finished off the remaining beer, they came down from their forward-observation-post to the parking lot of the enemy outpost. Jack pointed to an overhead line attached to the corner of the building. "There's your telephone line. If we pull the truck close enough, you can get up on the roof and reach it with a pair of diagonals."

Next, they walked over to the office window.

"See what I mean," Albert said. My truck bed can go right over the top of the window frame. I can knock the glass right out with the rear bumper."

Jack peered in to see the safe. It was not in view of the window. "Where's that sucker at?"

"It's just behind those file cabinets. It's small. There's plenty of room there to get it out."

After looking it over a minute, he said, "Okay. Let's check out the escape route." They walked to the left of the building to the end of the parking lot. There was a fairly large area of mowed lawn, and beyond, dense oak tree forest, interspersed with pine trees. Jack scanned the area before him for a moment, and said, "We can fit your truck through there." He pointed to an opening in the thicket. They walked through it. Judging from the street lights showing through the trees, the road was about one-hundred and fifty feet away if you followed a slightly wayward path wide enough for the truck. "As long as you don't hit any trees, this should be a pretty easy back door out of here. What do you think?"

"Sure. I'm a good driver. No problem."

They returned to where the truck was hidden in the woods on the other side of the main road.

18

Fatal Implications

Jack sat on the edge of the bed strumming his guitar. His other hand worked at stretching fingers that doggedly resisted all efforts in translating the black dot chord diagrams for "Hey Jude" to the real world of a fret board. He stopped what he was doing at someone gently tapping at the door. It surprised him to see Audrey outside the window. He leaned his guitar against the bed. The volume of Beatles hits that had been propped open across his lap, crashed to the floor as he quickly rose. He started to pick up the songbook, but decided against it in his haste to let Audrey in. He swung open the door. "Come in," he greeted with exaggerated nonchalance.

"Hope you don't mind me dropping in on you. I haven't heard from you. I was just wondering how you're doing." She made a shy smile as she entered. Her sheer, tight fitting dress accented her shapely figure, her black flowing hair offset against the red material. She handed him a brown bag with cord handles. It was full of pears. "I didn't know what to get you."

"Wow. Pears. I love pears." He held the bag by the handle up so he could have a good look at the contents of what must have been a dozen or more of the fruit.

"They're locally grown."

He looked at Audrey a moment, not certain what to make of her visit, less certain what to say. "I would have called you, but I don't have a phone. Sit down," he indicated toward the bed.

"I can't stay long. I'm doing some chores in town." She stepped over and sat down. Leaning, she picked up the song book from the floor giving it a curious once over.

"Get you a drink?"

"Sure. Something *without* alcohol."

He sat the bag down on the counter top, and opened the refrigerator. "Something *without* alcohol," he repeated her words to himself as he glanced inside. The utter lack of anything to serve someone for whom he felt very eager to please, stared back at him from the space between steel racks that held only two bottles in a six-pack carton. He had served the last of his Coca-Cola to Audrey to go with her rum on her initial visit last week. "You know, in Germany, beer is considered a food," he promoted his only beverage.

"I'll take one, if that's all you have."

He opened the bottle with his P-38. "Did you want a glass?"

"No. That's fine." She set the book back down on the floor as he stepped over to hand her the bottle.

"Forgot to get one for myself," Jack muttered. He returned to the refrigerator and took out the last beer. Again using his P-38, he easily popped off the bottle cap.

"What's that?" she asked.

"You mean this?" He held up the tiny but consummate tool that had opened hundreds of cans of C-rations in Vietnam, and was still going strong. He stepped over and handed it to her. "It's called a P-38. In 'Nam it was indispensable. It's the infantryman's combination can and bottle opener, letter opener, screwdriver, hole-puncher, fingernail cleaner, you name it."

Holding the small object by thumb and forefinger, she viewed it from all angles. "It can do all that?" She looked impressed. "I've never seen one of these before. Guess you camped out a lot when you were there?" She handed it back.

"Camped out?" he laughed. "I wouldn't really call it that. I mean it wasn't like the Boy Scouts. We lived in the jungle like animals is more like it."

She flinched at his words, asking, "Got any pictures of your time in

Vietnam?"

"Sure." He stepped over and quickly retrieved his photo album out of a cardboard box of his things in the corner of the room. He sat down next to her and opened the album so the large portfolio lay open on both of their laps. "The first couple of pages are the base camp. When I first got there, I was taking pictures of every corner of the place. I must have a hundred pictures I took in just one week. Most of them are still in a shoe box."

"I know what you mean. When I went with my folks on vacation to Yellowstone Park, I took ninety percent of my pictures the first day. After that, you start getting used to the scenery, and it all doesn't seem so photogenic anymore."

"Well, you never got used to that place." A day didn't go by without sights and events that would have been a war-photographers dream, he thought. But when you finally joined your unit in the field, you made an abrupt transition from the tourist mode of constantly shooting pictures, to that infantryman mode of constantly shooting your M-16 at that ever fascinating scenery surrounding you. Jack did not know how to explain this in anything less than a thousand words.

As she alternately muttered, Wow," then, "That's really something," after viewing each page of photos, Jack would slowly flip to the next page. His urge was to narrate, but he decided to simply let her ask questions if she wanted. After all, he had carefully printed names and places on the bottom border of each picture.

"What's 'KIA' and 'WIA' that's after the names? Like this one," she pointed.

Leaning towards her to see the picture, he was a little at lost from her question, because he had never thought much about the fact that almost every photo of one of his buddies had one of those acronyms following their name. This picture was of Clemens, his jungle fatigue pants saturated with mud from their day of humping the paddies. He stood before a bombed out hootch, bandoleers of ammo crisscrossing his chest, his utility belt festooned with hand grenades, and his M-16 at arms length. He was bright-eyed and smiling beneath his steel helmet, like anyone who had only four days left in the field. After the nickname "Wild Man" was a dash, and the letters *KIA*.

"Either killed in action, or wounded in action." That lump began rising in his throat until he could not speak for a minute. He wanted to tell Audrey that this was probably the only picture in existence of Clemens wearing a steel helmet, for two reasons. One was he had never worn one until several days before this picture. He always wore his floppy jungle hat instead, like most of the guys in Fourth Platoon. But if it was your last week in the field, it had become a ritual in their company to switch to the added protection of the steel helmet, and for some, if you could stand the heat, a flak jacket. Simply, you didn't want any bullets or shrapnel to take you out with only several days before your wondrous departure on the Silver Bird. The other reason being, this was the last photo *ever* taken of Clemens. He stepped on a booby-trap, with fatal implications, the day after Jack had taken the picture. "I guess you still harbor a lot of bad memories about the war."

Better yet, he thought, my mind is a *harbor* filled with a flotilla of war ships that are Vietnam memories. They're continuously firing heavy salvos in every direction, and have brought along enough ammo for a very long stay. "You got that right," he replied.

"I can't image what it would be like being over there."

"You just take your malaria pills every morning, and at night go to sleep adding an 'X' on your mental Tour-Of-Duty calendar."

"You kept track of an entire year in your head?"

"You bet. Everyone did. Right down to the minute. You could ask anyone, 'How short are you?' Without missing a beat, the guy would say, *'Ninety-three days, two hours and fourteen minutes.'*"

"Really!"

"'Course he had to look at his watch for the minutes." Jack did not see any reason to mention it, since it was only a curiosity to him, but after leaving the 'Nam, he now kept an approximate mental calendar of the days since he had returned home - three years, one month and some odd days. If he knew what day it was, he could do the days too. And if he were wearing a watch, he might even be able to narrow it down to the minutes. Flipping to the next page, he came upon pictures he had taken during the company's Vihn Hoa stay. Mia would be gracing the next several pages. Audrey was silent for a long time as she looked, then asked, "Who is this girl?"

"That's Mia." He never went on to explain the coincidence to anyone, that MIA also spelled out *missing in action* in military abbreviation.

"There's a lot of pictures of her. She an old girlfriend?"

"Well, I wouldn't call her an *'old'* girlfriend."

"You mean you still have contact with her?" She looked curious.

"Kind of," he admitted.

"How many other women are there in your life?" Audrey stared at him.

"Just her. Just Mia. I got the papers from Skye for the divorce. I signed everything and licked and put stamps on the envelope."

"That's good to hear. But where do *I* stand?"

"I didn't think, I mean I don't know. I didn't even expect to see you again."

"You know, I don't just cavort with anyone. What do you think I am?" She rose to her feet.

He closed the photo album, and moved it from his lap to beside himself.

Audrey looked at him. "You know, when I first saw you in the restaurant, there was an aura around you." She took a sip of her beer.

"An aura? I'm not sure what that means…"

It's a glow you. In my culture, when you see an aura around someone the first time you meet them in person, it means they're important to you."

"A glow?"

"Yes."

"Oh, I'd been drinking before I came into the restaurant. That's probably why I was glowing so much."

"It's not something you joke about. It's a very meaningful in my culture."

"I don't know anything about that kind of stuff. Sit down would you. You're making me nervous."

"That kind of *stuff*? As in?" She sat down beside him again.

"You know, hocus-pocus, witchcraft, ghosts. Stuff like that."

"Auras don't fit into any of those categories."

"Like I said, I don't know." He felt like perhaps he was being a jerk.

"There's a lot you don't know. You don't even know about your own self."

"Maybe not. But I've had twenty-two years of getting familiar."

"Doesn't matter if you've had a hundred years. You can still be a stranger to yourself, if you aren't solidly grounded. Let me have your hand." She sat her beer down on the floor, and reached towards him.

He extended his right hand.

Audrey took his forearm and turned it so his palm faced up. She studied it for a minute. Shaking her head, she said, "Your lifeline is nothing to write home about. Here, turn your hand sideways with your thumb stretched out as much as you can." When he did this, she pressed hard with the ball of her thumb on his wrist closest to the base of his hand. "That war really bothers you, doesn't it? It affects your very existence – you can't even sleep at night." She released his forearm and stared at him, almost accusingly.

"Yeah." He rubbed his wrist where she had pressed.

"There's one thing about it that stands above all else in your mind."

"Really? I mean are you asking me or telling me?"

"I'm asking, but I think I already know. You ever kill anybody?"

"A basketful. Never kept count," he replied casually.

"Let me have your hand again."

He lifted it for her.

This time she pressed her thumb on the inside of his wrist, intermittently repeating this every several inches, finishing off at a point half the length of his forearm. She opened her eyes that had been closed all during the probing with her thumb. "You saw the bullet from your rifle going into someone's body, killing them?"

"Sure. At least a couple of times I can recall."

"You're certain of that?"

"Well, now that you mention it, you rarely had a clear view of the enemy. Charlie was real good at staying out of sight. If you saw a movement or heard a branch rustle alongside the trail, everyone in the squad fired at once. It was like that most of the time. Even when we caught the VC in the open, it was hard to tell who shot who when there was a half dozen machine guns firing on full-automatic at the same time."

"You never killed anybody," Audrey declared. She reached down and picked up her drink without taking her eyes off of him. "And you never will kill anyone."

"How can you tell that just by pushing your thumb on my arm?"

"I don't know how to explain it. It's a *gift* I was born with."

"Wow! I mean really, Wow! This is incredible what you're telling me."

She smiled. Lifting the bottle, she took a sip.

"If what you say is true, do you know what it means to me?"

"It is true. Believe it."

"Pheew." He did not know what else to say. He felt the load shift in that steamer trunk full of war memories he dragged around behind himself. It tipped over, the lid popped open and some of the contents spilled out. These were major in content – huge weights of guilt.

"That what I told you, I know in my heart. But what I don't know, and my heart needs to know is, is it that Vietnamese girl or me?"

Jack felt his face become hot. It startled him when someone knocked. He looked to see two young men outside the door.

Audrey did not join him in looking out the window.

"You're going to have to make up your mind you know?"

He returned to meet her gaze, still staggering from her one, two punch of hocus-pocus, now this. "I, I."

"When you do, give me a call." She got up, stepped over and plopping her unfinished bottle of beer down on the top of the washing machine. She went out the door, leaving it open behind herself.

He followed, calling out the entrance past the two strangers who had stepped out of her way as she walked away, "Come back!"

She disappeared around the corner.

"Goddamn it! These women are driving me crazy?" He looked to the closest of the two, at the edge of the single cement step, still leaning out of the way in the wake of the excitement with Audrey's departure. "I've tried bullshitting my head off to keep the peace, but that caught up with me. This time I'm being perfectly honest, but apparently that doesn't work either. I don't know what they want!"

The young man with shoulder length hair made a confounded look, and shrugged.

"What do *you* want?"

"I, I ju-just saw the *'for sale'* sign on your car. The lady who answered the door told me I would find you here."

"Oh." Jack stepped back inside for a second and grabbed the keys that hung from a hook on the side of the cabinet over the sink. "Come on." He brushed past the kid and his baseball cap wearing companion who was at the top of the steps. They followed him around the house to where the GTO was parked. Jack noticed a U-Haul truck in front of his old place across the street. A man was carrying a large box up the sidewalk towards the house. In the drive was a woman taking a lamp from the back seat of a car. A little girl appeared running from the backyard. "I told you to stay where I can see you," the lady called. "Now get over here and help me with this stuff."

"How much you asking?"

Jack turned from the scene across the street to look at the kid standing behind him by the car. "Uh, seven-hundred. You want to take it for a spin?"

"Like to take a look at it first." He was already walking around the side of the car, examining everything along the way.

"Got a few scratches, but nothing a little touchup paint can't fix," Jack promoted.

"How many miles you got on it?" the kid with the baseball cap asked.

"Fifty-three some odd thousand."

"Three-eighty-nine horse isn't it?"

Was. I took out the three-eighty-nine and put in a four-hundred. It's a used engine but rebuilt. He went to the front and lifted the hood. They both joined him in looking over the engine.

"My cousin has a '69 goat. It's got a factory four-hundred."

"That's one ugly car – the engine trying to make up for the ugly." He stepped around one of them to the driver's side, opened the door and without getting in, reached through the steering wheel, inserting the key into the ignition. He made a quick turn of his wrist. The engine roared to life. Stepping back around front, he reached to the carburetor linkage and pulled it several times making the engine reeve commendably.

"Sounds good," the long haired kid cried over the engine roar.

His friend went around to the rear of the car. In a minute he returned. "There's black soot on the exhaust pipe," he reported. "The rings are probably shot."

"The engine's in good shape. Soot on the exhaust can be from the previous engine."

The kid reached and ran his forefinger beneath one of the valve covers. Withdrawing it, he displayed his grease smeared finger for all to see. "What's this? I don't know Sid, I wouldn't give over six-hundred," he said to his friend.

At a "shake down inspection" in basic training, the drill sergeant was standing there in his starched and pressed uniform displaying a dusty forefinger between them, after dragging it across the top of Jack's foot locker. "Drop for twenty push-ups!" He had barked.

Jack slammed the hood down.

Jumping backwards just in time, the kid cried, "What the hell you think you're doing? You almost hit me!" He rushed over, his hands now closed into fists, posturing angrily.

Shoving the teenager back by his right shoulder so hard he fell on his ass to the ground.

"That's my good buddy. Nobody hits my buddy without me getting involved," the other one strode towards him.

As soon as he was in arm's reach, Jack swung and hit him. Blood gushed from his eyebrow and ran down his face. He cried out in pain. The guy's friend, now back on his feet, stepped forward threateningly.

Holding both fists poised in the ready, Jack warned, "Both of you better get the hell out of here before I really hurt you."

With one of them partly blinded by blood running down an eye, and the other still picking gravel out of his bloodied hands, they looked at one another with equal understanding, turned in unison, and went to their car.

Jack leaned into his car and turned off the engine, taking his keys out. As he slammed the door, he noticed their car had backed-up to about a block down the street, instead of leaving down the main road. They both glared at him through the windshield. Tires chirped. The car sped towards him. He could not get out of the way because he was still alongside his vehicle. He turned in time to see the passenger door fly open, a second later bouncing into him hard enough to send him sailing forward. The door slammed shut just as he was sliding head first across the gravel.

"Fuck your mama!" the passenger yelled out the window as the car sped away.

Back inside, he closed the door behind himself and locked it. "I'll kill those motherfuckers if I ever see them again," he swore to himself, his voice trembling. Finding his valiums, he tossed two of them into his mouth, washing them down with the rest of the beer Audrey had left on top of the washing machine. He undressed from his shirt. It was torn and bloody. Looking down, he saw his upper chest was red from a large area of abrasion. His knee hurt badly. First taking off his shoes, he next removed his pants. Pieces of gravel scattered to the cement floor. He reached and found several more pieces embedded in his right forearm. This was the arm he had thrown forward to protect his face when he saw the ground rapidly rising to meet him. Jack stepped into the shower. He did not come out until the hot water heater had drained itself completely onto his bruised and bloodied remains. When he had finished his shower, he went into the living room with his towel and began carefully drying himself while looking out the window. His thoughts drifted to Audrey. Was she the one? How about Mia? Was he going to keep her in holding pattern for still another relationship that might not work out? Wasn't it getting a little late in the game for Mia anyway? He patted a section of towel over the left side of his chest. It hurt like hell.

19

Hot LZ

I told you about him," Albert reminded. "He was also with the Ninth. I met him on a mission in the Plain of Reeds. He's been back a year, but he's still there."

"I remember now," Jack replied. He sipped coffee from a Styrofoam cup. "Siegfield, right?" He turned to look when Albert did not answer after a minute. He saw that his good buddy's teeth were bared as he intently glared straight ahead.

"Sieg*freid*! Tim Siegfreid. We called him 'Sieg'. Come on. Get out of my way before I run your girly ass over," he swore at the sedan in front of them.

"I usually start passing on the left shoulder if they don't move. That scares the hell out of 'em enough that they'll move out of your way."

Albert grinned at the encouraging words, veering to the shoulder. A storm of dirt erupted from beneath his left wheels as they bounced along the dirt median. Gravel began pelting the side of the car as they accelerated past it. Jack held on tight to his coffee. The man driving the car looked on with surprise as they traveled alongside, but was blocked from moving over by a car in the slow lane. They were so close that Jack could have had an intimate conversation with the man if his window were down. The old man looked shocked at this beaten up truck plowing through the dirt and gravel at sixty miles an hour, inches from sideswiping him.

Jack wondered what the old man's expression would be if he had any idea that the driver was an unemployed, suicidal helicopter door-gunner, and the guy riding shotgun an unemployed, recently divorced rice paddy humper who had given up on therapy, and was the one who had encouraged the driver to pass on the freeway median. But what they were doing probably said as much. Tires screamed as the sedan braked. It came to a stop in the middle of the fast lane, allowing Albert to swerve back onto the pavement.

"Better get over partner," Jack alerted. "Scottish Flat turnoff rapidly approaching at two O'clock."

"I know," Albert replied. He cut in front of another car in the slow lane. A horn blared. In seconds they were speeding up the exit ramp. It climbed significantly more than the interstate that continued over the West slope of the Sierra Mountains. Albert did not slow for the upcoming intersection at the top of the overpass. Soon tires screamed as he ran the stop sign, cranking hard to make the right turn. Coffee swished onto Jack's lap. "Imagine putting a stop-sign in a place like that," Albert marveled, jamming his foot into the gas pedal as he guided his truck down the two-lane.

"How'd he lose his leg?"

"What else? Took a round from a VC fifty-one caliber dropping into a hot LZ. Got him in the thigh. There wasn't much left, so they had to amputate."

"I saw a guy get his head blown clear off from one of those dudes. Threw his leg in the pond huh?" Jack chuckled.

"I swear to God, anytime he wants me to come over, that's what he does. Throws his leg into the fucking pond."

"And you fall for *the leg in the fucking pond* every time?"

"So, what am I going to do, ignore him? He's one of us man. He wants to get my attention."

"Maybe you should visit him more often. Then he wouldn't feel inclined to throw his leg in the pond for attention."

"Problem is, every time I visit him, he starts on some crazy rant, and I get all bummed out. Doesn't do either of us very good. Watch for an oversized, olive-green, camouflaged mailbox on the left. You can't see the driveway until you're next to it."

"Where'd he get the M-16? They wouldn't let us bring them home."

"I don't know. Probably when he was in the hospital at Fort Ord. If you have the bucks, you can buy an armored- personnel-carrier from some guy in Supply at the base." Jack watched the heavily foliated shoulder of the narrow road until he spotted the mailbox Albert had described, just beyond a cluster of manzanitas about a hundred feet up ahead. "Slow down, here comes your turn." He pointed.

Tires screeched as Albert again cranked his steering wheel hard, sliding at a perfect ninety degree angle onto the gravel driveway. Jack quickly finished off his cold coffee before the rest of it sloshed out as they bounced along the pothole pitted driveway. An old two story sat before th in a grove of Ponderosa pines. A huge oak tree shaded the lawn that was more weeds than grass. Albert slammed on his brakes, skidding to a stop just before the verandah.

"Pretty isolated here, isn't it?" Jack remarked, letting his cup fall between his feet to the floor.

"Seig looked long and hard for this place. He wanted some place that reminded him of the U Mihn Forest, without the bullets and mortars. He fell in love with that beautifully forested region of planet Earth." Albert cut the engine.

"The good ol' Forest of Darkness." Jack remembered well that tract of dense jungle in the southern lying tract of 'Nam, a place that defined in dozens of deep shades of green, the very edge of reality, that staged more than the commonplace mayhem he experienced in jungle warfare.

"Likes lots of trees huh?"

"The main idea is he doesn't like lots of people."

"Man after my own heart."

The screen-door at the front of the house flew open, and a young lady in shorts and a halter top appeared.

"That's Anita, his wife." Albert hopped out of the truck. The rusty hinges of the passenger door shrieked as Jack got out on his side. He caught up with his friend at the dilapidated wooden steps to the verandah.

"He's around back," Anita motioned with an exaggerated glance, her long black hair swaying as hurried down the stair between them. They turned and followed. "He stopped shooting. That's only because he ran out of ammo. He was shooting into the forest, but nothing was there, just some birds. He drank a lot of whiskey."

They came within view of a small pond where someone was sitting in a lawn chair. When Anita came to a stop, Albert said, "This is Jack. He's one of us."

She glanced over her shoulder. Making a brave smile, she said, "Pleased to meet you. Thanks for coming." She looked back towards the man in the chair. He was slumped in the chair facing the pond, back-dropped by a pine tree covered ridge. An M-16 lay across his lap. One leg of his jungle fatigue pants went flat at the knee, and had been coarsely slit open the rest of the way down. "Albert's here," Anita called. She strode down the hill towards him.

The man looked around. His beard was shabby and so large it hid his neck at front. "What the fucking...? I didn't call for any air-support," he slurred.

"You crazy fuck. You don't need air-support," Albert walked up to him. "You need a new brain is what you need."

"So, who you got with you there. The fucking Wizard of Oz?"

"He's been known to run with that crowd," Albert replied, glancing to Jack with a grin. He did not enlighten Seig on the allusion he had stumbled upon. "This is Jack. He was a grunt in the Delta."

"Ground-support. That's what I need. Not fucking air-support, but *ground-support*."

"From the intelligence report I got, what you need is the kind of support that'll hold you upright."

"That's the only time you come and visit me, is when the ol' lady calls you and complains that I throw my fucking leg in the pond."

"Just give me an invite. You know I'll come over."

"An invitation! Anita, did you hear that? Set the table for crumpets and tea. This son-of-a-bitch needs a formal fucking invitation to visit his war buddy."

Albert began taking his clothes off. When he was down to his underpants, he walked to the edge of the pond. "Where'd he toss it?"

"Over there," Anita pointed.

He carefully stepped into the water, walking slowly until he was waist deep. He looked over his shoulder.

"Little farther. To your right."

"Goddamn it's cold. What do you do, sit here and throw ice cubes in the water all day?" Albert cried. He disappeared in the water that made a mirror reflection of a partly cloudy, but otherwise pale blue sky. Resurfacing after nearly a minute, he shrugged his arms. "Why don't you get one of those wooden legs so it'll float when you throw it in the pond?"

"You're in the right place. Just keep looking," Anita called.

Albert submerged again. Shortly, he surfaced. He raised the plastic leg triumphantly over his head. Anita clapped. Trudging through the water, Albert sloshed back onto shore and dropped the prosthetic on the ground before Seig.

"I don't want that son-of-a-bitch. Give it back to the fish."

"Listen. If you throw that leg into the pond one more time, I'm going to throw you in with it." Even dripping wet and in his underpants, Albert looked menacing enough to carry out his threat.

"There's a goddamn friend for you," Seig muttered.

"Thank you," Anita said to Albert, approaching with his pants and shirt draped in an arm. Giving him a once over, she burst into laughter.

"Next time, *you* go diving for the leg," he grumbled. The mountain air was turning chilly as the sun began its western descent behind nearby hills. Albert shivered.

"Take your cloths and I'll go get you a towel," Anita said.

"I don't need a towel," he replied, allowing her to hang his thing over an extended forearm.

"You'll catch a cold," she insisted. Hurrying off, she went up the slope of the hill to the house. By the time she returned, Albert had put on his pants and proceeded buttoning his short sleeve shirt.

"Here." She handed him the towel. "At least dry your hair." She held a fifth of whiskey in the other hand. Several plastic cups inserted into one another, were turned on-end over the neck.

Albert took the towel and gave his head a quick, vigorous wiping.

"I really appreciate you coming to the rescue."

"Hey, I got a good one for you. Where do you find a dog without any legs?" Seig asked while fastening his leg back in place.

"I don't know, where?" Albert replied.

"Right where you left him."

Albert did not laugh.

Neither did Jack, even though he thought the joke was pretty funny.

"He tells that one all the time," Anita said. "I brought you some whiskey to warm up with." She held up the bottle.

"Sure, I'll have some," Albert said. He tossed her the towel.

"You want some too," she asked Jack.

"Yeah. Please."

"My leg's wet," Seig complained. "It smells like frog shit."

"Here. Over here," Seig called. "I'm in imminent danger of sobering up as a result of all this trauma."

"You don't need anymore," she said. Stepping over to a wooden picnic table, she set the cups down and filled each of them from the bottle. Albert picked up his boots and went to the table, sitting on the bench at one side. He dropped his boots to the ground. Jack went over and sat across from him.

"You going to join us?" Albert called to Seig.

In a moment, he came staggering in the direction of the table. The shoe of his prosthetic leg made a swishing sound as he walked. He plopped down next to Jack. "I'm just going to drink from the bottle if you don't give me a cup," he warned.

Looking at him askance, Anita turned and went to the lawn chair. She picked up the rifle he had left leaning against it, and started towards the house.

"Go ahead. Take it. I don't care," Seig yelled. "I'm out of ammo anyway. And the war's over, at least for me, for now." He turned and looked at Jack. "What's your name again?"

"Jack." He shook the offered hand.

"What division were you in?"

"The 9th. 3/60th, 'A' Company."

"You were in the 9th man! That was my division."

"I told you that," Albert exclaimed.

Anita soon returned to the gathering. "Here you are," she exclaimed angrily, her Spanish accent pronounced more than ever. She plopped the plastic cup down on the table.

Albert picked up the bottle and poured a little bit into Seig's cup.

"Come on, I've got a hollow leg that it all goes into." He glared.

Picking up the cup, Albert handed it over. "That's all you get."

"He's drinking day and night, day and night," Anita reported.

"You should leave him," Albert said. "He obviously doesn't appreciate you. I'll leave my ol' lady, who doesn't appreciate me, and we'll run off to Vegas together."

"No deal. If I run off with you, or anybody, I want to go to Rio."

"Go ahead, both of you. Get out of my sight," Seig muttered. Instead of drinking from the cup Albert had just poured, he picked up the bottle and guzzled from it. Letting it down to the table surface, but still gripping it by the neck, he looked around at the others and said, "I come home and everyone is singing along about 'tying a yellow ribbon around an old oak tree.' Big homecoming for some dickhead convict. Meanwhile, I'm doing my patriotic duty, and end up getting my fucking leg blown off. Where's my yellow ribbon?" He looked at the bottle before himself a moment. His eyes watered. "All you got to be is a convict, all four limbs intact or not, and you're a fucking hero when you come home."

"He's feeling sorry for himself. He's always feeling sorry for himself," Anita sighed. Walking down to the edge of the pond, she sat in the lawn chair. She leaned forward and buried her face in her hands.

Seig's shoulders began to shake as he sobbed.

"Some friggen party huh?" Albert said, his voice thick.

"Really," Jack replied, fully understanding why it was so difficult for Albert to visit his buddy.

Albert raced up behind a car, the only one around for a half mile of freeway, and started tailgating it. "So, when we going to do the warehouse job?" He asked, speeding along only several feet from the rear of the station wagon. "Move out of my way you stupid motherfucker!" he blurted. The car finally merged into the slow lane allowing Albert to resume the speed to which he desired.

"Soon. I've been waiting for the moon to get its act together to our advantage. Or if we can get a cloudy night, so that the moonlight is blocked."

"The front of the building is all lit up anyway. What does it matter?"

"Can't do much about that. But I'm more concerned about our getaway. If someone spots us, we need to disappear into the darkness of the distance."

"You grunts think of everything," Albert smiled. He came up behind another car that was abiding the speed limit. "After we're done with that job, when do you want to do the one in Sacto?"

"What's with all this sudden ambition?"

"I'm broke man. I'm reduced to stealing money from Judy's purse just to buy booze. I don't get a monthly disability check like you." The car held its course despite Albert's continuous tailgating.

"Well, it's not much, otherwise I wouldn't be living in your basement," Jack said. "I'm with you. Really. In fact I've been meaning to talk to you about an idea. What do you think about us hijacking a helicopter for the bank job? You know, like one of those news copters. That way we could get in and get out in a matter of minutes, *and* not have to concern ourselves with the cops chasing us in a car."

"I can't fly a copter man. And you can't either. Unless you've been hiding something from me. Get the fuck out of my way you piece of shit," he swore at the car.

"I mean *with* the pilot. We hijack him to! Imagine, a chauffeur driven helicopter. We'll set him down right in the parking lot. I'll keep him at gun-point while you run in and submit your request for a very large withdrawal. Be a lot better than a car for the getaway."

"All right! You know me and helicopters man. This son-of-a-bitch isn't going to move." He grit his teeth. Swerving into the slow lane, Albert speeded up, passing the car so close that he had to swerve away from it a second before hitting the sedan's side mirror with his front left fender. "Think we can hijack a copter for the warehouse job?" He happily sped along on open freeway, his foot all of the way down on the gas. The truck engine whined loudly. Jack wondered how long it would be until a rod came flying out of the block.

"A *safe* in a light observation helicopter? Even the minimum cargo weight for one of those suckers has to be five or six hundred pounds at the most!"

"Oh, yeah. I wasn't thinking."

Jack reached and turned up the radio at a familiar tune. The song resonated from the speaker at the middle of the truck's dashboard. "Mia used to love this song," he exclaimed. "This was our song." He joined in with the chorus of *Live for Today* by the Grass Roots.

"You're not still hung up on her, are you?" Albert asked.

"Sure I am. Why not?"

"Well for one thing, you've got something fairly serious going on with someone else. Right?"

Jack shuffled his feet nervously, folding his arms, and unfolding them. "We've only been on three dates and already she's starting to get on my case about stuff."

"Like because you're married?"

"No, that's not it. Audrey knows the score. I told her I'm going to get a divorce as soon as I can afford it. Among other things, she keeps telling me that I have a death wish. Everybody thinks I have a fucking death wish."

"All anyone had to do is get in your car with you to figure that out."

"You should talk!" he retorted to Albert, who was barreling down the freeway doing eighty-plus. Cars were moving out of his way, one after the next so that he did not even have to slow down. A whining noise, accompanied by a vibration beneath the floorboard hinted of a worn U-joint stressed to its limit.

"She's making some pretty heavy demands on me."

"Such as?"

"Such as, she wants me to chose between her and Mia."

"You told her about Mia?"

"Yes."

"You got more balls than I thought. Or you're out of your freggen mind."

"Probably the latter."

"So, what now?"

"I don't know. I'm crazy about her. I'm more crazy about Mia though."

"You can't even afford a divorce much less the expense of bringing Mia to the United States. Besides man, she's a gook."

He swallowed. After glaring at Albert for several seconds, he turned and looked out the side window. They were traveling through the rural community where Jack had grown up. He did not notice the scattering of houses tucked back away from the freeway among the pine and oak tree covered hills, some the homes of good friends during his high school days, people with whom he no longer associated. His parents house soon appeared where it sat on a hilltop. Amber light from a setting sun flashed against its large living room window that commanded a view of the lower foothills.

"You okay buddy?" Albert asked.

Jack ignored him. Across the section of frontage road they were speeding past, appeared a row of rural mailboxes, one of which, incidentally, he was losing patience. If it didn't produce him a long overdue letter real soon, he was going to hand-deliver it a cherry bomb.

Even after three years, his feelings towards Mia had not waned. In fact, he felt more certain than ever she was the only person in the world for him. If he had the money, nothing could stand between his returning to Vihn Hoa to search for her. When the truck pulled up to the curb beside the house, Albert chimed, "Home sweet home."

Jack got out, slammed the truck door then walked off in a hurry.

"You still mad about what I said," Albert called.

Jack went down the cement steps and into the basement.

"This is me man," he cried, following Jack to where he stopped in the center of the room. "I don't care whether you marry your Vietnamese girlfriend or not. I'll always be your good buddy."

Jack stepped over to the sink to get a drink of water. Spinning around, he said, "You know I'm serious about her. And now this thing with the Americans pulling out, and the South Vietnamese civilians being persecuted by both sides. When I first met her, she told me that her father had been executed by the VC because he was a Văn Thiệu sympathizer. She's on that same 'hit list.'"

"I just can't believe you're so hung-up on her. You know it's just one-sided man. Vietnamese people don't fall in love the way we do. If anything, Mia's in love with the prospects of coming to the USA - not that I'd blame her."

Jack swung hard, his fist smashing into jawbone.

Albert sprawled backwards. He flattened against the wall, arms spread wide. The plaque of Jack's medals fell. Glass broke as it hit the cement floor. At once regretting what he had done, he reached to help his friend who was regaining his footing.

Withdrawing his arm before Jack could touch it, he stumbled towards the front door, where he stopped to wipe the corner of his mouth. Examining his blood smeared fingers, he said, "I would never hit you, no matter what."

"I'm sorry. Really. I'm sorry. It's like I lost control of myself," Jack stammered.

"You sure are out of control. You're out of line too." He glared sorrowfully.

"I guess it's time for me to break camp, and move on," Jack mumbled, looking down.

"You don't have to go anywhere. You know you're not the only guy around here who got fucked-up by that war. When you're done feeling sorry for yourself, let me know."

Holding a hand over the place he had been hit, he turned and went out the door, still open from when they had entered several minutes earlier.

Jack began to tremble. He looked to the floor at the frame of medals laying sideways against the wall. The colorful ribbons with their brass and silver emblems were in disarray amongst the shards of broken glass. One of them knocked free of its felt mount, lay on the floor several feet away. He stared at the scene for a moment. "Fuck it!" he exclaimed. "That's just fine with me!" He bent down and picked up the frame. As he lifted it, several chunks of glass fell to the floor, breaking into smaller pieces. He stepped over to the kitchen sink and tossed the broken plaque of medals into the garbage can. "Imagine people giving their lives for trinkets. Just fucking trinkets," he muttered. He found his bottle of Valiums in the cabinet, took three and washed them down with a glass of water. He turned from the sink, looked down at his Purple Heart still on the floor, took careful aim with his foot and kicked it. It shot like a hockey puck, ricocheted off the wall, and disappeared under the bed. "Score!" he cried. Going to the bed, he sat on the edge of the mattress, and took off his shoes. He dropped to his back, wondering, how did it all get this way? When I got back home, I really believed I would be waking up every morning giggling with joy over my good fortune. That last day in 'Nam when he had opened his eyes after being blown out of the tree, and found himself badly wounded, despite the terrible pain, and the scene of the wounded and dying around him in the field hospital, he realized, this is it - the Million Dollar Wound! Soon would be the mythical ride on the Silver Bird back to "The World," the place where rivers flowed with cold beer, beautiful women grew on trees, good paying jobs were there for the asking, as long as you asked in a nice tone, and the war remained safely on the other side of the world where you had left it. He sobbed.

* * *

From his coconut tree vista Jack could clearly see the tracts of jungle, rice paddies and network of canals that had provided so much obstacle to finally render Fourth Platoon's maps and compasses useless. Just several miles away, he could see the sugarcane field for which they had spent hours in the one-hundred and fifteen degree heat hacking with machetes and stomping a path. Here they found not the enemy headquarters' they expected, but rather a small sugarcane crushing factory converted to hospital. By all signs, it had been used by the NVA and hastily abandoned a short time before. There was the brief hilarity at the sight of a top-heavy load of equipment laden men using rifle butts for paddles, clumsily making their way across the narrow canal. Laughter from those on shore quickly turned to shock as the sampan capsized and the muddy waters swallowed Anderson and Hersh.

Their bodies were later recovered far downstream. Somewhere between here and that canal crossing is where the ambush occurred. This time the platoon got off light with only a single WIA. Traveling another hour in search of their point of extraction, the jungle finally closed in on them. Regardless of the aid of maps, compasses and radio communications, Fourth Platoon finally declared itself lost. Fortunately, among their ranks was someone who had spent his childhood climbing trees. Looking forward from his palm frond perch, his heart lifted at the sight of the Vam Co Dong River, much closer than he had expected. A south by southeast tack would have them there well before nightfall, forgiving anymore surprises. Along the mangrove tangled banks of the Vam Co Dong, the riverboats would extract the platoon and take them back to division headquarters' for a badly needed stand-down. Before slipping back through the fronds and sliding down the tree trunk, Jack took a last look around. Somewhere out there, much farther than vision or view allowed, were the rice paddies of Kien Hoa Province where they had set down into a hot LZ last month. His copter was downed when a B40 rocket made a direct hit on the engine housing. Everyone on board survived, but not without the broken bones and bruises you would expect from a two hundred foot freefall into a rice paddy. He was lucky enough to walk away with only a hurt back. What hurt worse was it did not stand up to the merit of a Million Dollar Wound. Just weeks earlier was the incident in the U Mihn Forest, he remembered well. The riverboats had unloaded the platoon. After a short while, as the flotilla rounded a hairpin curve in the canal, a sniper fired at one of the boats from the dense jungle that lined the canal. With them trapped on a finger of land, flanked on both sides by the riverboats, all hell broke loose. There were at least thirty of the World War II landing craft converted to troop-carrier riverboats. While the point boat, known as Zippo, melted all vegetation within thirty feet of the shoreline with its huge flame-thrower, the other boats blasted the jungle with their pointblank antiaircraft guns and sawed-off howitzers, sprayed bullets from dozens of swivel mounted machine guns, lobbed mortars and churned out grenades from automatic launchers. Jack's platoon, mistaken for the sniper, fell recipient to this wrath from two sides. The roar and explosions of incoming was so loud it drowned out repeated cries of "Cease fire!" from the platoon's radioman. As bullets streaked overhead and the ground shook from grenades and mortar rounds, some of the men began frantically digging into the soft earth with anything from bayonets to helmets. But even if perfectly good shovels had been handy, it was too late for digging foxholes. The friendly-fire claimed the lives of two of them.

The more he dwelled upon his experiences in those deep swamps and dark jungles, fiercely defended by machine gun toting little men who, magically sidestepped daily drops of thousands of pounds of American bombs, the greater became his uncertainty. Such as, Jack wondered, *what role do a soldier's maps and compasses play in a country where the very war in which he is fighting cannot find something as simple as its own battle lines?* He turned to look behind him. Beyond where the Vam Co Dong emptied into the Mekong River, and several hours east by riverboat lay the base camp. Here presided a few days of relative safety among the luxury of barracks and mess halls. This was what he had to focus on for now. Besides, in the more immediate scheme of things, this was all he lived for; warm food and a full night of sleep, uninterrupted by bombs and bullets. As for the big picture, he counted himself among those numerous others who were not fighting a war, so much as fighting to stay alive for the designated 365 days.

"Better get down from that tree," the lieutenant yelled. "You don't want one of our aircraft to mistake you for a sniper."

As he began sliding down the tree, there came a short whistle, and an explosion. Jack opened his eyes and saw the blurred underside of the coconut tree high above. He opened his eyes again to discover one man at his head and another at his feet loading him into a helicopter. The next time he opened his eyes, a young lady in white uniform was looking down at him. He lifted his head with a start, glancing one way and the other. There were beds filled with wounded men everywhere. "We were worried about you. You've been delirious," she said.

He looked down to see his knee wrapped in bandages, and back to the nurse.

"We did what we could for your knee. They're transferring you to the hospital in Fort Ord, California for more treatment. Do you remember what happened to you?"

He thought for a minute and shook his head. "I'm going home?"

"Yes, you're going home," she smiled.

The fact that he had been wounded so badly, with an injury that would most likely follow him through life, could not dampen his sudden joy. He wanted to thank her personally for the news, but was so choked-up he could not speak. He had a ticket for flight on the Silver Bird.

* * *

What troubled Jack most, was not what he remembered of that incident, but rather what evaded him. He remembered opening his eyes after falling from the tree. Upon regaining the wind that had been knocked out of him, he looked up. There was the out of focus underside of the coconut tree he had been knocked out of by the concussion. That's where everything went black when he tried to remember.

He had attempted to move, but a sharp pain shot through his leg. He passed back into unconsciousness. Now he remembered this for the first time. Also, for the first time, outside of what he had seen in his nightmares, he clearly recalled the sound of others crying in distress, and not being able to bring himself to look at what was right next to him. Jack turned in bed and folded up, wrapping his arms around his knees. His left knee hurt with the pressure, but he squeezed even tighter. The pain became so intense that with his eyes closed, he could actually see the beast. It defined an arabesque pattern of scar tissue, peppered beneath the surface of his skin with grain-size pieces of shrapnel too small and deep to remove when they had operated. Each piece glowed red, radiating the pain into a collective throb. Dirt clogs fell from the sky. They pelted the earth around him. He again squeezed his leg until the pain forced him to let up. It was my fault, he cried. If be-known, I had not been daydreaming for so long, the VC would not have been able to use me as a bearing to precisely site mortar round that landed right in the middle of the platoon. Two men had been killed, and one had lost an arm due to his stupidity. He had always known this, but had avoided the thought anytime it came back to haunt him. If I really had amnesia, as diagnosed, it was sure a convenient one, thought Jack. The sky rained with fist sized chucks of earth. They pelted the ground all around him. He squeezed his knee. But this time he could not avoid the rouge thoughts. He had turned his head to the side, and recoiled to see the arm laying next to him. It was severed at the elbow. Not far beyond the arm, laid out on his back was "Easterbunny" wailing in pain. The medic busied himself wrapping the bloody stump of Easton's arm with gauze. Jack shuddered. He realized how powerful his feelings were for those guys.

The scene of the ribbon of winding river as seen from mid-span on the bridge flashed before him. He leaned forward, the toes of his shoes extending into midair. The grip of a single hand on a parallel bar of the railing behind him was all that separated him from becoming at one with that scene. I can put an end to all this pain forever, he assured himself.

Jack felt cold so he pulled the sheets over himself. After what must have been hours, he woke in a cold sweat. It was still dark out. He kicked away the sheets, peeled off his tee-shirt, and drifted back to sleep. He bolted upright to the scream of a siren. "Jesus, a red alert!" he cried out loud. Jumping from bed, he started to run for cover. He looked one way, then the other. Spinning around, he pulled the twin size bed away from the wall tipping it on its side. A mattress won't protect you from a direct hit, but it'll absorb the flying shrapnel. He rushed to the corner of the room where a bunch of his things from the house were piled, pulling out his shotgun. He quickly found the box of shells, and ducked behind the upturned bed. Taking a shell out of the cardboard box he shoved it into the breach. With a smart jerk of his arm, he snapped the single-shot rifle into the locked and loaded. Another siren wailed. Reflections of the flashing red lights of the fire truck played through the windows and upon the walls as it sped past the house on the main road. He shuddered at the similarity between this siren, and the one at the top of the communication tower at Dong Tam. For the most part, he was in his element when all hell broke loose. But if all hell was not breaking loose around him, it occurred to him that it might be breaking loose within.

Jack sat on the floor from where he had been crouching, leaned backwards against the upturned mattress, and let his rifle down so it lay across his lap. But the enemy *is* out there, he felt certain. There were all the people that he foolishly thought he could trust: Skye, Roma, Jim, his dad and his VA doctors, not to mention all of the other noncombatants in his world. And to add to the indignity, Albert had apparently joined their ranks. If you can't depend on their simple-ass trust, then it came down to *you or them*. Drifting off to sleep, the sheets and bed cover that had fallen in a pile on the cement floor that were Jack's only cushion. When he woke, light was coming through the front windows. The cat meowed at the door. He got up, taking the shotgun with him, and let Shadow out. "Don't be gone long buddy. You're the only friend I have left," he called behind the cat that made a last glance at him before it ran out. He closed the door, and went to the sink, filling a glass from the tap, his rifle ever in hand. He gulped down the cool, refreshing water, then filled another glass and quaffed it down. Leaving the empty glass on the counter, he stepped over to the window for a look. It was quiet outside. Nothing stirred except Shadow, who was stretching her claws on the trunk of a pine tree in the middle of the yard. "It's *too* quiet," he whispered to himself. His stomach audibly growled. He went to the cabinet and searched for something to satisfy his hunger. There were at least a dozen cans of pork and beans in his stockpile. "Breakfast!" he exclaimed, and leaned the rifle against the counter so it was close at hand. After opening a can, he found a spoon, and began eating as quickly as he could gobble the food down. He occasionally glanced out the window as he ate. When he finished his meal, he went to the corner of the room where he found what he was looking for, his combat boots. He sat on the edge of the bed. Pulling one boot over a bare foot, he cinched each set of eyelets carefully from the bottom up, until the boot fit securely all around. He tied the remaining length of leather straps by wrapping them tightly around the top of the boot once, finally tying a bow knot. After putting on his other boot with the same amount of attention, he stood. This was the first time he had put on his boots since returning from the war. Such instant familiarity with a simple comfort invigorated him. Jack bounced a little to check the fit. "Perfect," he said. In war, you can have all the ammo, food and tactical advantage on the enemy in the world. But if your boots don't fit you properly, you're out of luck. Imagine plodding through knee deep rice paddy mud, and right in the middle of assaulting an enemy bunker in the wood line, one of your loose fitting boots is sucked off? Or try to imagine a six or eight mile march through the steaming jungles in boots too small for your feet. Then the shit starts flying and you have to sprint for cover to keep from getting mowed down by a machine gun nest?

Stepping over to the window, he looked out to make sure no one was around. He opened the door, glanced both ways, and went out. Dried leaves were plentiful beneath the nearby oak tree. Stooping down, he gathered a pile of them in his arms. Bringing them back to the front of his hideout, he scattered them over the sidewalk. If anyone approached, he would hear the leaves crunching beneath footsteps. A door and two windows facing the backyard were all that made him vulnerable to the outside world. No other route gave passage to his basement shelter. He had held a much less formidable defensive perimeter than this on numerous occasions. Jack got another idea. He went to the back of the room and tore a flap of cardboard from one of the boxes in which his things were stored. With a ball-point pen, he sketched large, heavy letters that spelled out "TO DIA." He fastened this sign to the glass section of the door, warning to all the world. Feeling very tired, he returned to his place behind the mattress and laid down.

The headquarters' radio operator had alerted him of enemy movement in his watch area, information passed on from an ARVN outpost. Possibly NVA troops. He gazed through the rifle slit of his small bunker. "God don't let it be NVA," Jack whispered to himself. The Tet Offensive had nearly wiped-out all organized Viet Cong activity in the Delta, but the vacuum had lately been filling in with North Vietnamese Army regulars. With the emerald screen of surrounding jungle, you could not see beyond five feet in any direction. Meanwhile, his apprehension grew in proportion to the increase in radio chatter from the other outposts. Various sightings amounted to heavily armed men in long columns wearing brown uniforms and small conical hats. Yes, that's what the NVA looked like. The pit of Jack's stomach was a ratchet tightening another click with each additional sighting reported. The numbers were stacking up to what amounted to an entire battalion. Very likely they were positioning themselves for an all-out attack on the base camp. "Lima Papa Three. This is Sierra Fox Trot, come in." The radio operator's tone sounded urgent.

"This is Lima Papa Three, over," he spoke just above a whisper.

"You have orders from higher up to un-ass, pronto! Do you copy? Over."

That several hundred yards back to the safety of the base camp might well have been a hundred miles with enemy everywhere. But taking that risk was better than finding yourself caught in the middle of a shooting contest between the NVA and the base camp, Jack considered. "That's Rogered. Over and out." They were not going to give anything away over the radio waves, but the command center was calling in all of the listening posts so they could start the artillery and air-strikes. He had to hurry. He started gathering his things, when he heard what must have been several of them. Normally you had to strain to hear them crawling through the underbrush if it were Viet Cong. These were footsteps. The NVA rarely crawled. They were too close for him to make a run for it now. Jack grabbed his rifle and sat on the ground in the corner of the bunker so that he faced the only entranceway. He had concealed the opening with fresh cut palm fronds, but now cursed that he had not replaced the old ones on top of the bunker. After several days, they were starting to turn brown. Though the earthen roof protruded only several feet above ground, if you were close enough, you could easily spot it without the cover of good camouflage. Finger trigger readied, he checked and double-checked with the feel of his thumb that his safety was clicked onto fully-automatic. The sound of men crashing through the dense jungle startled him. Light exploded into his dusky hideout. Two AK-47 barrels appeared pointing directly at him. They rattled loudly, fire spitting from their muzzles. Jack jumped. He looked frantically around himself. Recognizing the interior of his safe little hovel in the good ol' USA, he breathed relief. His tee-shirt was soaked with sweat. Taking it off, he wiped sweat from his face with a dry end of the shirt, and tossed it to the floor. He would not have known if it were day or night if it had not been for the sunlight coming through the windows. He had no idea of the hour though. But he was thirsty, and hungry.

"Hello! Hello! Are you in there?" He heard someone calling. "Jack. Are you in there?" It was Judy.

Jack stayed hidden behind the upturned mattress as she started banging on the door.

"If you're in there, unlock the damned door. I need to do my laundry!"

He remained perfectly still at his place on the floor.

"Damn it!" she exclaimed.

The sound of her footsteps walking away relieved him, but he waited a few more minutes just in case. Sure enough, she returned.

"I know he's in there. His car's out front," Judy said. She banged on the door. "Jack. Open up! What's this sign? It says, 'TO DIA.'"

"In so many words, in Vietnamese, it means 'Keep out, enemy-held territory.' Just let him be," he heard Albert tell her. "He's bummed out. Jack's going through some weird shit right now. He needs to be alone for awhile."

"I don't care about his weird shit. I just want to do my laundry!"

"Come on. You can do your laundry in town. After a few days he'll be okay and you can have your washing machine back."

"I want him out of here," she cried. "You tell him to find another place to 'get through his weird shit.' I've got enough weird shit around here already without Jack adding to it."

Jack listened carefully as they started walking away.

"Are all you Vietnam veterans this screwed-up?"

He heard her in the distance as the screen door slammed shut at the rear entrance to the house. When he was sure the coast was clear, he went to the cabinet over the sink and grabbed a can of pork and beans. Instead of using the handy kitchen can-opener mounted to the side of the cabinet, he opened it with his P-38. He got a spoon and ate straight out of the can. When he was done, he rinsed the can in the sink and filled it with tap water. There was nothing left to drink in the fridge. As Jack gulped down the water from the can, wishing that he had some beer instead, he started chuckling to himself to remember what Litely used to say when they would be in some jungle backwash having their C-rations for dinner. *"James, the gentlemen have expressed a desire to rough it tonight,"* he would call out, as if to a servant, in a passable aristocratic accent. *"Please serve the Dom Perignon in pre-used C-ration cans rather than in the usual crystal."* Jack was still hungry. He looked to the right of the sink on the countertop and saw the sack of pears. "Almost forgot about those dudes," he said, taking the topmost piece of fruit and finished it off as quickly as he could chew and swallow the not quite ripe fruit. He tossed the core into the sink. Wondering about his little buddy, his only friend left in the world, he peered out the window to ensure no one was around and opened the door. "Shadow. Shadow!" He called. Looking around the yard he waited a minute, and called again. There was no sign of her. He waited a few more minutes, but the cat did not appear. "She'll come home when she gets hungry," he muttered to himself, closing the door. Returning to his place behind the mattress, he straightened his bedding that was in a pile on the floor and laid down. The cement floor was hard but felt cool. He liked the coolness, and felt more secure and relaxed when he was close to the ground.

Mia clung to him with her slender arms where they lay on her small mat and wood slated bed. It was in love-making as it was in all aspects of their relationship that she knew how to please him. A little adjustment in her position here, a little there in selfless response to his every need. Once he had been fulfilled, she sighed with mutual satisfaction, even at times complimenting his stamina. Mia said she would get him a beer. As she stood, he noticed she made a quick wrist action. Something plopped down on the bed next to him. She dashed for the front door. Jack reached to find what she had dropped. Picking up the metal object, he held it up for examination in the dim light. He gasped to see that it was a grenade - without the pin. Flinching, he opened his eyes. Looking around himself, the familiar setting of his room assured him that he was halfway around the world from that land where live hand grenades had a way of showing up in the most inconvenient of places, delivered by people you would least suspect. He wanted to go back to sleep, but even though he felt like he could use about another twelve hours worth, he was afraid of a sequel to the nightmare he had just had. He moved his head around a little on the arm that had become a pillow, and pulled his legs into the fetal. That's when he noticed he was wearing his boots. Starting to take them off, he reconsidered. You never know when the shit might start flying. He lay motionless for a long time trying not to think too much. But here was a lot to think about. For instance, he wondered, when will this fucking pain go away? He also wanted to know if he would ever be able to enjoy life the way other people seemed to. He knew without doubt that a wife, a nice house and a job did not necessarily add up to happiness. At least not for him. How about Mia? He felt certain *she* could make him happy. Even in the middle of a war zone, she made him happier than he had ever been with anyone. He got up. Finding his photo album, he brought it back to his place on the floor. He opened it to the picture of his favorite person in the world. It was the one with Mia peeking over the top of sunglasses that she held daintily with a thumb and forefinger at the end of her nose. In the background to her left, at the east end of rue de Jardin, Jack's gaze settled on a stretch of wood line. A movement startled him. Out of the dark jungle appeared the figure of a man, a rifle bursting with fire as he ran towards the town center. Behind him were more, all firing their rifles as they poured onto the streets of Vihn Kim. Shortly, the town swarmed with black PJ wearing little men, shooting and throwing hand grenades everywhere. Fiery balls exploded from the doorways and windows of restaurants and stores. Fragments of glass and furniture flew onto the sidewalks and street. People fell to the ground maimed and bleeding. Jack slammed the album shut. He drifted back to sleep. Villages were overrun; helicopter hit hot LZs; platoons were ambushed; base camps were rocketed; casualties mounted - the usual. A droning sound woke him. He felt a sting on his neck and swatted hard with his palm. The buzzing sound slowly faded away into the dark. "Fucking mosquito!" he cried. Jack remembered in 'Nam how he would slather every exposed part of his skin with bug repellent, three times a night, and they would still bite him. Motherfuckers were at one with the enemy, *their* arsenal comprising of such high-caliber weaponry as malaria and Dengue fever. As he was drifting off back to sleep, he heard it returning.

Listening, he not moving until he felt it lite on him again. This time it wanted blood from his face. Jack slapped. "Ouch!" he cried out. But at least I got rid of the little bloodsucker, he reveled - until he heard it buzzing away. Jumping to his feet, he leapt over and threw on the light switch in time to see the insect fly in between the cloths hanging in his improvised closet. He slid the hanger of one garment after the next along the length of pipe that he had converted to a rack, searching for it. As the weight of his coats and shirts shifted to one side, the single nail supporting the pipe on that side gave way. His rack of cloths collapsed in a heap. Spotting the mosquito flying overhead towards the front of the room, he yelled, "Motherfucker! You motherfucker!" He chased it to where he saw it land in the sink. Running to the kitchen counter, he looked to see it had taken refuge part way down the drain. "Clever little motherfucker huh? Watch this!" he exclaimed in premature victory, suddenly twisting the hot water tap all the way open. It flew out of the sink just ahead of the steaming water. Jack spun around and went after it. He followed, hopping and slapping his hands in midair, trying to get the evasive insect in flight. It returned to the back of the room where his clothes were on the floor. "Looking for your old hideout huh?" He lunged towards it as the mosquito circled. It finally lite high on the wall. He reached, slapping his palm hard. When he withdrew his hand, he looked to see with glee a black spot amidst splattered blood on the surface of unpainted sheet rock where the mosquito had been. "That's *my* goddamn blood, and I don't want anyone to have it except me!" He cried. Taking a minute to get his breath back, he heard what sounded like a waterfall. He gasped, running into the kitchen area. The sink was overflowing, steaming water cascaded to the floor. Lunging to the sink, he turned off the tap. Glancing down from where he stood, Jack saw that the water came up about an inch around his boots. He looked around to see that the water was flowing out the slit at the bottom of the front door. It'll take care of itself, just like the good ol' rice paddies, he thought, sloshing his way. He went back over his bedding where the mattress had staved off the deluge. It had soaked up the water that had flowed that far, fortunately keeping it from his bivouac. Jack laid back down on the floor. But every time he closed his eyes, the dirt clogs began falling. Now, he clearly remembered the incident. Would it replay in his mind forever? Would he ever forgive himself? He decided what needed to be done. Going to the back of the room, he sifted through the pile of his one-time neatly hanging wardrobe, where he found something appropriate for his final mission - his Army Greens.

* * *

Pulling off on the gravel shoulder just before the entrance to the bridge, Jack parked the car. An hour at least preceded sunrise, and there was no traffic. He started to take his keys from the ignition, but said, "What's it matter?" He walked with the nonchalance of taking a stroll to where he figured was mid-span, to the place where he imagined the other 'Nam vet had jumped. He intentionally chose this side of the bridge. In early morning hours, the wind moved from the west, up canyon. If he jumped from the windward, the other side of the bridge, he stood the risk of drifting in mid-flight, perhaps smacking into a supporting girder, cracking his head open or breaking some bones, spoiling what otherwise could be a perfectly good suicide jump. Climbing over the railing, he stood with the toes of his boots hanging over the edge, a one-handed grip on a parallel bar of the railing the only thing preventing his fall into the abyss. In daylight, you could see the river looking like a section of twisted white ribbon because of the rapids through this part of the canyon. Sheer rock walls jutted upward from the narrow sand and gravel shores of the river. As the seven-hundred foot canyon rose, it became wider, but not to any extreme. Even at the top, on either side, the ground did not level off, but became steep sloping pine covered hills. In the days he had trekked those endlessly flat tracks of jungle and rice paddies, he had just as clearly visualized a thousand times over, this rugged hill country that was his home. His fingers were becoming slippery with sweat and he felt his grip loosening. "All I wanted to do was *come home,*" he cried into the darkness. "All I wanted to do was *come home,*" echoed in the canyon, as if the abyss itself were mocking him. Jack thought about what Audrey had told him about him never having killed anyone. *Did she know how much that meant to me? Of course she did.* The breeze that came up from behind him carried a fresh scent. The recently burned tract of forest in the canyon, he realized, was now regenerating. What he smelled was new pine growth.

In a mop-up operation after an Arch Lights attack in the Giong Trom District of Kien Hoa, he had marveled at the completeness of devastation as elements of the 3/60th Regiment swept through the five square mile area the B-52s had leveled. Plodding through a stretch of obliterated jungle, he came upon a dirt bunker. "Fire in the hole!" he yelled, lobbing a concussion grenade into the rifle-slit to destroy it. He stepped out of harms way in five seconds and watched as the several foot thick layer of roof lifted into the air. To his surprise, a black PJ wearing man staggered backwards within the now exposed opening in the ground, dirt clogs raining down on him. Jack fired at him with a full burst from his M-16. The emaciated looking and badly tattered man threw his arms in the air. When the medic examined him later, the only thing he could find wrong was that his ears drums had most likely been perforated, and one of the rounds from Jack's M-16 had nicked his forearm. The platoon's Vietnamese scout interrogate him. The man told that he had been left behind by his Viet Cong battalion after an attack by American jets a month and a half earlier. The napalm they dropped had incinerated the hamlet where the VC unit was bivouacked, burning to death all of those in his squad as well as the villagers. He had escaped with his life by jumping into a nearby canal where he stayed submerged with only his nose poking out of the water for air, until it was all over. He lived on fruit that he gathered and a bag of rice. For a month and a half, he took up residence in the bunker where Jack had found him, hoping his unit would return one day. This man had survived a B-52 attack, a concussion grenade that exploded at his feet, a magazine full of M-16 rounds at pointblank and a napalm attack. Jack remembered the great sense of admiration he held for that scraggly little man. Talk about walking eye-deep through hell. If he had been a commanding officer, Jack would have put the guy in for a Medal of Honor, enemy or not. Rather than for heroism, the medal would have been for surviving the most incredible of odds. *And here I am blubbering all over myself for being divorced by a girl I didn't even love, and losing a miserable job or two,* he wondered at himself. His grip was becoming so weak on the rail that he had no doubt that a good gust of wind would quickly make up his mind for him about jumping.

It wasn't just the marriage gone wrong and the failed attempts at employment. That goddamned war wouldn't leave him alone. He imagined taking advantage of the time and place and dumping that weight he was dragging around.

He visualized simply reaching around and squeezing a quick-release that connected a tow rope to a body harness. Beneath him, the metal-banded steamer trunk covered with colorful stickers bearing the names of dozens of Mekong Delta staged military campaigns disappeared into the void. After several seconds there was a loud splash. A geyser of water rose in a column, not unlike that made by a mortar round hitting in a flooded rice paddy. But that was only an image. It's not all that easy, he knew. The real trick would be to gradually dump the contents as the occasion permitted. It might take a long time. "Okay, count me in for the long haul," he said to himself. He closed his eyes and took a deep breath. Swinging with his free hand, he grabbed on to the railing, pulling himself in. Securely taking hold of the rail, he climbed back to the safety of the other side.

Jack parked the car in front of the house. Leaning back for a moment in the comfort of the bucket seat, he focused on trying to control the trembling. I guess that was something I needed, he thought after a few minutes. There's nothing like a good talking to yourself - with a little bit of incentive to listen - to put things into perspective. As he got out of the car, he noticed the sun was just coming up. He walked around the house. Fragrance from the thick lawn in the backyard greeted him. He paused a moment and inhaled. When he came to the door, the warning sign that he had displayed startled him. The guy who did not think he could *come home* had put it there. Once inside, he closed the door, and pulled the cardboard flap out of the window. Ripping it into quarters, he tossed the pieces to the floor. He tipped his bed back upright. The edge of the mattress was still wet. Looking around himself, he noticed at least the rest of the water that had run out of the sink to the cement floor had now dried. Looking behind the bed, he stared a moment at his lair in the corner, the bedding and pillow on the floor, and his loaded shotgun. He picked up the rifle, carefully leaning it against the wall. Jack draped the bedspread over the part of the mattress that was not wet, and tossed the pillow on top. Shoving the bed to its place against the wall, he sat down on the edge of the mattress and rested a foot on his knee to untie the straps of one of his boots. When he finished, he stood and took off his clothes. "God I'm tired," he exhaled, collapsing backwards onto the mattress. Wearing only his underpants, he stared at the ceiling with its exposed wood beams. It looked like the ceiling of one of the many bunkers in Dong Tam, with the exception of all of the nails sticking through the overhead planks. The main difference is, with a bunker, there is no floor overhead, rather several thousand pounds of sand bags. He always felt safe in those combat engineer built bunkers - safe as one could expect to feel in the middle of a besieged base camp, surrounded by the enemy-held jungles of the Mekong Delta. He wondered if this onetime dependency on bunkers for refuge from the falling mortars and rockets, had not grown into some kind of permanent addiction. It occurred to him that Albert, and the others who still wore their combat boots, were stuck in bunker-mode. You never know when you'll be shaken out of your sleep in the middle of the night, and have to run for cover. He knew that he would give anything to return to those cowboy boot wearing days of his youth.

"Jack, you in there?"

He opened his eyes thinking, *I must have been dreaming. I thought I heard Albert calling me.*

"Jack? Jack, you in there?"

It *is* him, Jack realized. He sat upright. It's Albert! He did not speak for a second, finally saying, "What's the password?"

"Fuck you in the left ear."

"Step forward and be recognized."

"You okay buddy?" Albert asked as he entered looking around at the disheveled room.

"I've been better. But I'm okay."

"Really?"

"Really." He got out of bed and went over and offered a hand to his friend. "I want to apologize for, you know."

Albert pulled him close, giving him a squeeze. Jack wrapped his arms around his friend and hugged him just as warmly in return. After a moment they stepped back from each other. Albert gave him a once over. "You look like shit."

"That doesn't even come close to describing how I feel."

"Hey. I got some good news. We don't have to rob no warehouse or bank. I just got a job." He made a dramatic pause. "At the sawmill. They've got three more openings. I told the foreman that I had someone else that needed work. He told me to bring you by on Monday."

"Tomorrow?"

"Today's Saturday," he chuckled. "Losing track of time huh?"

"What's the job?"

"'Sorter.' That's someone who checks out the quality of the wood before it goes on for final milling. Just takes a couple of weeks of training. That's what I'll be doing too. You hip? Pays seven bucks an hour to start."

"Sign me up!" Jack looked around for something to give in appreciation to mark the occasion. He was all out of booze. Noticing the bag of pears still on the counter, he took one out. "Here, have a pear. It's locally grown." In afterthought, he grabbed another one.

"Here, this one's for Judy."

"Thanks," Albert grinned. "I'll bring down some beer later tonight, if you want."

"Can't wait. See ya then."

A pear in each hand, Albert went out the open door.

Jack stood in the doorway, watching as his war buddy walked to the back door of his house. He shifted one of the fruit to the other hand, opened the door and went inside. Looking around the yard for Shadow, Jack gave up after a few minutes. "First things first," he said to himself. After a long shower, he commented on his stubble to himself in the mirror, *"You look like you've been on a three week long mission."* He shaved and splashed on a lot of aftershave, finally spraying a good dousing of deodorant before getting dressed. He wanted to make an impression. When Jack went out to his car, he glanced across the street at his old place. He saw the little girl who now lived there sitting on the steps to the front door. There was a cat in her lap. He blinked to see the cat she was petting was Shadow. *"So that's where you are, you little two-timer. True to your gender,"* he muttered.

* * *

Audrey was wiping the counter surface when he walked in to the restaurant. The cook leaned his head out the service counter from the kitchen smiling when Jack seated himself at the dining counter. "Hey Jack! How's it going there?"

"Hello Stan." He smiled back.

"How's that goat. Still eating gas, tires and oil for lunch?" He looked to Audrey. "Get it. Goat, GTO - Gas, Tires, Oil."

"You're the cook here. You should know about greasy things for lunch," Audrey said.

"Ha ha ha. That's pretty good," he laughed. "Any luck selling it?"

"Took it off the market. So, how's everything in the restaurant world he asked, pulling the coffee cup Audrey had placed on the counter for him. "Thanks," he said.

Good. Great! I love this job. I really do. I mean really. Where else do you find a job where you're surrounded by beautiful girls. And you know Woody, he may be an asshole for a boss, but he only hires the ones with the big personas." Stan cupped hands over his chest to make his point.

Audrey shot a look at him.

He made an innocent grin, drawing his head back into the kitchen. "Well, got to check out the storeroom. We've got mice in there getting into the cracker cartons. I'm going to catch those sneaky little suckers and cut their heads off with a spatula to go with tomorrow's chili. Ha ha ha!" He turned and walked out of the kitchen.

"It might be a tough job here, but at least you've got good company," Jack said to Audrey.

She rolled her eyes. "He's not going to the storeroom to hunt sneaky little cracker connoisseurs. He's going there to smoke a joint. When he's not burning the food or telling dumb jokes, he's in the storeroom getting stoned. Janet too. While I'm here running the whole restaurant by myself, they're in the storeroom smoking dope."

He looked around to see a couple at a table by the front window. They were the only other customers in the place. "It's not as if you're in the middle of rush hour."

"So, what'cha have? You are here to eat, or did you come to talk?"

"That's why I'm here - to visit you. Got a menu?"

She took one from a holder at the end of the counter for him. "*Visit* with me? You're going to have to do better than that. You *know* why I'm so upset."

He squirmed in his seat. After a minute, he began to peruse the menu.

"I don't know why you have to waste your time looking at it. You know that menu by heart - if you have one of *those* things," her last words muttered under breath, but loud and clear.

"I keep hoping you guys will add something good to it. Just wishful thinking I guess." He noticed the menu shaking, and lowered his trembling hands against the counter so it would not be so obvious. *This is the moment of truth*, he thought. *She expects me to make up my mind about Mia before I leave here. What's the matter with me? I knew what I was getting myself into as soon as I stepped through the front door.* Already knowing what he wanted to order, Jack slid down in the seat so he could hide behind the menu pretending to read it, in actuality, buying time for the right thing to say.

Audrey continued wiping a counter that did not need wiping.

"I've decided," he finally said.

"You've decided?" She poised motionless.

"Yeah. I'll have the southern fried chicken with mashed potatoes."

She glared at him.

"You have that available, don't you?"

"Yes we do. Southern fry, with mashed," she called over her shoulder to the kitchen.

"Did you forget? He's in the storeroom getting stoned," Jack said, reaching

225

for the creamer. He poured from the stainless steel container until the level of coffee and cream mix rose to the brim of his cup. At the evening sun dropping into the front windows, Audrey held a palm before her face to shield the light. In a moment, its trajectory leveled over the top of his shoulders. She moved a little so that his head eclipsed the glare. Accordingly, he moved, unleashing it back to her face. Each time she moved, so did he, keeping the sun in her eyes. He wondered about this girl. Maybe he had found his *match*, the evidence of her power consisting within the realm of the glow known as an aura; his within the glow known as a Sniper's Sun. Whatever was happening between the two of them, he had not known such feelings, perhaps since falling in love with Mia. He stared at this beautiful girl with the sun glaring in her face, her eyes shaded by her palm. "Albert referred me to a job at the sawmill. I'm going there on Monday."

"I'm going to go get Stan out the storage room so he can make your meal," she said and walked off.

Jack stirred his coffee and returned the spoon to its place on the counter. When Audrey returned, he asked her to go out to movie with him. "A film called The Godfather is playing."

She nodded from her place behind the counter. "I heard that's a good movie." The sunlight came into her eyes again. Jack moved in such a way in his seat to create a shadow for her from the direct light - a Sniper's Sun.

Notes to the City of Truth or Consequences

Do any of you in service to the citizens of Truth or Consequence, you city officials know what it's like to feel inclined to hunker down, day and night in the trenches like in a war zone in your own home, and do any of you care?I live on Main Street in the historical District. I've traveled and lived in towns around the world for over fifty years. I've seen that usually, any city's historical district is regarded sacred turf. A town's historical district is it's face to the world. Apparently, not the case here. When my wife and I settled here twenty years past, after a year we felt obliged to build an eight foot high stucco wall facing Main Street to somewhat divide and protect us from the two lanes of lunatic traffic. Any day of the week, all hours, gang-bangers with subwoofers so loud to rattle windows into the wee hours; retarded morons on Harleys doing twice the speed limit, repeatedly revving their extremely loud pipes for attention (see me, hear me...); pickup trucks sans mufflers drag-racing along side one another up Main, down Broadway. The elderly and disabled of our little town are afraid to cross the street at the risk of life. Shop owners cringe at the level of street noise least tourists are discouraged from lingering long, never to return in a town under siege of those dangerously brain dead motorists. Earlier this year, I was arrested for kicking the wheel-well of a car that nearly ran me over while I was walking across the Compass Bank parking lot. Seems us pedestrians are the bad guys in a town being doggy done day and night by moron motorists.

Oh Lord, give me an oversized, gas guzzling pickup truck with huge tires, a Harley motorcycle that makes more noise than a 747 on take-off, a car wired with thousands of dollars of subwoofers boom, boom booming down the road (African drumbeats replicated), and co-habitants of my environs will bow in fear and respect. Welcome to Truth or Consequences.

About the Author

I've published many short stories and four books. A Sniper's Sun will be my fifth. I have an MFA education in Creative Writing from Colorado State and taught writing and literature at university level. I currently am working on a sixth book, and volunteer to facilitate writing workshops for war veterans in my home of New Mexico.

Made in the USA
Columbia, SC
01 March 2025

54556298R00128